BEYOND CUTTING

A Viv Fraser Mystery

V. Clifford

This is a work of fiction. Any references to real people, living or dead, real events, businesses, organizations and localities are intended to give the fiction a sense of reality and authenticity. All names, characters, places and incidents are either the product of the author's imagination or are used fictitiously, and their resemblance, if any, to real-life counterparts is entirely coincidental.

Published by Inverardoch Press
Copyright © Vicki Clifford 2013

Cover Photograph © Copyright Ian in Warwickshire and licensed for reuse under this Creative Commons Licence

ISBN 978-0-9927377-0-2

Chapter One

Out on the pavement, high tenements exclude much of the promising sky that Viv Fraser had seen from her window, six ancient floors up. A nippy wind gusts around her as she hitches her rucksack over her shoulder and pulls her jacket up close to her neck. Looking left and right she's damned if she can remember where she parked last night. As the memory surfaces she sets off with her head down in a futile attempt to avoid the cold. She trots through the Grassmarket into King's Stables Road where the impressive bulk of Edinburgh Castle casts its shadow across the street, cursing as she spots her little maroon MG wedged in by other cars. The worst thing about living in the West Bow is finding a parking space. It's a daily routine that she could do without.

As she draws closer she swears again quietly under her breath: it's even worse than she thought. She has no idea how she'll get her car out short of rubbing lard on the bumpers of the Beamer and the Volvo. The MG is temperamental and today is no exception. After she has turned the key for the fourth time the engine catches and she revs it until it sounds convincing. Chastising herself for keeping the car, she reconsiders whether it still has any of the merits she once believed it had. She glances round to see if anyone's watching. Her first nudge is tentative, but as she gets into the swing of it the BMW takes more of a bumping than she means it to and slowly it begins to shift. The switch on the radio is equally temperamental, but this morning Radio Four crackles into life. For once, she might hear *Woman's Hour* through to the end. The discussion, on Augustine and Rousseau, reminds her of all those contemporary 'confessions' that should never have made it to print. At least Augustine and Rousseau had controversial things to say, and were not full of vacuous clichés. She listens to the debate as she crawls through bumper-to-bumper traffic on the Southside. Everywhere she looks there is bargain shop after bargain shop: a depressing sight. She finally makes it to one of the main routes south from Edinburgh. Her first clients are in the Borders. Forty miles and she'll be in Earlston.

Listening to three academics not getting to the point just isn't doing it for her, and her mind returns to this morning's conversation. Jules, an old friend and editor at a newspaper that Viv occasionally writes for, had telephoned to call in a favour knowing Viv's familiarity with the gay scene. 'A bit of quiet research': Jules had said it was to be handled with 'sensitivity'. A schoolboy has gone missing and Jules is keen that Viv find out as much as she can. Viv had recognised the face that Jules was talking about from a news clip on Breakfast TV, and was disturbed that she couldn't remember exactly where she'd seen him before. As she whistles an old Eddi Reader tune the face of the missing boy floats through her head, but she shakes it away: there's her holiday to think about. By Sunday she'll be up on the West Coast driving through Assynt: Stac Pollaidh, Suillven, Canisp – extraordinary hills, each rising from a landscape as beautifully bleak as imagination could allow.

Viv has been making this trip to the Borders for over a decade. Her townie friends are amazed that she's prepared to drive this far 'just to cut hair'– a sign that they've no understanding of the relationship that develops between hairdresser and client. Viv's clients want to know that they can trust her beyond a decent haircut. She's privy to many secrets: pants and socks on the floor, girlie mags by the bed, kitchen roll in the loo, bank statements lying on worktops. The women she's seeing today are familiar with her and she with them. They're comfortable with one another . . . well, most of the time.

Over the years, Viv has skirted the tricky topics of fox hunting and getting 'good help'. These girls no longer consider her as 'help'. Viv has more qualifications than they could claim between them. So it's difficult for them to ask her to use the tradesmen's entrance, although there are some who might try.

Once she's driven out beyond Dalkeith her breathing slows. She'll barely see another building above one storey for the rest of the journey. When she reaches the steep brae up onto Soutra, the terrain changes, becoming bleak and inhospitable. Even the tough old Romans struggled with this moorland but they weren't as tough as the monks who built the hospital at its highest point: archaeologists have found indications of a learned group who healed travellers over centuries as they moved between north and south. On the south side of Soutra the landscape stretches out – it begins to roll, becoming gentler and less violent.

On this familiar journey Viv passes through Lauder, a typical Scottish market town with one main street. The Tolbooth, the town's grandest building, houses a clock in its tower which she usually relies on, but not today – most of it is obscured by polythene and scaffolding. Viv doesn't get it when planners bang on about the vernacular buildings of Scotland. This county architecture is all slightly different, evolving as it has, through generations. As she nears Earlston she notices a dusting of snow on the Eildons. Walter Scott country. Poor wee Walter struggling around this landscape with polio; can't have been much fun. Still he made up for it on the page.

On reaching her destination, Viv inches up the drive, just containing a longing to spray the meticulously raked gravel over the pristine lawn. She looks up at the front elevation of a gentrified farmhouse: its stone façade belies generations of dissatisfaction, each alteration attempting perfection. The shutters excluding life and light on the upper floors make the house appear closed for business, which much of the time it is, now that the children have been exiled to the Home Counties. Viv reflects that bricks and mortar are all very well, but they're no solution to the happiness question.

Before the car draws to a halt a pair of pugs bolt out of the front door and snarl at her tyres, which is par for the course. As soon as she extricates her legs from the bucket seat they're all over her like a rash. Lou Lou jumps inside sniffing like the bloodhound she'd like to be. It's as well the dogs make a fuss because their mistress never does. After retrieving a compact case and the pug from the car Viv negotiates dods of dog poo, finally reaching the door, which as ever is ajar. She could have been off with the silver many times if she'd a mind to. This open door policy is a puzzle to her. Is it a conscious act of wisdom in that, if burglars want to they'll get in regardless, or is it simply neglect?

She scrapes her boots on an oversized coir mat sunk into a shallow well in the vestibule and strolls through a cavernous hallway, panelled in light oak up to the dado rail. The cloying scent of hyacinths mingles with that of furniture polish. She spies the blooms on a side table contained by a discreet wire – an obstacle to their naturally wayward behaviour – and muses on how distinctly we assert our need for control. The walls are lined with paintings of hunting scenes and portraits of Margie's family who, in their heyday, held positions of some social importance: years of coal smoke have dulled their lustre, but they remain an intimidating sight. She glances up into the eyes of a stern old man and notices that the painter has given his hands a delicate femininity, which isn't echoed in his chiselled face. By the time she reaches the kitchen the smell of hyacinth is making her gag. Closing the door behind her she calls out, 'Margie, it's Viv!' Nothing.

It isn't until Viv has set up her gardener's sheet on the floor and found the extension cable for her drier, that Margie strolls in with a pile of washing teetering on one arm, her face its usual picture of disappointment, a far cry from her self-assured relations in the hallway. Viv finds Margie's inertia criminal. Living in a big house with a husband who bores for Britain isn't much to be proud of, but now that the kids are away at school she's no excuse not to get a grip and create a new existence. Viv reminds herself to stick to what she's being paid for.

'Oh hi, Viv. How are you?' No interest in hearing the answer – just going through the motions. If Viv said, 'I've had a shit morning,' Margie would just say, 'That's nice.' Sadly there's no opportunity to test this, as Tosh arrives, setting the pugs off into paroxysms again.

With a hand balancing her towelling turban Tosh negotiates the delicate task of air kissing Margie, bypassing Viv, before they decide the order of play. Tosh says, 'I'm out to lunch' – not even a hint of irony from someone who has never been anywhere else. Viv disguises a smile beneath a cough. She knows Tosh's husband Perry who happens to be Jules' boss. He's a fair man whose tolerance for his wife's trivia is already stretched. Margie doesn't seem to mind who goes first and, the tailor's dummy, Tosh takes a seat, unwrapping her turban to allow her dark, poker-straight hair to fall over one of those faces whose individual features are unremarkable, but add up to a picture of a Renaissance mistress.

Viv, embarking on her first miracle of the day says, 'A little or a lot?'; much hysteria has been caused in the past by 'too much coming off', and Viv is more cautious than most hairdressers: the repercussions of bad hair days are untold.

Of no one in particular Tosh asks, 'D'you think the time has come? I'm sure I saw a grey hair the other day.' This is not a new question. Then, not missing a beat and without so much as a glance at Viv, she brushes an invisible speck from her shoulder, 'Just the usual, thank you. Are you well, Viv?'

'Yes th. . .'

But Tosh is off into a diatribe about her gardener. Viv may as well have vaporised.

She feels a perverse pity for them. All that money spent on public school education, to teach them that they are privileged. Lies, all lies. Their journey through boarding school leaves each with an aching void that has no hope of being filled. There can't be anything worse than investing in the belief that 'one' is privileged when it turns out to be the emperor's new kit. The investment might as well have gone up the lum. Out of these two only Margie has been touched by humanity, and she's pretty inconsistent, especially when Tosh is around.

Margie offers Viv coffee and Tosh blinks in surprise, as if the offer is a breach of allegiance. They see Viv as another sort, but are no longer sure where to place her. 'What exactly is a PhD?' Margie had asked. Not many people know. And they certainly can't get their heads round a hairdresser being a Doctor, unless it's one of those barefoot kind. They need her – she's the best there is north of the border – but this blurring of the boundary is tricky for them. But not only tricky for them – people are always baffled when Viv has to explain what she does; their fondness for fitting others into neat boxes doesn't work with her, and it causes them more than a little discomfort. Viv's careers, in hairdressing, academe and now an occasional guest column on a

Sunday magazine, courtesy of Jules, has had even her closest friends shaking their heads in disbelief.

While Margie continues to stroke her pile of cotton sheets as if they might purr, Tosh, hair now finished, in an act of vandalism runs bejewelled talons through her beautiful blow-dry, then kneels down to tie her shoe lace. She flicks Lou Lou roughly out of range causing Margie's eyebrows to reach for her hairline. As Margie sits down she says, 'I saw a strange thing this morning on my way back from the village; a man was dumping black sacks in the lay-by. I tooted because I thought it was Jock MacCallum, but it was just someone with the same kind of truck. Anyway he shot me the most vicious glare.'

Viv wonders if looks can be vicious and decides that if they can kill then surely they can be vicious. After too much comment on the general rudeness of some people the inevitable school talk begins. Viv is always astonished by this. It's not as if they aren't intelligent women, but the chat on this topic always takes precedence over current affairs. Margie's hair is a frizzy mass that is unwilling to be tamed by any product from African wax to Araldite, but somehow Viv has managed to create a shape that survives despite Margie's neglect.

The morning passes, each is happy with her hair, neither of them a risk taker, and once their next appointments are made – no mean feat given the fishing season has started – Viv is on her return journey.

She can't believe it when she reverses into a prize parking place in front of her stair, then curses; she never gets this space when she's in for the night. Standing on the pavement she stretches her neck and notices a 'For Sale' sign attached to Ronnie's window. He lives in the flat next door to her and is a perfect neighbour. It would be a pity if he moved out, but perhaps she could buy it? Viv rents her flat and, if she could afford it, would gladly make this investment. She retrieves the mail from her pigeonhole then bounds up the eighty-six steps two at a time, thinking this could be her only exercise for the day. Breathlessly she taps on Ronnie's door. Silence. He usually works from home, but you'd never know it. She'll try later.

She rings the estate agent while the number is fresh in her mind; the price is scary, but might be doable. Her answering machine registers three messages. The first is from Paul, a friend who only rings when he's having relationship issues. He can definitely wait. The second is another from Jules. Viv hasn't heard from Jules in a while and had wondered if she was out of favour: two calls in one day spells 'desperate'. The final call is from Perry, Tosh's husband and Jules' boss. He pleads, 'For God's sake Viv do us all a favour and ring Jules before she kills us all.' Now for her emails. Jules, true to her word, has filled her in and attached a photograph – Viv recognises it. It is the face from the news report this morning. Viv returns Jules' call and gets Alice, her long-suffering secretary.

'Hey, Alice, is Juliet around? She left me a message to contact her.'

'Sure, I'll put you through.'

Within seconds they are connected. 'Viv! Thank God. Where the hell have you been? I've left at least a dozen messages. Even Perry said he'd try.'

Viv shakes her head, amazed at Jules' shift from heaven to hell in so few syllables, and replies, 'Not far since we spoke this morning, but you'd have to be ringing the right number.'

Viv smiles, visualising some poor sod whose answering machine is choked with irate messages from an unknown crazy woman. 'Okay, what's so urgent?'

'Well, for starters the young man that went missing from St Jude's. His school blazer has turned up, down by the Water of Leith . . .'

'I'm guessing he wasn't with it?'

Jules is not in the mood. 'Very funny, Viv. He's head boy and loves the blazer. Apparently it has all kinds of coloured braiding and leather patches on the elbows. His parents are keen on doing the reward thing, but at the moment I'm interested in his extra-curricular activities. Get what you can . . .'

'Hold on a minute. I've got a busy week!'

'It's night work, Viv, no excuses.'

After a long pause Viv asks, 'What is it you'd like me to do?'

'The word is that he prefers boys and could have got himself involved in stuff in, the gay underworld. You . . .' Viv cringes. Jules obviously skipped classes on political correctness.

'And what? You think guys in gay bars'll talk to me? You're more nuts than I thought. Do the words "sore thumb" make any sense to you? They'll no more talk to me than to . . .'

She can't think of anyone and huffs and puffs a bit more. Jules waits until she hears the quality of sigh that she's hoping for.

Sure enough Viv exhales emphatically and concedes: 'Okay, I'll give it a go.'

'Great, I'll need all you can get by noon Thursday.'

'It's already Tuesday. Not hoping for much are you!'

Viv ruffles her fringe, thinking it's time it was cut, as she mulls over where the likely haunts would be for a young man with a penchant for other young men on a Tuesday night. She is familiar with Edinburgh's gay community, although it has been a while since she was out and about herself. Many of the bars are open all hours, so she showers and changes into leather jacket and jeans, then decides against the leather, it's too stereotypical. Instead she grabs a warm wool jacket and locks up. She hears Ronnie's laboured breathing as he pauses before tackling the final few steps to their landing.

'Hey, Ronnie, what's happening? I saw the sign.'

Ronnie is the shyest man she's ever met, but somehow they've got through that. Viv never tries to finish his sentences. Occasionally his stammer has stopped her waiting for an answer, but she keeps smiling; her body language lets him know when she's in a hurry. This afternoon she's not in such a rush to keep moving and eventually he says, 'Got a bit of a legacy. Would like a garden.'

'I'll be sorry to lose you – are you sure you won't miss the hustle and bustle of the Bow?'

He looks confused, as if it hasn't occurred to him. Viv restarts her move towards the stairs. As she leaps down she dodges the worn step and wonders for the thousandth time why out of eighty-six steps only one should be so much more worn than the others.

Viv decides to leave the MG, knowing she'll never get parked on the north side of town. She heads up the West Bow, onto George IV Bridge, straight down the Mound via the Playfair Steps, and passing the elegant classical buildings of the National Galleries reaches Princes Street. This street was once the envy of many European cities, but is now full of bland chain-stores, each one an insult to the splendour of its neighbours on the opposite side of the road. Up Hanover Street, a short jog on George Street, skipping between parked cars in the centre of the road, then into Howe Street – takes ten minutes tops.

She pushes open the door and a warm, over-deodorised atmosphere hits her. The place is begging for a blast of fresh air. It's busy. As she squints into the back room she decides that if Jules' information is good the men here are a couple of decades too old, but she orders a half of cider anyway. It's barely two o'clock and one guy, hanging onto the bar, looks as if he should head for bed. Sidling alongside him she says, 'I'm looking for my brother.'

'You and me both.'

No slurring. Hopeful.

Viv tries again. 'He's beautiful. Darkish hair. Tall. About so high,' holding her hand above her own head. He turns and looks her up and down.

'A lot like you then.'

She doesn't expect this. Gay men can be antagonistic towards lone women invading their turf. Viv continues to build her fantasy 'brother' with another lie. 'He hangs out with a young crowd. Not many in today.'

'We'd all like to hang out with a young crowd, dear.'

He sneers, showing overly white porcelain teeth that should have been made into teacups. They slip as he yawns, and, self-consciously, he raises his hand to cover his mouth before slumping back onto the bar. He should definitely go home; he can't be good for business. As she moves off he murmurs: 'Day time, you'll have more luck in Copa Cabana.'

'Cheers!'

Copa Cabana is a new bar at the east end of town within easy walking distance. Setting out at a brisk pace Viv takes in the grandeur of Edinburgh's New Town. This wasn't called Great King Street for nothing. To the uninitiated these buildings look identical, but everywhere there are discreet architectural details: astragals each slightly different, urns and pillars; all a testimony to neo-classical symmetry.

Approaching her destination, she negotiates her way anti-clockwise round Drummond Place, a splendid square with gardens in the centre for the use of its residents. A disappointing sign reads 'No Dogs or Ball Games'. Beyond the square lies the entrance to Edinburgh's gay ghetto – Broughton Street, where more pink pound is spent at the weekend than any other area of town. Viv's destination is close, but hasn't managed a premier spot. As she waits at the traffic lights to cross Picardy Place she can see young men entering and exiting Copa Cabana and her spirits rise.

This bar isn't at all like the last one. Here there is a huge plate glass front, wooden flooring and leather furniture framed with stainless steel: designed for exposure not discretion. The bright halogen lights are a secondary source of heat, which after a whole evening must be torture, but are a bonus to her now. Women are welcome here so she looks less conspicuous as well. Taking off her jacket and sitting down she peruses a menu. A panini would be welcome. The waiter who comes to take her order barely looks in her direction. She doesn't believe he caught what she said, but within a few minutes he's back with her glass of cider, a napkin and cutlery, so there must be something on its way.

After a long draw of her drink she scans the room for prospective interviewees. The waiter, as camp as anyone she's seen in a long time, is entertaining three young guys at the end of the bar. If this were not a known gay establishment, she would have thought they were simply three football fans, their Hibs colours a convincing disguise. On closer inspection they look underage, but most people do now. She'd better tread carefully; mustn't alienate them before she's got what she needs from them.

The waiter, responding to a shout from the kitchen, minces off to collect what Viv hopes is her food. Sure enough he twirls round the end of the bar and ceremoniously places a full plate in front of her. This exhibition was certainly not intended for her amusement – the young guys laugh uproariously and the waiter, satisfied, makes a low bow. The bread smells great and she tucks in, but before she's finished a woman sits down opposite her and smiles: 'D'you mind?' Viv smiles back through a mouthful of mozzarella cheese, which has taken on a life of its own. Grabbing the napkin she struggles to contain it, and blushes like an adolescent.

Viv is usually comfortable in gay bars; as a trainee hairdresser it was one of her initiation rites. The first time fellow juniors took her out on the town, a town a whole lot different from any Edinburgh she could have conceived of, a woman asked her to dance, and she had yelled, 'There's NO WAY I'd ever dance with a dyke!' It's mortifying just thinking about it. The woman had subsequently come to the salon to have her hair cut and said to Viv, 'I only wanted to dance.' They both laughed at her panic and became friends.

Now, Viv is relieved that the woman sitting opposite, mucking about on her phone, doesn't make any further attempt to chat, but wonders why she chose to sit there given the empty seats elsewhere. Feeling better after food, Viv heads over to the bar. She hears the barman saying, 'O-M-G!' Then as she gets closer, 'W-T-F?' Get used to it, Viv. The Atlantic has become like a puddle. As she nods to the group, they glance at one another, look her up and down, then snigger, before one of them asks what they can do for her. More sniggers until she replies, 'I'm looking for Andrew Douglas.'

This puts their gas at a peep. Their frivolity drops a few leagues.

'Who's askin'?'

Viv turns to look behind her and says, 'I don't see anyone else, do you?'

'Witty, very witty. Why do you want to know?'

'Let's say, I'm making it my business to know. When was the last time any of you saw him? I'm not asking for the good of my health.'

Of the three, the one who has spoken is the tallest, over six feet. He looks the least healthy. Skinny, with pale grey skin and a fair portion of acne, which doesn't bode well in this world where youth is only half of the equation. The other two are about five eight, with clear glowing skin, perhaps the residue of winter sun. Middle-class skiing? School chums? None of this sits comfortably with the football colours.

Ignoring the tall boy Viv sets her gaze on one of the others. 'So you know who I mean?'

This boy is not so brave and quickly looks away. Then, returning her stare, he holds it defiantly. He pushes an invisible strand of hair back from his forehead – a movement more camp than she'd expected from his muscular frame. Still looking directly at her, he says, 'What if he doesn't want to be found?' His accent cultured but not public school.

'Well, that would be interesting and I'd respect that. But there's a reward for information about his whereabouts.' Viv smiles encouragingly.

The tall boy's face twitches a humourless smile into a look of possibility.

'How much?'

Viv doesn't actually know the amount, but she's been here before and responds with, 'Plenty.'

He smirks. 'You're taking the piss.'

'Come on guys. When or where did you see him last?'

'You're wasting your time, missus.'

His accent is an attempt to be more working-class than he is: condescension oozes from the title.

'It's Doctor, actually.'

Viv's PhD was completed exactly because of her contempt for Ms, Miss and Mrs. Not titles, but categories designed to expose a woman's 'station'. Pulling her Doctorate out of the bag usually raises a few eyebrows and on cue the tall boy raises his, then with a return to a cocky smirk says, 'He's not dead . . . but maybe not as healthy as he'd like to be.'

'Any idea where I might find him?'

'You could try the Colonies.'

She's doing well so far but keen not to push her luck, dips into her pocket, pulling out a ten. He snorts. She extracts a twenty and puts them together. He stays silent. When she pulls out another twenty he puts out his hand. Once he's got hold of the money he lifts a pen from the bar and writes on the back of a coffee menu and slides it along to her. It's an address, most likely false.

Chapter Two

If she jogs she could be at this address within fifteen minutes. Viv, feeling the three sets of eyes on her back, leaves the pub, relieved to be away from the testosterone-laden atmosphere. But before she crosses at the lights she ducks down and doubles back, looking into the bar. As she thought, the tall skinny guy has one hand shielding his ear while his iphone is pressed against the other. The address he's given her is bound to be useless but she has nothing else to go on so it's worth checking out.

Before she steps up her pace she flips open her mobile and presses Jules' number. It's busy so she sends a text instead. From what little the boys have said Andrew could be alive or they could have fed her a load of baloney. As she's turning the corner into Broughton Street she glances back and spots one of the boys, the one who didn't speak at all, walking quickly in her direction. As they make eye contact he shouts, 'Keep walking!' Slightly bemused she continues and when they are halfway down Broughton Street he shouts again, 'In here!'

She turns, retraces her steps and follows the boy into yet another gay bar. This one is tiny, with salsa music, but not many people. Its décor is arty and shabby chic; the Copa Cabana, by comparison, tries too hard. He beckons her through to a small room with a barrel-vaulted ceiling, and pulls out the chair next to him. Viv takes a seat opposite. She checks their proximity to other patrons – all okay. He, oblivious to his surroundings, blurts out, 'Everything Tommy said back there was true. Only, I think Andrew really would like to be found. The flat will be clear at this time of the day – and certainly now that they've been warned.'

'D'you know what's going on?' Viv tries not to sound too keen.

He shakes his head, unwilling to make eye contact.

'Only that there are drugs available if you'll play their games.'

'What! We talking sex for drugs? Surely not hard?'

'I don't know. Uppers, I expect.'

This could mean anything. Most illegal substances will give you a high before you hit the deck.

'Any names?' She's tempted to ask for his name, but worried that it might shut him up, she holds back.

'No, I saw Andrew leaving the pub with an old bloke. Really not his scene; he always has young boys around him. I've only seen him once since and he was off his face then as well. He asked me to go back to the flat with him. I didn't go. There's a limit, but Andrew's forgotten what it is.'

Viv lets him run on while filling in the gaps in her mind. This is not sounding like a nice place for a middle-class boy, or any boy for that matter. Viv looks round, surprised that no one seems worried that they're not ordering anything. She reaches into her pocket, but he stops her, 'No, thanks. If I didn't think he needed help I wouldn't say anything. Helping a mate doesn't have a price. We're not all like Tommy.' His phone rings. His answer is positively upbeat. 'Hey Ruthie.' Whatever 'Ruthie' said, his voice drops. He turns away from Viv as if she might hear. 'No.' He seethes. He blinks and his jaw tightens in frustration. 'Which bit of no…?'

The caller hangs up. Viv raises her eyebrows, but he stuffs the phone back into his pocket without reference to the call.

Viv stands and nods, 'What's your name?'

He doesn't answer. She shakes her head and says, 'Thanks.' Then as she walks towards the door he calls out. 'Pete.'

She nods again, not sure whether to believe him, then makes her way back out onto Broughton Street.

The Colonies aren't far, so she heads downhill turning left on reaching the clock at Canonmills. She slips onto Glenogle Road, and walks toward

Stockbridge, before continuing along beneath a high wall where she stops to read the address.

Beyond where she stands are rows of Victorian terraced houses. But to her right, set back from the road, is a three-storey block of flats with a flat roof. Built in the nineteen eighties, it is surely an embarrassment to its architect. The residents' car park is between her and the front entrance.

She strolls across the tarmac, down a path of concrete slabs, idly looking up at the windows above. At the entrance sit two derelict planters. At eye level is a panel of buzzers; the one that she is looking for has no name against it – she feels for the postie.

Her finger is on the buzzer for longer than is polite. No answer. She presses the button again. Nothing. Then again. And again. She's nothing if not tenacious. As she glances round looking for another entrance she hears footsteps from inside the building. Viv makes a pretence of checking names, but the exiting man brushes past without even giving her a look. She jams her boot in the door just before it shuts. Inside there's a corridor to the left with a glass door at the end, which probably leads out to the back. The staircase is directly opposite and there's a flat to the right and left of it. She assumes the address that she's been given is on the first floor so she takes the stairs.

Each door has a tarnished metal plate with a number on it. Finding the one she's looking for, she knocks and isn't surprised when there is no response. Then, hearing the slightest of movements, she draws closer to the door when the sound of retching reaches her, followed by the flush of the loo. Viv turns as the neighbour across the hall comes out of her door and locks up behind her. She looks Viv up and down then asks, 'Can I help you?'

'Um, I'm looking for someone.'

The woman snorts: 'I wouldn't go in there if I were you. They're a bunch of raving paedos if you ask me.'

Viv hadn't asked, but it's helpful to get an idea of whether there's good will between neighbours: evidently not in this case. In an attempt to humour her Viv says, 'D'you see much of them?'

'Not if I can help it. The noises from inside make me sick, laughing and screaming at all hours. I don't think any of them know the meaning of the word work. The police do nothing.'

If this is true, it won't mean the cops don't keep an eye on them.

The woman hesitates. 'You from the police then?'

'No.' Viv hears her own defensiveness and softens her tone. She'll not get info otherwise: 'Too bad. Someone ought to do something.'

While they stand on the landing there's no further sound from inside the flat. No one has come out of the bathroom as far as she can tell.

The woman calls back over her shoulder. 'If I could get them out I'd be able to sell my place. No one will buy it with that lot there . . . big fat bastard.'

Viv sighs and whispers to herself, 'Say it as it is, why don't you!' She tries knocking again. No luck. Still, at least she's out of the wind and patience is supposed to be a virtue. Taking a seat on the top step she checks her messages then rings Jules back. The stair is clean, no graffiti and the floor's pale green mock marble surface matches the walls. It doesn't smell too bad either, which is a stroke of luck. After leaving a message giving Jules what she's up to she tries knocking on the door again. Another small sign of life: a groan, but life nonetheless. She knocks again. On her third knock she hears a noise, but even with her ear to the door she's unable to make it out. It definitely wasn't an invitation. Too bad. She tries the door handle; it's her lucky day. The door opens into a warm carpeted hallway with four flush wooden doors: two on the right, one on the left and one directly ahead.

'Hello?' The hall floor is littered with blankets and sleeping bags. Pushing open each door, she repeats, 'Hello!' No one answers. Finally, in the last room, she makes out the shape of a body curled in a foetal position, beneath a pile of bedclothes. The room smells of stale sex and God knows what else. Crouching beside the figure she quietly says, 'Hey.'

She hopes to God this isn't Andrew; this one doesn't look as if he'll survive. His skin is translucent – not good, especially coupled with blue lips and vomit round the mouth and on the tee shirt. His breathing is shallow; she goes down onto her knees and puts her ear to his chest. Without thinking about it, she's dialling 999 and asking for an ambulance. As she rubs the back of his soft chilly hand she takes in the little there is of the room. The cheap voiles covering the windows look clean, but there is nothing on the walls; no paintings or posters. Everything apart from the floor is pretty bare. It seems an age before she hears the approach of a reassuring siren.

When the paramedics enter, they look at her as if she should be scraped off their shoe. She doesn't explain who she is, just what she found when she came into the flat. They don't question her beyond asking if she has a name for the young man or any contacts. She reports that she has nothing, but that she heard someone retching and decided to try the door – which sounds thin even to her ears. As the paramedics are busy getting the stretcher set up, Viv tries to work out what actually goes on in this place. It's a viper's nest, den of iniquity, call it what you like, but the stench itself is a guarantee that the windows are never opened: it certainly isn't anyone's home.

On the way out one of the paramedics asks, 'You coming along?'

'No, um, no, I'll come up later.'

He looks at her, recognising the lie, and nods. Every room has been slept in apart from the bathroom, and even in here she can't be sure. There's a pillow lying beneath the kitchen table. The food in the fridge is all the cheapest 'value' labels. The chances of this being a crime scene seem pretty strong so she lifts things with the sleeve of her jersey pulled over her hand. She's intrigued that there are no unwashed dishes, only a damp cloth over the tap.

Inside a small wooden cabinet by a king-size bed, she finds masses of ribbed condoms. That there are condoms at all is a good sign. Safe sex. Also there are well thumbed 'top shelf' mags and DVDs. The CID guys that she knows have a priority list: stuff that's not worth bothering about and stuff that is. She's guessing this is the former. Further raking around turns up a thick folded piece of paper. It's one of those letters that doesn't need an envelope, with perforations that you tear. It has the logo of HM Prisons on one side and the name Alexander MacDonald on the other. She slips it into her pocket.

There isn't any sign of sniffing material: the odd bottle of poppers, but no white powder. This doesn't mean they don't have it. Viv is suspicious that there's so little junk lying around: every home has junk. There aren't any bags or rucksacks, which is strange, given how many people seem to sleep here.

This isn't a home. It really could just be a camp. This is quite scary. She decides to head home. Apart from the letter she leaves it as she found it.

Crossing the car park, she spots the woman from the flat next door walking towards her, laden with groceries. Viv stops and asks if she can give a hand with her bags. The woman screws up her eyes, but hands her a carrier anyway, and in her Edinburgh accent says, 'You get what you wanted?'

'Not really, I came to look for a young man, and I'm not sure what I've found. Have you met the guy who owns the flat?'

'Yes! Fat bastard.'

Not helpful, but Viv perseveres.

'You don't like him, then?'

The woman is hostile. 'No and neither would you if you met him. He's here in the daytime, but always out at night. There's no mail for him apart from wee thin parcels and it doesn't take a genius to work out what might be in those.'

When Viv cocks her head the woman says, 'Well it must be films.' The accent on the last word is almost comically heavy.

Viv makes no response and the woman continues, 'That said, he wears a uniform of some sort. He's had long times on the sick. The local pharmacy delivered his medication then. He's disgusting; a fat, ugly pervert exploiting young men . . .' Her sentence trails off.

'What?' Viv raises an eyebrow.

'Some of them come here in school uniform.'

Viv makes a face and the woman says, 'I see you've not the mind for it either.'

Once they reach the front door the woman roots around in her pockets for a key. She must only be in her fifties but she's slow for that. The crows-feet round her eyes show she's had some laughs in her time.

Upstairs, Viv lays the carrier bag on the floor and turns to leave. 'Thanks.'

'Surely it should be me thanking you.' Less hostile now. Perhaps even a touch of friendliness?

Viv smiles and retraces her steps.

Within half an hour she's home. She grabs what little there is in her post box and takes the stairs, checking to see if there's anything of interest. Her *Hairdressers Journal* is the only thing worth keeping. Time for research. A steaming mug of industrial strength coffee and a packet of biscuits are all she needs to keep her eyes on the screen for a couple of hours. Retrieving the letter from her pocket, she reads the HM Prison slip. Alexander MacDonald makes good money. With a dash of creativity she gets into the correct website to gather more information about MacDonald. The Saughton Prison home page is rather smart. Viv used to pass the prison every day on her way to school. She goes down a few blind alleys before finding the staff list, but once she's in her eyes come out on stalks. There's an Alexander MacDonald who is a prison psychologist. Do prison psychologists wear uniform? That would be rich.

Perhaps there's more than one Alexander MacDonald? After trawling for a further twenty minutes she finds another. 'Bingo! Mm. A senior officer. He looks gay. So no prejudice there, Viv.'

She'd better be careful. They could both be gay. She smiles, recalling the one in four statistic. Wondering how the poor young bloke from the flat is doing, she reaches for the telephone, but her hand hovers over it. They will only give her information if she turns up; too easy to fob someone off on the phone. She's suddenly struck by the contrast between her own tiny, but homely flat, which could never be described as minimalist, and the state of the one she was in earlier. It was like an unloved hostel. Maybe that's what it is. Curious. The intimate bits and pieces of a home were missing. Not even computing equipment, no printer or wireless hub, no telephone or ornaments. There was electricity, that's for sure: the fridge was on, and the big screen TV was set up with DVD and video recorders. Strange. Everyone has a mobile phone. But do they all use laptops? It's easy to tap into wifi from a neighbour without them even knowing. Most homes these days can't function without a computer. She'd counted at least nine sleeping bags and one king-size bed, and would lay bets that the sales particulars for the flat didn't claim that it would sleep quite so many.

She has ways of finding exactly which Alexander MacDonald resides in that flat, and sets about putting her mind to rest. Viv's computing skills were honed at university, which she hadn't expected. She'd made friends with a

Hungarian woman whose knowledge of the web had made Viv's look positively infantile. The information age offers up untold riches when used with what Gabby, the Hungarian, called 'creativity'. Many clicks later Viv discovers what she had secretly hoped not to. The prison officer's pay slip that she has in hand corresponds to that of Her Majesty's fifty-six-year-old psychologist. This could get interesting.

The man in the photograph staring back at her from the screen looks older than his years, more like a convict than he should, and not exactly a picture of health. The prison issue uniform does nothing for his waxy tattie complexion, his screwed up eyes or multiple jowls. Not a bonny sight. Who in their right mind would have intimate relations with this apparition? Who indeed? Perhaps he doesn't participate; he might just enjoy the Pullman seats. Yuck! She shudders at the idea of one of those young chaps from the bar with him. Enough. Time for a shower.

Letting the power and the heat of the water do their work, Viv turns her mind to what's next. First stop is the Royal Infirmary to see how the unknown chap is doing, but before that she'd better have food. Her kitchen is compact: swinging cats are definitely in danger here. The hummus is on its sell-by date, so she slaps some onto a thick slice of bread and eats it on the way downstairs.

Living in the Old Town is like being in the bohemian quarter of any European city. In the sixteenth and seventeenth centuries these buildings were constructed to cater for numbers not aesthetics. Although her top-floor flat towers above the Grassmarket and has magnificent views across the south of the city to the Pentland Hills, the lower you go inside the stairwell the darker it is, and at the bottom the light is so poor that anyone who isn't familiar with the idiosyncrasies of the flagstones is in some peril. Viv knows them well and skips out the front door onto the West Bow.

The street is bustling with early evening drinkers. The real ale pub next door attracts people who rarely venture from the security of the New Town – men in suits with ties loosened, and women, also in suits, stand outside in the cold, all drawing on cigarettes as if their lives depended on it. Maybe they do? Viv assesses this crowd and although she's never had rose-tinted spectacles, she compares them to the young man in that nest in the Colonies, The New

Town is the epitome of precious and she's often thought it should be called Parvenutown. Again she decides to leave her car in its treasured space and hails a taxi at the top of her road. The hospital is a jog too far. Besides, she'll have to watch her time.

The Royal is an old name for the new hospital recently built to the south-east of Edinburgh, in an area called Little France. A place less like France she'd never set her eyes on. Apparently the area got its name in the sixteenth century, because Queen Mary, also Queen Consort of France, housed her French workers at this side of town in the lee of Craigmillar Castle. It was probably once a lovely country hamlet.

When Viv leans forward to pay the driver she's surprised that it's a woman. It's unlike her to have missed this, and she reminds herself to keep her wits about her. She hesitates at the automatic doors before entering – her discomfort at being in a hospital always makes itself known. She checks the overhead signs for the male unit. There are lots of visitors outside the ward doors. It may look state of the art, but it smells like any hospital and runs just like its Victorian counterparts. Sure enough, a bell goes and the visitors walk through. Viv attaches herself to a family, to look less conspicuous, but as soon as they reach their son's bed she's on her own.

Confidence is everything. Viv has always found it difficult to play the role of carer. At first she thinks she's out of luck, but then spots a boy without any visitors at the end of the ward. He looks frail, and has a drip attached to his hand. His eyes are open.

'Hi.'

'Who are you?' Wary.

'You probably won't remember me, I'm the woman who rang for the ambulance.'

He lifts his head to get a better look at her then drops it back onto the pillow. 'You had no business doing that.'

His voice is weak and his eyes fill up. He closes them and tears run down the side of his face into his ear. Viv pulls up a chair. She hadn't expected to be greeted with open arms but is surprised by his tears. She whispers, 'You weren't really trying to kill yourself, were you?'

He doesn't answer and she doesn't push him. The noise of chatter in the ward is phenomenal. She reflects on how difficult it is for the sick to get any peace. He tries again to lift his head but fails. 'What were you doing at Sandy's?' Although he's weak, he's still curious.

'I was looking for Andrew.' There's no sign of his recognising the name so she adds. 'Andrew Douglas?'

She watches as a flash of something crosses his face and he hesitates before saying, 'You mean Drew? I don't know his last name.'

She's no idea where to go next, but nods in agreement and he continues. 'Never seen him in the flat during the day.'

His eyes show suspicion and she quickly asks, 'So you've seen him recently?'

He screws up his eyes and in a wary tone asks again, 'Who *are* you?'

'I'm his sister.' Her lie flawless. He sighs and she continues. 'I need to find him. Or if not him Sandy.'

'You know Sandy then?'

'A bit.'

An insufficient answer, but it's all she's got.

'Sandy won't be around for a while. I think he's gone back to his wife's. He needs looking after.'

The sarcasm is heavy. Viv is intrigued by this.

'Well, I'll just have to concentrate on finding Andrew . . . Don't suppose you'd know where Sandy's wife lives?'

'In the prison quarters, but I haven't a clue where that is.'

Viv knows the prison officers' houses are at Saughton Mains, within walking distance of the prison.

'Was Andrew with anyone when you saw him last?'

'Yup, we were boggle eyed because the bloke was too old and Andrew . . .' He stops and shuts his mouth.

'I know about his lifestyle.' Viv speaks gently.

'Well, the guy was older; good looking, but older. They left the flat after picking up . . . Actually . . . maybe you should go.'

She doesn't move, but asks, 'Drugs? Was Drew picking up drugs?'

'You'll have to ask him.' He closes his eyes and turns his head away.

'Can I get you anything?'

He doesn't respond. John Black is the name above the bed.

As she heads back along the corridor her nose is assaulted again by the cocktail of cleaning fluid and poor, over-cooked food. She wonders how anyone could get well in such a place. Spotting a taxi through the automatic doors she breaks into a run, her hand in the air. She jumps in and slams the door.

Chapter Three

'The Copa Cabana!'

This time Viv does look at the driver, but he doesn't return her interest. She feels invisible and that's just fine. He does a U-turn and heads back into town. The roads are quiet, most commuters returned home for the night.

Nights at Copa Cabana are always busy. She pushes and elbows through the throng until she reaches the bar. Who'd believe that anywhere would be doing such lively business on a Tuesday night. The barman, with a clean shirt and jeans, acknowledges her order of a half of cider with a nod and a wink, which reminds her of Benny Hill, saucy but not sexy.

Viv squeezes back into the crowd looking vainly for somewhere to stand without being jostled. She spots Pete who nods and raises his glass slightly. She still thinks he must be under-age, but can't believe they would take the risk in here. The cops will be on to their every move. In fact as she stands with her back to the wall she sees two officers at the door showing the security guy a photograph. Her heart stops. Behind them she spots a face from her past. God! Liam the Creep.

Liam was a trainee in a salon where she worked. His flat, unprepossessing face hasn't improved – still the pinnacle of a hunched body that moves as if it's three decades older than it is. It must be difficult to be Liam among hosts of beauty queens. His gait is what her mother describes as 'ten to two feet'; it's a walk that provides him with the attention he seeks. He couldn't care that it's negative attention; attention is attention whatever kind it is. He never had chums until he started throwing money around, too much money to be legal – tips for washing hair were not that good.

Viv slides down the wall before Liam spots her. She's head and shoulders below everyone else when she notices she's being watched – by the same woman who sat next to her before. From her hunkered down position she raises her glass, as if to say, I've no idea what I'm doing here. The woman smiles then turns back to her friends. Viv watches them. She can't imagine why such an odd crew should be here, but then remembers her own relief at not being surrounded by heckling hets. One of them is wearing old-style lesbian gear, the sort that would have been worn at Greenham Common: a big Ban the Bomb tee-shirt over a big tummy and baggy trousers. Three have grey hair and are overweight. The redhead, who just smiled at Viv, is wearing jeans and a tweed jacket and is about the same build as Viv, toned but not skinny.

The lights are killing, their intense heat creating a broth of sweat mixed with too much deodorant. The voice of Laura Brannigan is so loud everyone is shouting to be heard. Viv's penny drops. No wonder it's busy: it's an eighties night.

The gay bars of Edinburgh are home to every profession, and Copa Cabana is no exception. QCs mingle with shop assistants and bus drivers, and it wouldn't be the first time if she bumped into one of her lecturers from university. She's even seen the occasional unsuspecting husband of a client: those ever so hetero-camps who if they don't touch can't resist looking.

After her cider is gone she slides back up the wall in the hope of catching the eye of her young accomplice, but he's busy waving to attract the barman's attention. The redhead on the other hand sidles closer, and in a raised voice says, 'Hi! My name's Sandra. What brings you here again?' Viv notices a slight lisp.

'Probably not the same thing that's brought you here. The name's Cath.'

'Is that right? And here was I thinking I'd found Viv Fraser.' The redhead's smile looks genuine.

Surprised to hear her name, Viv has to work hard not to show recognition. 'Sorry. You've got the wrong girl.'

The redhead smiles again, 'I don't think so.' And nods in the direction of the door. 'Liam over there said your name's Viv.'

'I wouldn't believe all, in fact I wouldn't believe anything that Liam says.'

The redhead shrugs and turns, about to go back to her friends, then stops. 'He wouldn't lie to me.' She winks at Viv and Viv snorts as the redhead continues. 'I wouldn't be so sure that we're not here for the same reason.'

The heat is suffocating and Viv glances longingly at the exit. She knows she can't call it a day yet. Should she go to the loo, splash water on her face and be more assertive with the young accomplice? Yup – the loo wins. The women's toilets are rarely a priority in a gay bar, but these aren't too bad. Directing the cool air of the hand drier up onto her face, she's almost ready to face the crowd again when the redhead comes in and nods to a young girl, who hasn't yet started drying her hands. Red nods more vehemently. The girl shakes her hands and gives Red a death stare – a sure sign that she didn't attend a local comprehensive school, where death stares were purely for saps – before stomping out.

Viv tilts her head and grins, 'We must stop meeting like this.' She says this to make sure that she leads the conversation.

Red takes something from her pocket; a movement that has Viv on alert. But Red flashes a CID badge and smiles, obviously anticipating Viv's surprise. 'What exactly are you here for, Viv?'

'Well, that would be telling, wouldn't it?'

'Shame if we can't help each other.'

Viv isn't stupid. She's helped the police before, but there's rarely been any pay-off and she isn't inclined to help them until it becomes necessary. If Red were not standing between her and the door she'd be out of here.

Red interrupts her thought process. 'I'm looking for information on Andrew Douglas, and it sounds to me as if you have been asking similar questions . . . Now why would you be asking questions about Andrew?'

Viv quietly treads water, grappling for an answer. The boys have fairly been yapping. As a way out she says, 'If I hear anything I'll let you know.'

As she steps towards the door Red goes into her pocket a second time. This time she pulls out a card with her number on it and hands it to Viv. 'Not difficult now that you have my contact details. We might be on the same side.'

'I doubt it. But I'll keep it in mind.'

As she approaches the outside door she hears Liam's unmistakable shrill tone.

'Vivian!'

Her skin crawls. Not even her mother calls her that, unless she's out of favour. She steps up her pace and is out onto Picardy Place flagging a taxi, turning briefly to see him watching her from the door.

He'd have made a terrible hairdresser – too self-obsessed. To be confronted with one's own image nine hours a day means seeing each blemish magnified for the same length of time. Liam's constant preening was sickmaking. A hundred quid went missing from Viv's purse. It was found in Liam's shoe and he was sacked on the spot. So there's no love lost between them. She wouldn't trust him as far as she could spit, and imagines it's mutual. He'll not forgive her for ruining his 'career prospects' even though he'd never have made enough money cutting hair, at least not compared to dealing. In a perverse kind of way he owes her.

Tired, and with the prospect of a hair day tomorrow, she heads for home feeling as if the Andrew Douglas story has begun to grow legs. She sticks the taxi receipt in her back pocket and pulls out her house keys. The lock on the outside door is sticking and whilst she's shoogling her key around she senses that she's being watched. There are loads of flats on the other side of the road so it's not unlikely, but it's the wrong feeling. The heavy clunk of the stair door behind her is reassuring, but doesn't stop her from doing the steps two at a time for the second time today. Safely in her own flat and with the door double-locked she sighs, glad that she has no one to minister to but herself. Stripping everything off and tossing it on top of an already bulging laundry basket she steps into the shower and scrubs as if she's lousy.

After another session on the net, looking for anything about Liam, she finds a couple of mentions on Facebook, but sadly nothing incriminating. She must be looking in the wrong places. Too tired to do any more she heads back to the bathroom, carries out her teeth-cleaning ritual and collapses into bed.

She sleeps right through, but wakes feeling tetchy. It's Wednesday and her first client is in Barnton. The journey won't take long, so she turns over in the hope of having a few more minutes. Not a chance. Once she's awake, she's awake. She throws the duvet back and opens the window a couple of inches, which lets in a rush of cold air.

Back in the shower, the face of John Black keeps floating before her eyes. She shakes her head and blows out a spout of water. She can't help thinking that there are too many young men like him. If only they weren't ashamed of their sexuality. Fear of being found out keeps them in the shadows, and there are plenty of unsavoury types who know how to exploit them there. She's reminded of the photograph of Alexander/Sandy MacDonald. You couldn't get more unsavoury than that.

Rubbing her hair with a towel, she notices the familiar blinking light on the answering machine. She anticipates Jules and sure enough there are two messages from her; one asking how it's going and another saying to watch out for DC Nicholson. Viv pulls out her wallet and checks the name on Red's card: DC Nicholson. Good old Jules.

She dresses to meet hair day expectations. People want their hairdresser to look like a hairdresser and who is she to deny them this? Her wardrobe has always been on the verge of maverick, stylish but definitely maverick. Today she hauls out a pair of cream corduroy jodhpurs, a cream moleskin shirt and a tweed jacket that has never seen the kind of hack it was designed for. She remembers buying it ten years ago, maybe more, from a school exchange. Best three quid she's ever spent. On the inside there's still a faded name tag, the jacket tailored exclusively for its first owner.

Once her hair is dry she fingers a bit of gel through it – unkempt is the look she wants. A cursory look in the fridge forces her to forego breakfast. Her system can't cope with an assault this early in the day anyway.

Going through the usual routine with the MG she wonders what it would feel like to have a car that was warm and co-operative. The MG had seen better days before she bought it, but it was this very unreliability that had attracted her to it. Viv has an ascetic streak – Presbyterian. Things shouldn't be too comfy. The MG could never be described as comfy.

The rush-hour traffic has slackened off and her dread of a hill start on the West Port is alleviated when she doesn't even have to slow down. As she sails down Morrison Street and through Haymarket the car sounds guttural, as if its exhaust has blown. People are looking, even more than they would normally. She gasps: there is black smoke in her rear view mirror. 'Shit!'

Her first client isn't known for her tolerance. Too bad. Viv didn't start her day with the intention of bugging Jean Johnston. Pulling in to the kerb opposite Donaldson's School she looks underneath the car as if she knows what she doing. The exhaust has split, leaving one section trailing on the ground. She recalls there's an exhaust place not too far from here so she gets back in and limps the car another mile or so into Roseburn. As she lifts her work kit out of the boot she's greeted by a man in blue overalls.

'Doesn't sound too well,' he says as he smiles and takes the proffered key.

She's resigned to whatever has to be done and replies, 'Just do what you need to do and I'll pick it up later.'

'We'll need contact details.'

She fishes out a battered old card, making a mental note to have more printed, and hands it over. Then goes back onto the main road and hails a taxi.

Jean, without grace or subtlety, looks at her watch as Viv enters the porch three minutes late. No greeting other than, 'Go straight up. I'll bring my coffee up.' Her voice clipped public school.

No question of Viv having coffee. Squeezed between the shower cabinet and the basin Viv sets about shampooing Jean's hair. The routine is without variation: one wash and a lick of conditioner, avoiding the roots at all costs.

This is a difficult job for Viv. For years she's had to field Jean's questions about other clients. Only her strict policy of confidentiality has saved her skin. People, especially Jean, enjoy gossip and Viv had been frequently accused of being this source, until she actively put a stop to it. The question she hates most is, 'Don't you think?' This isn't a real question, but a means of gaining Viv's allegiance in order that Jean may say, ' Viv said . . .' Once Viv got wise to this she started saying, 'Actually, I've no idea.' No more reasoning with her. No more, 'Well, I can see both points of view.' Just a blunt, 'No I don't.'

This was harsh but the only way to break the pattern. The consequences went beyond breaking the cycle of gossip; it injured the congeniality that allowed them to bear the hour, occasional hour and a half if it was a day for highlights, that they had to spend in each other's company. In Viv's ideal world control freaks like Jean would move on. If only Viv wasn't so good at her job – mobile hairdressers with Sassoon training are thin on the ground in Edinburgh. Once she takes a client on it seems impossible to lose them. Viv takes a deep breath, heartened by the fact that very few clients are like Jean, then heads upstairs.

Jean's only having a cut today. So once Viv has set up, Jean takes a seat and looks straight through the bedroom mirror. No eye contact; in the huff. That's fine with Viv; the less she has to chat the better. After about ten minutes of layering, Jean says, 'It didn't lie very well last time. I think you'd cut too much off that section.'

Viv picks up the section that Jean's pointing to and holds it up at ninety degrees. She can tell immediately that she wasn't the last person to cut this, so says, 'You haven't had it trimmed in the village, have you?'

At first Jean doesn't want to admit it, but can't bring herself to lie. Feigning deep thought she then admits, 'Oh! I might have had a little trim for the Oban Ball.'

Viv bites her lip and nods, 'I'll do what I can to build up the weight again, but if you must have it cut in the village it would be better if you ask them to leave weight round your recession areas.'

The use of the word 'recession' makes Jean flinch. Her hair is, without doubt, her crowning glory: if it's not working, life's a disaster and not much of a bowl of cherries for those around her either.

'I'm not thinning, am I? I thought only men thinned. God, what would I do?'

Viv doesn't answer; she's won her point. Once she's finished cutting they go through the usual product consideration. Not once has Jean agreed to do something different, so Viv, biding her time, keeps her hand on the tin of spray. Right again. Halfway through the blow dry the telephone rings, so Viv puts the drier off and waits. She looks round the beautiful bedroom: a four-poster bed with fine muslin drapes edged with down. A matching walnut dressing table and chest of drawers smell of lavender polish, now slightly masked by fresh hairspray. The door to the double walk-in dressing-room boasts a full-length mirror. In fact she counts six mirrors in all in this room – narcissistic or what? The magazines on the bedside cabinets indicate who sleeps where.

Viv always turns her phone off while in with clients. Basic manners say there's nothing so urgent that it won't wait half an hour. As Jean chats to her chum without so much as lifting her eyes to the heavens in apology, Viv taps her foot. After five minutes Viv looks at her watch. The banal chat continues. Ten minutes later she thinks, fuck this, and starts packing up her kit. Within seconds the telephone is back in its cradle. Viv doesn't say anything but continues packing.

'What are you doing?'

Viv doesn't answer. Too angry to speak she keeps her head down as she winds up the flex on the drier. Once she's gathered scissors, comb, brushes and spray she does a final scan of the room. 'I'm done here.'

'But you've not finished . . . my hair.' The final bit of the sentence trails off as Jean notices the look on Viv's face. 'I'm sorry, but I coul . . .'

'Don't.' Viv puts her hand up to stop any further crap and makes her way downstairs to the front door. It's always locked and she has to wait whilst Jean fishes about in a china bowl to find the key.

'What about our other appointments?'

'I think we're done here, Jean. The village can take care of you . . . Don't let them forget that recession area.' A cheap parting shot that she regrets before she's reached the gate. Viv knows that Jean's behaviour stems from insecurity. So did Hitler's.

Chapter Four

It's quite a distance to the main road, but a brisk walk will soon get rid of the build-up of steam. If this episode had been a first Viv probably would have waited, but Jean doesn't know the meaning of the phrase, 'pissing on one's own bonfire'. Once Viv's onto the main road she rings the garage. They've managed a temporary repair and she can pick it up now, but it'll need some money thrown at it before it will pass its next MOT. No surprises there then.

Queensferry Road is busy and now that the Barnton Hotel is closed it's more difficult to get a taxi. She walks east for ten minutes before she sees the welcome orange light of a cab. Minutes later she's back at the garage with her credit card at the ready.

Viv throws her kit into the boot and drives off down towards Stockbridge. She dumps the car in a residents' bay anticipating a ticket but if she doesn't get coffee soon she'll flake out. The café is busy and she has to share a table. The woman opposite, reading a book, is vaguely familiar, but Viv consoles herself with the notion that most people seem familiar in this small city. The uncertainty is removed when the woman tilts her head and tentatively says, 'I think we've met.'

Viv, on hearing her distinctive accent, is prompted. 'Yes, I think it was at the National Library . . . No, no, it was at Central, at the Crispin lecture.'

'Well done!'

It was a good lecture, but although the detail of 'The Scottish Home' is now vague in Viv's mind, one aspect of the evening isn't vague: this woman opposite had the courage to question the lecturer's dogmatic theory. Viv smiles, 'I remember you gave Josh Crispin a hard time.'

'You have got a good memory. He was being far too black and white.' She flicks her hand as if shaking him off. Her Scottish accent betrays a faint hint of eastern Europe, borne out in her broad angular cheek bones.

Viv loves Stockbridge. It's full of intellectual worthies who are committed to keeping their little grey cells alive, and this woman is one of them. Viv discovers that the woman had been a lecturer in Scottish history, and although she's fascinated to hear more of the woman's work she suddenly catches sight of a clock above the counter. 'Oh God, I'll have to go. Nice to meet you again.'

She reaches her car and beams – no parking ticket. Lucky.

Her next client, Jinty Stewart, is an angel, and deserves the fine Georgian building that she lives in. Viv needn't have had coffee because it's always on offer at Jinty's. They've known each other for a decade and love each other's company. Jinty is good-humoured, generous, stylish and has impeccable manners. The notion of spending time on the telephone when she has a guest would be anathema to her. She sees Viv as a guest, that's the difference. The benefit of top-drawer women, which has nothing to do with their birth, is that they treat everyone with respect. Viv has heard her chatting to the gardener as if he's Prince Charles. Jean could learn much from Jinty.

Jinty's hair is much admired and she tells everyone it's her hairdresser's talent. Viv in turn says it's Jinty's wonderful head of hair; and that even a monkey could make it look nice. She's being overly modest, but doesn't know anyone who she'd rather compliment than Jinty – clients like Jinty keep Viv animated about cutting hair. They hug and rub each other's backs as they walk through the hall. The house is like the Ashmolean, full of eccentric bits and pieces, and every time Viv comes there's a fresh feature. Today a new chandelier almost blinds her with its sparkle. It's a monster of a thing, which in anyone else's house would look kitsch, but here it works a treat. Jinty points at it saying, 'We had to have it. You understand, Viv, life in this house is never about need. Coffee's on.'

Viv can always drink more coffee, especially when the maker is an aficionado. Sitting at the kitchen table Jinty fills Viv in on what's been happening in the last three weeks. Rory, her son, has an eating disorder – a nightmare. Viv imagines him creeping around the kitchen with a bucket of Haagen Daz in his arms, but that's not how it works with him; bulimics and anorexics find ways to control their every movement.

'His teeth are much worse. They seem more discoloured every time I look at him. He's becoming like a stick insect. His father is as bad as ever about it. This business about Andrew won't help.' Jinty shakes her head.

Viv, drawing in breath, recalls where she's seen the young face from the TV yesterday. It was here, but not recently. She remembers Andrew and Rors sitting at the kitchen table eating peanut butter sandwiches. Jinty notices her distraction, 'Are you okay?'

'Yeah, yeah. It's just that I'm intrigued about Andrew.'

'We haven't seen him for a long time. What do you think has happened to him?'

'Wish I knew. We are talking about the same Andrew Douglas whose dad, Andrew Douglas senior, once tried to . . .?' Jinty nods, looking embarrassed. So Viv continues. 'But this isn't getting your hair done.'

There's a photograph of Rory on top of the fridge – Viv had forgotten how good looking he used to be. She has heard Ror's history and sympathises with Jinty for having to play piggy in the middle. Rod, her husband, is a judge in more places than the High Court and Jinty has been defending Rors since he was born. Although she knows that you can teach an old dog new tricks, she's lost the will to keep trying.

'Let's head upstairs and get your hair sorted out. At least I can do something to improve that.'

Jinty smiles and pushes herself away from the table. They meander up a wide elegant staircase, lined with an eclectic mix of Scottish landscapes, to a first-floor bedroom. The light is flooding in through a break in the cloud and Jinty pushes one of the shutters closed so that Viv won't have to squint to do her job. Once Jinty's in the chair the atmosphere calms and Viv tells her about a book she's been reading, *The Scots and Slavery in the West Indies*. Jinty says in passing, 'Oh, remind me next time to show you my family slave lists.'

'What! You've actually got the original lists? How old are they?'

'I'm not sure. I haven't looked at them for years.'

Viv puffs out her cheeks, thinking how lucky she is to have such an interesting client. She runs the comb through the back of Jinty's thick fair hair.

Jinty has a natty little bob with a touch of graduation at the back that accentuates her already lovely head shape. She deals with it well herself: no worries about meeting her in the supermarket and being embarrassed. Viv sections it cleanly at the nape and cuts precisely half an inch off the base line before tackling the layers. Their conversation ranges widely and then Viv tentatively says, 'I walked out on Jean this morning.'

'Wow! Good girl! I don't know what's taken you so long. You should have done it a decade ago. She's a social climber who needs her cage rattled. How do you feel, though?'

'Not as good as I thought I would, but good enough.'

She smiles into the mirror; Jinty smiles back at her and says, 'Be proud. She's been pushing the wrong buttons in you for too long. She's only one of the snipers, but at least losing one is better than none. How many to go?'

Jinty is always in Viv's corner; she knows what it has cost Viv to keep her mouth shut so many times.

'Word will get round, in fact I'm amazed you hadn't heard before I arrived.'

'Don't go wasting energy on what people think. They'll think what they choose . . . whether you worry about it or not.' Jinty's gaze in the mirror is serious for a moment.

'Hey, that's my line. Still I anticipate a full answering machine when I get home.'

'I think you'll be surprised. People aren't as stupid as they look. They're perfectly well aware how difficult it is to get a decent haircut this side of London. You are a diamond and they know it. Poor Jean.' She says this last without conviction. Jean's reputation for unmitigated manipulation goes before her. She's managed to bug everyone at some time or another.

When Viv has finished the blow-dry, which has enough product on it to survive a tsunami, she packs up her kit, while Jinty stands with her arms crossed, looking out of the window. Casually she says, 'We're having a few for drinks this weekend. Don't suppose you'd like to come along?'

This is a common invitation from Jinty, who has a social calendar that would put our monarch to shame. Thinking through the logistics of the rest of her week Viv says, 'Can I ring you and let you know? Its just that . . .'

Jinty stops her and says, 'It's okay, Viv, you're allowed to say no.'

'No, it's just that I'm working on something that has taken a twist and I might be caught up.'

'Very cryptic. Ring me.'

With a cheque for fifty quid safely in her pocket, Viv skips down the steps towards her car.

One more call, in Tollcross. It's a top-floor flat, but as long as she convinces herself it's good for her health she takes the steps two at a time, her kit bag knocking against her knee as she goes. Annie is an academic, on sabbatical this year, so Viv's appointments with her have been easier to fit in. In the past Annie's been grumpy about having to rush back after work, or even worse take up her precious Saturday mornings having her hair cut. Viv had hinted that she could get it cut in St Andrews where she works, but that went down like the proverbial lead balloon.

'Hi Annie, how're you doing?'

'Great, thanks. Wish I was permanently on sabbatical. How are you?'

'Good, thanks. Oh God, there I go taking up Americanisms. You weren't asking about my moral welfare. I'm just fine.'

'Viv, I don't know anyone finer. By the way, someone stopped me in the supermarket the other day and asked for the name of the person who cut my hair. I said your list is closed. Is that right? Is it still closed?' Annie cocks her head.

'Yeah, it sure is. There's now a waiting list for the waiting list. Dead client's shoes. How's the book coming along?'

Once Viv has set up in the kitchen, she glances round the room while waiting for Annie to settle on the chair. With the gown safely secured, Viv sprays the short hair with water and combs it back off Annie's face. Not many women can get away with such severity, but elfin cheekbones in her small heart shaped face mean she's one of the few. The kitchen is a museum for Art Deco with original hand painted tiles and a dresser displaying crockery by Suzie Cooper and Clarice Cliff, including some of Shorter's famous fish. Annie and her husband Roy are obsessed by all things thirties and have gadgets for every conceivable use. Annie, remembering Viv's question, says, 'Very nearly there. The Ruskin Foundation want me to talk to them about it, which is a compliment, even if they are a bunch of stuffed shirts.'

'Last time I was here you were working on Ruskin's trip to Scotland. Effie and Millais were being naughty. It sounded as if it wouldn't bode well for Ruskin.'

'God, well remembered, and you're right it didn't. He and Effie, after a great scandal, divorced and she ended up with Millais. Ruskin couldn't consummate the marriage – although I'm not sure who was taking notes under the bed. Revolted by pubic hair apparently. Seen too many statues on his grand tour. Their match was never going to work. If he had been as wise in love as he was with so many other things he'd never have married her. Suppose you can't be good at everything. Ruskin really wanted a prepubescent girl. He'd be called a paedophile today.'

Viv snorts at the absurdity, not in the slightest shocked by the Victorians. 'The usual?'

'Sure. Can I get you anything before we start?'

'No, thanks. I'm already buzzing.'

They've been through a number of 'flavour of the month' cuts and Annie always goes back to her usual, a textured elfin look that's perfect for her delicate Mia Farrow features. When she has strayed from her tried and tested path she's always regretted it. People create warmth in different ways and Annie has always treated Viv as an intellectual equal, which isn't entirely true. They chat about books while Annie's hair takes shape, then it's time to pack up.

Back in the car she doesn't have far to go. Along a tree-lined Melville Drive, up through Buccleuch Street and round Forrest Road before she pulls over onto a yellow line and darts into the post office for a pint of milk. All the while musing on how much she loves learning about the human psyche when she's with her clients. Back out just in time to see a blue meanie coming round the corner. She feels such childish joy at defying the law for two minutes, but the joy evaporates as she circles round the Grassmarket. Mid-afternoon is never a good time to get parked. Then she spots someone's reverse lights halfway down and puts her foot to the floor. What a stroke of luck – it's in a residents' bay. Trotting back up the cobbles she looks up at her building, checking that the sign is still there. It is. She makes a note to take action. Inside, after a long morning of haircuts, she can't wait to get rid of the millions of tiny shards of hair pricking her skin.

As she stands with hot water pumping over her she's glad to get time to revisit the Andrew Douglas story. What was he doing in Copa Cabana? Who was he with? Will his father have changed? What could be underlying his disappearance? She slips into a long tee-shirt, determined to speak to those boys again.

Unable to put her thoughts in order she gets busy on-line. Her bank accounts will have to be juggled, but the purchase of next door looks doable. Writing out a note she slips onto the landing and puts it through Ronnie's letterbox. The sunlight is streaming through the cupola and she's tempted to hover in its warmth. She doesn't. Her sense of modesty wouldn't allow her to get caught on the stair in a state of such undress. Pulling on fresh underwear, old 501s and a black cashmere sweater she plays back her messages.

Jules is irate. ' Viv, ring me asap. There's been a development.'

The next message is from her mother, 'Vivian, I'm expecting you for tea, where are you?'

'Shit! Shit! Shit!' Glancing at the clock, she's never going to make it. Her mother's use of her Sunday name is not a good sign, so the quicker she faces the music the better. It's engaged. 'Damn!' Pressing 'ring back' she heads through to her bedroom and gives her hair a blast with the drier.

When she returns she punches in Jules' number on her mobile. 'Hey Jules, what's up?'

'God, Viv, you're so difficult to get hold of.' Jules' irritation ever present.

'I have checked my messages this morning. When did you ring?'

'Oh, never mind that. There's been a report that Andrew was seen in the petrol station just beyond Dalkeith, apparently with an older man. The woman behind the counter said they were like father and son. The guy I've got on this was ready to believe her. Yeah, sure! Get out there, girl, and do a bit of snooping.'

Viv stifles her own annoyance, not least at being called 'girl'. 'Jules, by now that woman will be making up stories with bells on specially for the press. It'll be a waste of time. I'd be better off following my own trail.' Maybe she could combine dropping in for petrol with her revisiting of the Royal and the Colonies. 'Okay, I'll do it. But I need to do my own stuff first.'

'As long as I get the information you just do as you please, girl.'

Yeah, as if. Viv knows Jules. She is like an itch; irritating and never going anywhere until it's ready to. The concept of letting anyone do as they please is completely alien to her. At the sound of her landline, Viv says goodbye to an already dead tone. Shaking her head she lifts the receiver.

'Hi Mum!'

'Hi, Viv. And to what do I owe this pleasure?'

No notion that she had called Viv in the first place.

'Just wondering how you're doing.'

'I'm fine, hen, just watching John Wayne, so don't let me keep you.'

Viv hears the dead tone for the second time in fewer minutes. Shaking her head again, she mutters, 'God! She's getting dottier and dottier!' She knows that her mum's memory isn't what it used to be, but that was crazy, even by her mum's standards. Her dad once said, 'old age was no place for sissies'. He couldn't have handled being old. She swallows the memory, doubting now that he had gone to heaven. The adolescent Viv had had to believe it. Then, lifting her old leather rucksack, she pats her pockets for keys and mobile then heads out into a wet, miserable night.

Viv decides to go to the hospital first and turns right, retracing her earlier steps through the Grassmarket. The MG hasn't started by the fifth turn of the key. Tonight she really can't be arsed with it playing up. She sits tugging her lightweight jacket round her in an attempt to resist the cold draught the car effortlessly admits. It needed a new roof when she bought it, but she hasn't prioritised doing anything about it. Now it seems a good reason to get rid of it. She is definitely beginning to crave the comfort of a breeze-free vehicle. Sixth try is successful. She still curses, hoping the heater will kick in sometime soon. Although Viv partly believes that discomfort is good for you, she also considers the desire for comfort a sign of middle age. Tonight she cares less about theories and just wants warmth. She doesn't get it in full measure until fifteen minutes later when she walks through the automatic doors of the Royal.

The loiterers inside are a different bunch from her last visit, but their determination to sneak out into the cold wet night for a puff is the same. The smells are also different; as over-sanitised as yesterday, but there must be different veg on the go. The bed that the young guy was in is empty, but there is a fat chap sitting by it. Interesting. She hesitates for a moment, then takes a deep breath and saunters up the ward. Shit! It's the psychologist she saw on the website.

'Hi, how is he?' She attempts to sound more confident than she feels.

'Who's asking?' He is wary, his eyes raking her briefly. West coast accent.

'Well, that's not very nice.'

She puts out her hand for him to shake, which catches him off guard. Automatically he takes it and they shake. It's now more difficult for him to be nasty – she hopes. He nods towards the empty bed. 'He's away for a shower. You the woman who phoned the ambulance?'

'Guilty!'

'He thinks he's getting out tomorrow, but I've got my doubts. Just as well you found him. I'll not ask how that came about.'

As they wait the silence builds. Finally John Black limps down the ward aided by a nurse. She hasn't seen him upright before and he is a pitiful sight: skin and bone, as if he's run out of blood. His deep-set eyes look dead, encased in dark circles. He could hardly look worse.

'You back?'

Viv smiles, amazed at how frequently people state the obvious.

'As you see. How're you doing?'

'As you see.'

'Touché!'

Another awkward silence follows. John finally breaks it.

'Think I'll be out of here tomorrow. If I've got somewhere to go.' He stares at the prison psych, who keeps his eyes down. 'It'd only be for a few days.'

Nothing. Viv notices the hint of a north-east accent.

'Please, Sandy?'

'You know how it is, John. You can't. Don't make things more difficult than they already are. Robbie will go ballistic if he finds out I've been here.'

Viv is fascinated by this revelation. There's obviously a favourite with power over him. Sweat trickles down Sandy's forehead. He reaches into his pocket, draws out a clean cotton handkerchief and blots his brow. Viv can't believe that this apparition has a jealous lover in the wings. Although he's not in uniform he's unmistakably Alexander MacDonald, and the way he wheezes he should be in the bed rather than on the chair beside by it. Viv hardly considers him capable of getting to the end of the ward, never mind getting his end away with young boys. Still, money is a powerful incentive when you've got a habit. John is still looking at him, hopeful of a reprieve, but MacDonald keeps his head down.

Viv interrupts their stand-off, 'John, where do you live?'

He bats away the question. 'What's it to you, and why are you here again? I've already told you Drew can speak for himself.'

At this MacDonald's head snaps up, 'What are you after?'

He looks accusingly at John.

'I've said nothing . . . have I?' A plea to Viv, who says, 'Nothing useful . . . Mr MacDonald, you wouldn't have any information on the whereabouts of Andrew Douglas, would you?'

He's surprised at her use of his name. 'As he said, what's it to you?'

For the first time he looks directly at her. She stares back, noticing his eyes, deep blue pools rimmed with darker blue, almost black, and edged with thick lashes that must have been the envy of many. Perhaps he did have something once, but it's long lost in a face that now looks Jurassic. He blinks first.

Occasionally, a loose truth works, so Viv says, 'I'm a journalist doing a story on young missing people; Andrew is missing.' She raises her eyebrows and tilts her head in a gesture hoping for appeasement. MacDonald starts to get to his feet and supports himself by pressing one incongruously slim, manicured hand on the bed. He doesn't speak. He pushes himself upright, and once he's shuffled past the central nurses' station, he turns and says, 'Leave it. You don't know what you're getting into.'

'Why? What is it that I should leave?' Viv calls after him. He doesn't even turn back; just keeps ambling up the ward.

John lets out a huge sigh. 'Now what?' Turning to face Viv, he shakes his head. 'What the fuck am I going to do?' When he swears it's as if it's unfamiliar; as if he's trying it out for the first time.

'Go home?'

His face contorts as if she's created a bad smell.

'You've no idea – no clue.'

The nurse stops by and reads his chart. She looks at them, knowing that she's interrupted something, but that's not her concern. She takes her time then asks John to get back into bed and get some rest. He complies. It'll be nothing short of a miracle if they let him out tomorrow.

'You're letting him out tomorrow, then?'

The nurse looks at Viv, then at John.

'Not that I know. He's to have an assessment in the morning . . .'

Viv catches John shaking his head, trying to shut the nurse up, but Viv is on a roll now. 'What kind of assessment would that be?'

John speaks up. 'None of your business. Now get lost. You've done enough damage for now.'

This isn't going to plan at all. Viv imagined at the very least finding out about the flat, so tries a different tack. 'Why won't he let you stay at the flat then?'

The nurse clips the board to the back of the bed and with a backward glance takes off down the ward.

'Sandy would let me stay but his crazy boyfriend is a nutter who has taken a dislike to me . . . not just me. He also likes to get his own way. There'd be such a row . . . Sandy's a good guy, but Robbie's bad news. Total bad news.'

'In what way?'

He sighs, 'Did I not tell you to get lost? Just believe me, he's bad news.'

'You could stay at mine.' This is out before she realises what she's said.

He narrows his eyes so that they almost disappear. Then his tone lifts. 'You serious?'

'For a couple of nights till you get sorted. You'd be sofa surfing.'

He looks puzzled.

'On the couch . . .' Her voice tails off as the prospect of sharing her space kicks in.

He notices and says, 'What's the catch?'

'You tell me. You've got nowhere to go and I'm offering you house room – two nights tops, mind.'

Viv fishes around in her jacket pocket and hands him a card with her mobile number on it. 'Here, ring me if they're going to let you out. Have you got any money?'

He looks away. Stupid question. She takes out twenty quid and says, 'This'll get you a taxi to where I live, but ring me first.'

He takes the twenty and mumbles a thank-you, before meeting her eye. 'I don't know anything else.'

'Fine. Ring me.'

She smiles as she walks back towards her car. This isn't the kind of thing she would do normally. In fact she hasn't had anyone to stay since Dawn left over two years ago. What's life for if you don't take the odd risk?

Chapter Five

The drive out to the petrol station seems like a waste of time but at least it will keep Jules happy. Besides, she's getting low on fuel and it'll give her time to think. Viv is surprised at how decrepit MacDonald is. He hasn't been good to himself and looks as far from her image of a psychologist as she can imagine. The gay world is more unkind to the ugly than the heterosexual, and she can't get her head round him being gay or having a wife for that matter. He strikes her as way beyond his sexual sell-by date. She justifies her ageism by saying out loud, 'Well, I'm just being honest.' As if this makes it okay.

The road is quiet at this time of night and the petrol station is deserted. As she gets out of the car she shuts the door, which makes a clunking sound it shouldn't. The seatbelt's caught in the door. As she bends to put it back inside a shadow falls over her. She looks up. There stands one of those guys you see on American TV who can lift a truck with his pinkie – tattoos, hairy hands and a five o'clock shadow that isn't designer stubble. The fact that he can move without sound is pretty scary. She almost smiles, but thinks better of it.

He growls, 'You all right, lady?'

'Yes, thank you.' She bristles slightly at his use of 'lady'.

He doesn't move, and when she tries to lift the petrol hose he puts his hand on her shoulder. 'You're not about to ask any questions in there, are you?' He nods toward the automatic doors.

'No, just in for petrol.' Her petulance rising.

'Be sure about that.'

Unambiguous. Viv fills the MG and saunters across the forecourt to pay. The woman behind the counter doesn't meet her eye, but looks beyond her through the window to Bluebeard, standing beside Viv's car with his arms folded. Viv, alarmed but also pissed off, thinks, how the hell did he know? Do I look that much like a journo? Just wait till I get my hands on Jules.

As she gets back into the car he stares, but doesn't say anything more. She drives off frustrated as he stands watching her. She pulls in at the first lay-by she can find. Her heart pounding, she takes a few deep breaths, and punches in Jules' number.

'Jules! You any idea what the fuck is going on here? I've just left the petrol station out by Dalkeith, and some bruiser gave me a warning.'

'The police?' Jules sounds unperturbed.

'No, not the police. This guy had more muscle in one pec than the whole force. I'd say he's his own personal Mafia. Asked if I was planning to ask questions.'

'What did you say?' Still perfectly calm.

'What d'you think I said? . . . I said no. There's a lot more going on than Andrew Douglas going missing. What is it?'

Jules doesn't address the question and instead says, ' Fancy coming into the office before noon tomorrow?'

'*No.* I haven't found him yet and I'm picking up some very unsavoury vibes from people who know him. I'm on my way back to the pub where his pals hang out. I'll check in later.'

Viv throws her phone onto the passenger seat and starts when it rings as soon as it bounces against the leather. She grabs it in one hand and with the other nudges the lever on the heater. She screws up her eyes at the phone display, the light too poor to make out the caller's number, but answers it anyway. She is surprised at the voice on the other end. It's the factor of her flat.

'Hello! Oh, hello. It's a bit late for you, isn't it?' She doesn't mean to sound rude, but worries that it does.

'I know it's short notice, Ms Fraser, but I was wondering if there was any chance that Dr Chapman could take a look round the flat. We think it's time for some up-grading.' Viv sighs with relief at his affable tone.

'Well not tonight, obviously, but it may be possible tomorrow. Yeah, yeah. Okay. I'll ring you tomorrow. Bye.'

She cuts the line and looks at the phone. Curious. Why would her landlady want to pay a visit to the flat now? Viv rents her flat fully furnished and has always been intrigued about its owner. Looks as if she's going to find out something now.

Trying to focus on what's next she slips the MG into gear and heads towards Copa Cabana. It isn't as busy as last night, but Viv still has to use a bit of elbow to get through to the bar. The barman tonight is more self-assured than the previous guy. He moves as if he's on a commercial: his jeans hang off his backside, his Jacob's ladder is exposed above the waistband of his Calvin Klein's. He has topped all this off with a black tee shirt at least one size too small, which does a grand job showing the muscle definition on his torso.

This Adonis shouts above the music, 'What can I get you, ma'am?'

His mid-atlantic accent has spent the odd year on Sauchiehall Street, but he's cheerful with a smile that reaches his eyes and lights up his pretty face.

'Cider, organic if you've got it.'

He raises his one eyebrow and grins. 'Good choice. Anything else?'

'You seen Andrew Douglas recently?'

'No idea.'

He gestures at the crowd. 'They could all be Andrew Douglas. How would I know?'

Polished.

'Well, he's young, good looking and missing!'

'You don't look like a cop.'

'Thank you, I'll take that as a compliment. I'm not.' Viv grins encouragingly.

'Others are asking the same question. He must be wealthy!'

He places her drink in front of her and takes the offered tenner.

Viv nods, 'Put one in the till.'

'Thanks, I'll do that.' His charm is flawless.

To avoid any more jostling she makes her way to the nearest free wall and looks back into the crowd. No sign of the young Hibernian supporters. She spots Liam's back and in a move that's becoming familiar she slides down in case he catches sight of her. The last thing she's up for is a conversation with the Devil.

'You trying to avoid someone?'

Speaking of the Devil, Red emerges from the throng. Viv looks her up and down. She's wearing the same kit as yesterday.

'Nice uniform . . . You live here?'

Red is unfazed. 'Could accuse you of the same thing. Now what say you we pool resources?'

'I don't think so. It's not good to mix motivation. I have a job to do and so do you, but they're very different.' Viv doesn't want to have this conversation, at least not right now.

'There are parallels, though.' Red perseveres. 'We are both looking for Andrew and

. . .'

'And what?'

During this conversation Viv spots Pete. They make eye contact and he nods toward the corridor where the loos are.

'Sorry – have to go.' She places her glass on a sill and leaving Red bemused heads to the loo. Viv's forgotten just how grotty pubs make her feel – even without the smoke. Once she's washed her hands, she presses the button on the hand drier. Dead. Unable to see a paper towel, she pushes her hands up beneath the drier again. Nothing. Water runs down her wrists and under the cuffs of her jacket.

Wondering if the men's loos are as bad, she turns into the corridor rubbing her hands on her jeans, and catches sight of Pete coming out of the men's doing the same thing. She's reassured that some men do wash their hands and says, 'No drier!'

He shakes his head. 'I had a text from him.'

They lean against opposite walls of a narrow corridor, with men squeezing past to visit the loo. It isn't the ideal venue for this conversation but Viv isn't sure what to suggest. 'Where is he? Is he okay?'

'Hold your horses. He didn't say where he was. He needs money . . . too much for me to get hold of.' They both fall silent as a couple of blokes in high spirits look in mock suspicion from Viv to her accomplice, then giggle their way to the gents.

'How much and did he say what for?'

'Five hundred. And no he didn't.' His harsh whisper is irritating but Viv knows she'll have to bide her time.

'Why would he ask you for that kind of money? I mean, do you have access to that amount of dosh or is he supposing that you'll raise it . . . How well do you know him anyway?' She looks at his tight white sports top. Its logo isn't one that she recognises but it no doubt sends the right message to those who do. His jeans hang off his taut athletic butt and he, like the barman, makes no attempt to pull them up.

'He knows that I'll do whatever he asks.' He sighs. Resigned.

'Why's that?'

'Why do you think?'

He looks at his feet and she thinks that his trendy trainers are an unlikely source of answers.

'Were you and him . . .?' She doesn't finish her sentence as the two blokes return from the gents.

'I wish. We've been through school together. Pals. Only ever pals.'

She hears disappointment in the 'only'.

Here definitely isn't the place to have this conversation and she says, 'You hungry?'

'Not much.' But realising the question isn't about food he adds, 'I'm happy to watch.'

'Okay,' she says, 'lead on.'

On the way to the door she senses Red's eyes on her back and turns. Viv taps the side of her nose – nothing if not competitive.

The east wind howling up Leith Walk cuts through her as she steps onto the street. Pointing to the trattoria opposite she says, 'That do?'

'Sure.'

He's not going to be good company, but it's not company she's after.

Once she's ordered and the garlic bread arrives his hunger catches up with him, so she hails another waiter and doubles the order.

'Was it from his own mobile number?'

'Yep, I think so. I didn't check.'

He slips his mobile out and scrolls through until he finds the message.

'No actually, I don't recognise these last three digits. Maybe it's the guy . . .' He stops.

Viv sighs, 'Look, we don't know each other from Adam, but we both want the same thing – the safe recovery of Andrew Douglas. Would you let me have that number? I may have a way of tracing the last call. It's not very accurate but it could tell us if he's still in the country.'

He looks shocked at the notion that Andrew could be abroad. The order appears, piping hot lasagne, and they are silenced for a few minutes while they blow and stuff it in.

This young man has got the love bug real bad. If Viv pushes the right buttons he'll give her the number. She says, 'We'll just have to hope that nothing horrible has happened to him.'

The colour, as she anticipated, drains from his face.

'You really think he's in danger?' He hesitates, then slips his phone out again. 'D'you have a pen?'

She roots around in her rucksack then hands him a pen and a card. 'Here.'

This middle-class boy has the features of a tearaway but is too well brought up to carry it off. He writes the number out and slides it across to her. But before tucking it away she says, 'Better give me yours as well.'

'No, I'll ring you.'

She sighs, 'It was only to keep you posted.'

Conceding again he recites his number and she jots it down.

Back in the flat it's cold. She's forgotten to close the bedroom window and all of the doors. Rushing from room to room she switches up panel heaters and draws the curtains. She changes into comfort kit, and boots up. Then, throwing a teabag into a mug she grabs what's left of a packet of chocolate digestives, staple food for an all-nighter.

Before making a start on her notes she glances through her emails. There's one from the factor offering a time for Dr S. Chapman to come and look round the flat at nine a.m. the following morning. Damn nuisance at the moment. Her first hair client tomorrow isn't until ten thirty and she'd imagined a long lie. She fires a quick email back, knowing he won't pick it up until morning, saying 'not convenient' and requests a time shortly after noon instead. The luxuries that email affords.

She goes over the events since Jules first rang her. Typically, Jules mentioned something about 'the gay underworld'. The type of comment only an outsider would make. For insiders it's simply their world. She recalls the detail of the first pub: the poor chap with the ill-fitting dentures, the tinted mirrors, the worn carpets – an old-style gay bar whose clientele reflected its origins, in an era when desires had to be hidden. The next bar was also a reflection of its clientele: most of them out and proud. With lighting too bright to be forgiving or discreet and big windows onto the street it's a fish bowl with nowhere to hide. Not to ignore the deafening music blasting from surround sound. Hardly ideal for those in the closet.

Viv shudders, unable to visualise Sandy MacDonald in this postmodern aquarium. The first bar, on the other hand, is right up his street. Fear of being outed is still a big deal. But where are the other deals done? She tries to walk in the moccasins of a dealer. Are the toilets a good enough place to pass on your wares? Probably. Dealing can be done anywhere there's money. If she's right, this is about drugs and not sex, but even as this goes through her head, she reminds herself that it needn't be either/or. The two are bedfellows. There's something tugging at the edges of her mind, but it's not willing to emerge yet. Red's presence is significant. She wouldn't be planted in a gay bar as often as she is unless it was worth Lothian and Borders resources. Yep. Must be drugs.

Her mobile rings and she jumps. She looks at the time on her laptop. Too late for a social call.

'Hello?'

No response. Only the sound of a car engine idling.

'Hello?'

She listens intently for anything she might recognise; there isn't much to go on. Whoever they are they hang up. She checks the number. Not one she knows, but mobile numbers have so many digits that she's become lazy and now only files the last three digits as an aide-memoire. Crossing her arms over her chest she rubs her hands up and down her arms. She shivers. Then pushes down the switch on the kettle and picks up a biscuit. Was that a real warning from Sandy? 'Leave it. You don't know what you're getting into.' What did he mean? If this is as big as he implied, how big is big?

Viv reads over the few notes that she's produced. It's not much to go on. Too much speculation. The only fact she's got is that Andrew is still AWOL. Remembering that she has the number Pete gave her she punches in the digits but is only invited to leave a message on a generic voicemail. She doesn't, since it's late. Time for teeth and bed.

Was it a dream or light edging through the gap where her curtains don't quite meet that woke her? She glances at the clock. Too early. She pulls the duvet over her head. Sleep doesn't come . . . too many visions of dry ice, disco dancers and Man Mountain standing over her with his arms folded, looking like a hostile Aladdin's genie. She doesn't feel that frightened, more exhilarated. She loves the thrill of the chase but what's not to like about poking around the human psyche?

Viv creeps out of bed and pulls back the curtains. Thursday. The earlier light has been exchanged for a grey, drizzly day. She pulls the duvet off the bed and wraps herself in it then pads clumsily through to the living room and boots up. While the computer gets going she drags the duvet behind her to the kitchen to fill the kettle. The thought of unwrapping herself and diving into the shower doesn't yet appeal.

Then she spots the piece of paper on the floor at the end of the hall. She has a letterbox, but no one delivers up here. Not if they can leave things in a pigeon hole on the ground floor. The postie must have gone to his union about how many stairs he has to climb in the West Bow. It's unusual to have something delivered. Perhaps it's a response from Ronnie. It's a folded sheet of standard A4; no envelope.

'BACK OFF PRINCESS!' In black felt tip pen.

So, not from Ronnie then! Viv isn't a woman of faint heart, but the hairs on the back of her neck lightly bristle. Whoever doesn't want her meddling knows exactly where to find her. How come? John Black has her mobile number but doesn't know where she lives. Man Mountain seemed to know who he was looking for when she turned up at the petrol station. Someone tailing her? Or mobile communication? Who could have alerted him?

She braves the shower and afterwards feels more able to focus on what to do next. Knowing that she'll have to face the music with Jules she decides it's better to get it over with. She lifts the phone.

'Hey Jules, no can do on the noon deadline.' Jules attempts to interrupt this speech, but Viv won't let her. 'I've got nothing to say that you haven't already heard. One thing though is whatever we're onto has caused someone to drop me a line.'

'What sort of line?'

'Certainly not the kind that you'd take kindly. A note through my door saying, 'Back off Princess', in capital letters. Nice to be regarded so royally. I have to figure out what my next step is, but I've got hair this morning and a meeting after that.'

'Okay, okay! . . . What kind of meeting?'

Viv sighs, 'I do have a life that doesn't belong to you. But if you must know it's with my landlady. Speak later.' She sighs again, but can't quite believe she got off so lightly.

Today's hair is in the penthouse office of a finance company – Morgan Clifford. Not just anyone's finance, but HRH the Queen's. Their offices have views across the north of the city but getting to see them is quite something: first there is negotiating a space in their underground car park, then the concierge, and finally two bolshie receptionists, one of whom thinks she's protecting the actual Crown Jewels. Once Viv is through each of these defences she sets up her mobile salon in a position where her client, Maxwell

Scott, can take full advantage of the view. He's a nice man, well read, polite, professional and willing to delegate power; a sure sign that he actually has power. He's a regular, a once a month man, so it's only a maintenance job. As Viv runs a clipper over the back of his neck the telephone rings so she switches off the machine. He lets it ring and says, 'It won't be as urgent as this trim. Carry on. Reception can field it.'

She carries on and they chat about whether the ISA is all that it's cracked up to be or whether Viv should put money into a slightly higher risk venture. Not that she's got lots of disposable, but what she does have she likes to work for her. Maxwell's chats have proved fruitful in the past so she always takes note whenever he comments on what's going up or down in the market. Their idle chat turns to family matters.

'How's Sonia?'

'Oh, fine. Spending lots, so she's fine.'

'You didn't imagine that she'd be low maintenance, did you?'

Sonia, his second wife, is known around town as the 'dose of salts'. If he's aware of this he's never said. Her previous husband died people say, of poverty, emotional poverty.

Max sighs and says, 'Off to China in the morning.'

'For how long?'

'Three days.'

Viv holds the clipper away. 'Wow! All that way for three days? I daren't ask what that'll cost.'

'The cost of not going would be so much more.' He changes the subject. 'Viv, have you ever thought of doing something better? I can't be the only client who's tickled at having a blue stocking to cut my hair.'

'Don't you worry about the colour of my stockings and finish your sentence. Better for whom? And who else would listen to your grumbles *and* cut your hair?'

'Oh, I didn't mean you could give me up.' He laughs.

'Besides,' continues Viv, 'I do use my brain. In ways that you don't know about.'

'Curious. What would make you spill the beans?'

'Nothing that you could give me.'

They laugh at the double entendre. Viv has seen him through a divorce, his two children married off and the birth of his first grandchild. They know each other pretty well. But however well people think they know one another there are always gaps. Some gaps bigger than others.

As Viv leaves his office the pretty blonde receptionist looks at her as if she'd like to kill her. She must have heard them laughing and has never quite managed to get the hang of Viv's relationship with her boss. What little conversation Viv has had with the woman has shown that she's the kind of person who can't allow someone to be more than one thing. Hairdressers are supposed to be thick and blonde. Viv defies both categories, which leaves those of shallow mentality confused and resentful. Tough! Viv smiles and flashes her security card against the laser, or whatever the funny blue light is that reads the card, before she walks out to the lift. The security in this building has been much tighter since the Twin Towers, but here she's a known face and no one gives her a second glance. The novelty of the boss's hairdresser coming in once a month has long since worn off.

The lift doors open and she steps out into the flickering lights of the car park. Someone must have activated them. Viv walks purposefully back to her car, but feels uneasy. She slows and glances round. Nobody about. Her own footsteps echo around her as she passes car upon car. She mumbles to herself, 'You're having a moment, girl.'

She steps round to the back of the MG to store her kit but gets a whiff of petrol, too much even for her old banger. Then she notices the flames licking the side of the car. Black smoke starts billowing up. 'Shit!' She runs, then dives to the ground. The place is filling with smoke. She hears the rev of an engine and the squeal of rubber and suddenly wide-eyed watches a car heading towards her at full pelt. She rolls and it narrowly misses her before disappearing into the smoke and screeching towards the exit. Viv leaps up but can't see anything. She hears the crash of the barrier as the car bursts through it. In that same moment the wail of the smoke alarm splits the air. And there's an almighty explosion as the petrol in her MG ignites. The blast flings her to the ground and she's showered by shards of glass and bits of metal. A voice reaches her out of the din yelling, 'Stay down!' And before she knows what's happening there's someone kneeling on her back and hauling her hands behind her, as handcuffs are clicked onto her wrists. Her captor pulls her to her feet. Her eyes are stinging and she coughs roughly as she inhales the smoke. She tries to shrug off her keeper, but he's gripping her arm and marching her towards the building. It's pandemonium. The police Special Unit have arrived and there are people in uniform running all over the place. She half-turns and catches sight of a firefighter in full gear pounding the remains of the MG with foam. The man yanks her arm again.

'Shit! Will you back off?'

This is all too Hollywood for Viv. The pain in her ears competes with the pain of this moron gripping her arm and she can't think straight. He keeps pushing her and she screeches, 'What the hell are you doing?'

'We'll ask the questions.'

A man in security gear joins them and says, 'Who are you?'

'A friend of Maxwell Scott's.'

The two of them look at each other and one of them speaks into his radio. Then, 'You'll have to come with us.'

'You're not giving me much option are you? Shouldn't you be more worried about that maniac in the car?'

'We're onto him.'

She has her doubts, but stumbles between him and his buddy, back into the building, leaving behind a throng of uniforms and blue lights. They climb the stairs to the first floor where Max is just coming through a secure door.

'Viv! For God's sake! Are you okay?' He spots the cuffs. 'Take those things off her, she's not a criminal.'

Relieved of bonds and captors, she rubs her wrists and shakes glass from her hair. Adrenaline courses through her and she hops from foot to foot as if she's just finished a run.

'Max. I've no idea . . .' She feels a lump rising in her throat and swallows it back. 'I'll tell you everything I saw.'

'Let's get you a cup of tea and a seat then we'll go over it.'

Slumped on a chair, she buries her head in her hands. Then she lifts her head. She's surprised to hear the voice of DI Marcus Marconi, one of a few police officers that Viv respects and who now heads up the National Task Force. They've met a couple of times, most recently at a conference on knife crime in Scotland. Their conversation that day established that they might, on occasion, be useful to each other. What is Marconi doing here? He looks equally surprised.

'Hi, Viv. I didn't expect to see you here.'

'You and me both.'

Viv turns to look at Max while Marconi introduces himself and his PC. Not sure who to defer to she directs her answers to Max, although he is no longer asking the questions. If she thought this would be over in a few minutes she was mistaken. A security breach and a 'car exploding' is a big deal in most people's books, but the location for this crime has caused huge complications. By the time Marconi has covered all bases and is convinced that she's not a suspect, she's knackered and begs to go home.

Chapter Six

She'll never have to worry again about the MG not starting. What remains of it will spend the next few months in police custody with a forensic team crawling all over it. Max brought her home, giving her an awkward hug before she climbed, without her usual bounce, upstairs. Hugs are never easy for Viv, but when she's distressed it's even worse. She had choked back another lump and assured him she'd be fine.

Locking her door she leans against it trying to make sense of her morning. She heads into the bedroom where she strips everything off. Tiny slivers of glass fall onto the rug. She kneels to gather them up while silent tears trickle down her face.

With the shower on full pulse, and the heat almost too much to bear, she allows the water to beat the tension out of her head. Is this what Sandy had in mind when he warned her off? Or is it a coincidence? How did they get into the car park? They must have followed her from home and sneaked in. So much for post-9/11 super security. An insider? This idea takes a stretch even with Viv's imagination. How could someone tail her without her noticing?

With the taste of shampoo in her mouth she throws her head back for a final rinse. She's not paid enough to put up with this sort of crap and she steps out of the shower intending to give Jules an earful. The sound of the door buzzer is the only thing between her and telling Jules to stuff it. She presses the button on the intercom.

'Hello?'

'Oh hello. It's Sal Chapman here.'

Viv can't think if she knows anyone by that name.

'And?'

'I've come to look round the flat . . . Is this a bad time?'

'Shit!' The penny drops. It's her landlady. 'No. No, it's fine. I'd forgotten the time. Just come up.'

Viv races back to her bedroom and throws on a tee shirt and jeans, quickly rubbing her hair with a towel. Too soon she hears a gentle knock and after a tussle with the locks swings back the door.

'Hi! Come in.'

Viv sticks her hand out to shake, and looks down into the most amazing green eyes. The woman returns her grip and beams up at her. Feeling her colour rising, Viv points to the sitting room.

'I expect you know your way round. There's not much to see.'

'I don't actually. I've never been here before. Too painful!'

Viv has never met this woman nor does she know her circumstances and, wondering what might have happened to her, she scuttles round rearranging things, tidying, pushing clothes into the laundry basket as if she's entertaining her headmistress. Her visitor notices and smiles, as if she would do the same.

'I'm sorry to put you out, but I think it's time I did some renovations. The place could do with central heating for starters, and if I remember correctly the oven's been dodgy for a while.'

'It doesn't worry me. I don't cook much. I had a relationship with the microwave, but that didn't last.' Viv notices the nervousness in her voice as well.

'Me neither. Jamie the factor is trying to keep me right. The place looks nice.'

It's Viv's turn to smile. She has done very little to the flat and most of the furniture was here when she came. She hasn't even given it a lick of paint. Pointing towards a Chesterfield with a brocade throw over it she says, 'Tea?'

'That'd be lovely. Thanks, but don't . . .'

'I'd love one myself. I'll put the kettle on.'

As she walks out to the kitchen she can't imagine why she's suggested tea, but it's too late now and pushing the button on the kettle, shouts, 'I've only got chocolate digestives.'

'Great. They've seen me through many a long night.'

This catches Viv's interest, and she wonders what kind of Doctor she is. 'Are you hospital based?'

'No, not a real Doctor at all. Only a PhD.'

'What do you mean "only"? I think a PhD is the real thing.'

Viv puts a tray on the ottoman in front of the couch. 'Take a look round while this brews.'

It's Sal Chapman's turn to look embarrassed. She says, 'You could show me.'

Viv gets up from her knees and shows her the bedroom. It's small with a deep recessed window. Like in the rest of the flat the curtains of dark red velvet are slightly shabby, but obviously good quality. The bed, an old Scottish double with turn of the century wooden bed ends, has white linen and a tartan throw folded at the bottom. Viv spots a stray sock peeking out from beneath the bed and edges it under with her toe. There are only four rooms, all in a row off the same corridor, so the rest of the tour doesn't take long. The tiny bathroom is entirely steamed up and still smells of eucalyptus.

'Probably needs a new extractor fan.' Sal sounds apologetic.

'No, the current one was disconnected.'

'Why? I'll have it fixed . . .'

'No. I couldn't stand the racket. I disconnected it myself.'

Sal looks mildly impressed. Viv considers her lie – she'd disconnected it because her former partner couldn't stand it. Viv revisits spaces where Dawn's possessions were in the flat. They'd never lived together. So there weren't many of her things, and strangely it's because there were so few that their absence is more obvious. Dawn's toothbrush had always looked lonely in a glass, Viv's electric one standing to attention beside it but without contact. It was a reflection of their relationship. If only Viv had realised. Aware of a voice, Viv shakes her head into the present.

'Oh. That's fine.'

Viv can't remember what they were talking about. Silently they return to the sitting room. Pouring tea into huge china cups and saucers with lilies of the valley painted on them, Viv is regretful that she offered it in the first place. As they sip in silence she notices that the wooden sculpture, cunningly placed over an iron burn on the carpet, has moved a bit, exposing a charred curve; she edges her foot towards it but catches her landlady watching. The morning is definitely catching up with her. Sensing her time is up, Sal says, 'I'm sorry to take up your time,' and gets up to leave. Viv jumps up too quickly and catches the edge of the tray, spilling the milk. She shakes her head and sighs, 'I've had a bad day.'

'Then I'm doubly sorry. Thanks for the tea.'

'No trouble. Nice to meet you Dr Chapman.'

'Sal. The name's Sal.'

Sal follows Viv down the narrow hallway. Then in a gesture as intimate as Viv can handle, Sal gently places her hand on the small of Viv's back. It takes all of Viv's concentration not to snake her body out of reach. Then they return to formality with a handshake, both avoiding eye contact.

Viv leaves the tea cups in the sitting room. She opens her laptop. As it's coming to life she rings Jules. Viv fills her in on what happened at Morgan Clifford's, surprised the news hadn't already reached her. Jules, a mistress of understatement, when it suits her, says, 'Viv, I think we should be cautious with this, it's a wee bit meaty.'

Unsure how much more meaty she wants life to become, Viv makes a non-committal sound. Morgan Clifford's must have friends in the right places for this not to have reached the wire by now. They won't want to be the centre of attention because of what will be interpreted as a terrorist strike. She lets Jules rattle on then gives her what she knows about Andrew Douglas. As she says goodbye she tries to imagine what could connect Andrew to the blast this morning.

Who are these guys that are willing to take the risk of blowing up a car? Although any idiot can set fire to a petrol tank. It was only a warning. Some warning! Maybe they're not local and don't have any knowledge of the prestige of Morgan Clifford. Or perhaps that's the point. Too much speculation. From what appeared to be a missing person investigation this is getting out of hand. If Andrew's involved in this kind of stuff who knows where it will land him.

The landline rings and she hesitates, recalling last night's silence. The answering machine kicks in and the voice leaving a message is familiar from earlier in the day.

'Hi, it's Marcus here. Could you give me a ring as soon as. Thanks.'

Viv takes out the card he gave her this morning. It's like her own business card – no detail beyond a name and number.

He answers immediately. 'Dr Fraser. Thanks for ringing back. Any chance you could get yourself down here? We need your help.'

She is taken off guard by his formality. 'I don't think there's anything more I can say.'

'You don't sound sure about that. I'll send a car for you.'

She thinks for a moment. 'Okay, give me ten minutes.' But spending the next few hours in Fettes isn't part of her game plan. She punches in Pete's number and bites at a ragged nail while waiting for an answer – she hates bitten nails and does her best to tidy it without taking it down to the quick. Eventually a nervous voice speaks. 'Hi.'

'Hi. It's Viv Fraser.'

'Thank God. Have you heard? They've found him. He's dead.'

'What?' She's silent. Then, '. . . Are you sure?'

'Well . . . that's what I was told.' His voice begins to crack.

'Who told you?'

'Thomas.' He sniffs.

'And how did Thomas know?'

'I don't know . . . I overheard.'

There's traffic in the background. Then, as if he's stepped into a doorway, all goes quiet. 'Where were you at the time?'

'Moonshine Café. We go there after schoo . . .'

'I'm not the police, and I'm not interested whether you're legal or not. I'm only interested in Andrew.'

She can hear him sniffling at the end of the line. Crying? The beeping noise of a pedestrian crossing and a change in his breathing indicate he's on the move.

'Where are you now?'

He manages, 'I'm on my way home.'

'Will you be all right?' She hears him sob. 'Well, I'll ring you later once I've done a bit of searching.'

She cuts the call and rings John Black. It goes straight to answering service. If he was getting out she should have heard from him by now. Glancing at the clock she decides she could make it to the Royal in twenty minutes, before visiting's over. Marconi's questions will have to wait.

At the Royal, as she's paying the taxi-driver, she spots Sandy getting into a car with a younger man. They look as if they're arguing, but she's too far away to hear. The young man slams his door. Not happy.

John Black looks worse than he did before. He doesn't even turn when she sits on the edge of the bed. Unable to work out if he's asleep she peers at the chart behind the bed. No use pretending she knows what any of it means. She stands and makes her way to the nurses' station. The same nurse as last time is on duty, but is busy with a patient on the other side of the ward. Viv stands around, knowing that no amount of trying to catch her eye will work. Eventually, having completed her task, the nurse saunters over and looks at her.

'It's John Black, isn't it? His visitors seem to think this is a hotel. You know I can't tell you anything unless you're family. Are you family?'

'Yes. Cousin.'

'Yeah and I'm the Virgin Mary!'

Her Irish accent gets stronger as she continues, 'He's not well enough to go anywhere. Had a blood transfusion today. We're hopeful that'll make him pick up.'

'Did you speak to his earlier visitors?'

'No, why? . . . I heard them arguing. Not John, he's too weak, but the other two. It's a bad mix.'

Viv isn't sure what she's talking about.

'D'you mean the couple?'

'No,' corrected the nurse, staring at Viv, who understands she needs to make a more educated guess.

'Drugs?' The nurse's solid frame looks as if it could withstand anything, but her watery eyes tell a different story.

'That's it. He's not the only one we've had. It's a really bad mix. I hope to God the police get to it before it does any more damage.'

'What is it? Cocaine and . . .?'

'We don't know yet. Of course the Hippocratic Oath isn't very addict friendly if you get my meaning. Doctors think they've got better things to do with their time than rescue "idiots",' she jabs the air with the quote marks, 'who take risks like these guys do.' She shakes her head, drawing in a breath, and, none too discreetly, looks at the ward clock.

'Do I get the impression that you don't agree with the Doctors?'

'I've a young brother with a problem. I see it from the other side.'

'The guys that were in earlier . . . did you hear what they were actually talking about?'

'The older fella was trying to keep the young one from being nasty to John. The young one kept saying, "It's your own fault. Nobody made you take it." The old guy told him to back off, but he wouldn't. John has barely the strength to eat or pee let alone argue. In the end I said they'd have to leave as it was time for his bath. I could still hear them at it at the end of the ward. I'm not one to make judgments, but that young one isn't destined to dine with St Peter. You won't have to worry about John dossing on your couch for a while. He really isn't a well boy. It was nice of you to offer though.' She turns away from Viv and steps back inside the low gate of the central nurses' station.

'What? He's not going to make it?'

'Stranger things have happened here. We'll see after the transfusion. I wish we could find his family, but he gives us nothing but grief. We know he's probably from Aberdeen – his accent's a bit of a giveaway – and he's also had unusual surgery. A plate in his head after a car accident, carried out at Aberdeen Royal. If you happen to find out about his family, it would be good to let them know where he is. I'd hate to think of them, you know, hearing the worst when it's too late.'

Viv, looking back down the ward to John Black, can't believe he could die. When she found him in the flat she thought he might be really sick, but the last time she saw him she thought he'd made progress.

The nurse is busy again with another patient, chivvying him with another type of crack. Viv admires nurses' commitment, when they're looking death in the face everyday. She couldn't do it, that's for sure. Deciding she'd like to sit with John for a few minutes she returns to his bed. He stirs, but even though his eyes are open they don't seem to register her.

'Hey. How're you doing?' She doesn't expect an answer and isn't disappointed when she doesn't receive one. He looks desperate. His eyes have sunk into black dents in his head, and his cheekbones, already prominent, appear to be skinless. How can this have happened in such a short time? Viv's bedside manner leaves a lot to be desired, but words aren't necessary at the moment. His lips are dry and his attempt to lick them is futile. She looks around for a jug of water and not seeing one goes back to the nurse.

'I'm looking for a jug.'

'The Doc's due back anytime.'

This is apropos of nothing that Viv knows about, so she takes the proffered jug and turns to fill it with water.

'It's okay for me to wet his lips? He's really dry.'

'Go ahead. It'll not do him any harm.'

Once back at the bed, she pours a glass and then tilts his head, slipping some water onto his lips then lowering him back onto the pillow. This role is unfamiliar to her. She can't even do this sort of thing for her mum. Sitting in silence she watches the shallow movement of his chest. Each rise looks as if it could be the last. He whispers.

'Robbie.'

She thinks he said 'Robbie', but can't be sure. 'Robbie, Sandy's friend?'

He nods.

She pushes. 'What about him?'

His eyes and shaking head indicate his frustration.

'Is he a dealer?'

He nods.

'And he's bad news?'

He nods again. When he closes his eyes she squeezes his hand and leaves. She prays he won't die.

At the front door she gathers her jacket around her, fending off more of that biting east wind. There isn't a taxi in sight so she steps back inside. No point in chittering outside when she can see the taxi rank from here. What to do now? Robbie seems to have made enemies with some of the young guys who use the Colonies flat . . . or should she say, have been used at the flat? Her skin crawls at the idea that Sandy is encouraging young boys to take drugs so he can have his kicks. How did he come to be with Robbie? She tries to think how they might have met and what the attraction was, but her imagination fails. Drugs, it has to be drugs. Sandy's job affords him ample opportunity to meet every kind of criminal. That must be it.

Waiting, Viv checks her messages and sure enough there's one from Marconi asking where the hell she is. She presses Reply: 'Hey! It's Viv Fraser.'

'I know who it is. Where the hell are you? We need you here right now.'

As he's speaking she spots a taxi – lucky or what? – and says, 'I'm on my way. I'll be with you in twenty minutes.'

'Don't make any detours.'

Dead tone. She says to the driver: 'Police HQ.'

Fettes' architect must have graduated summa cum Lego. A more functional, ugly building you'd be hard pushed to find. Its closest neighbour, Fettes College, built in the French Scottish style, is one of David Bryce's, and Edinburgh's, architectural gems. As she approaches the reception desk she does a double take. Sal Chapman slips through a door to her left, wearing what looks like an official card round her neck. What on earth is she doing here? Viv gives her name to the officer behind the desk and pointing to the door, asks: 'Where does that go?'

The officer looks at her warily and says: 'This way.'

She trots to keep pace as he marches up a flight of stairs and into a conference room. At least she's not in an interview room. When she enters, the three men present stop speaking and Marconi pulls out a chair, gesturing for her to take a seat. He sits at her side, but doesn't introduce her to the two other officers, who remain standing. With more than a hint of irony he says: 'Glad you could make it, Dr Fraser.'

'Glad to be of service, Detective Marconi.'

He shoots her a warning look. 'We need to gather more information about the explosion. Now . . . we understand that you were in the Morgan Clifford building for the purpose of cutting hair, is that correct? And here was I thinking you were some kind of columnist.'

His tone is patronising and her hackles rise.

He continues. 'Why do I find it difficult to believe that you were only cutting hair?'

She shakes her head. 'Because you've got a stereotypical view of hairdressers.'

'Convince me that I'm wrong.' His tone is sharp.

'As you see. I am a hairdresser who happens to dabble in a bit of story telling.'

'And the PhD, is that in hairdressing?'

She smiles. 'No, actually, anthropology.'

It's his turn to shake his head.

Viv continues, 'I know it's hard to believe, but trust me, I'm a Doctor – although not the sort who asks you to go behind a screen and take your kit off . . . Well, not unless the circumstances are very special.'

He clears his throat. 'Okay, tell us again everything that happened when you went into the building. Every possible detail.'

Being an anthropologist means that 'detail' is what she does. There was the walk from the car to the lift, her chat to Ron at security, the dirty looks from the receptionist, then the 'incident' in the garage. Her gut tightens as she reflects that she could have been blown sky high if she hadn't run for it. She remarks, 'Their security isn't up to much. By the way,' she changes the subject, 'what department are you in?'

'I head up the NTF, Northern Task Force. A new unit; the name speaks for its self.'

'So you think this has something to do with terrorism? You're barking up the wrong tree. It's . . .' She halts just in time.

'It's what?'

She looks at her nails, horrified at how ugly they look after her session of biting.

'You'll not find the answer there.' Marconi runs his hands through his hair, leaving it sticking out on one side.

Distracted by this Viv continues. 'No, but I'll maybe focus on what would be helpful and what wouldn't.'

'You could let me be the judge of that.' With a pen poised over a note pad he waits.

Viv knows a few detectives and hasn't yet found them too interested in sharing, which means she's been inclined to be the same. A vision of John Black helps her to make a decision. Marconi seems like a good guy. She may be wrong, but he doesn't display any of the machismo crap that detectives often do.

She goes on, 'I was asked to look into the disappearance of a young man who has gone missing.'

'And who asked you to do this?'

'Juliet Muir.'

He raises his eyebrows, clearly impressed. 'A hairdresser who writes for the broadsheets!'

She glares at him. 'Look, if you're going to get hung up on the hairdresser thing . . .'

'No, I'm sorry, it's just all a bit odd.'

Really losing patience now. 'Well, tough. You've probably already got a copy of my CV and my inside leg measurement, so don't pretend that you haven't got a clue about what I'm qualified to do.'

'Okay, okay.' He puts his hands up as he watches the colour rising in her cheeks. 'So you're investigating this missing man and you suddenly find yourself in an attempted . . . what?' He raises his hands as if he's about to give a sermon but stays silent.

'Look, I went into Morgan Clifford, as I do once every month, which, if you've done your homework, you will also know because I'm on the sign-in sheets, and met up with Maxwell Scott, as you also already know. I hadn't a clue I'd been followed. Someone had warned me that I was getting into something too big for me.' She leans back and runs her hands over her face and through her hair.

'And who might that have been?'

She ignores his question and says, 'I think that it was a warning to me. I don't think they were trying to blow up me, or Morgan Clifford. If they wanted me dead they could have easily done it outside my flat.'

He sits up. 'Yes, and that's my problem. They didn't. They waited until you were inside one of the most prestigious finance houses in the UK. Why do you think they did it there?'

'Less likely to be seen there than out on the pavement. It could be as basic as that.' Viv folds her arms and crosses her long legs. Marconi watches and flushes when she catches him looking.

'It could be. But you can see that it might not look like that to Morgan Clifford who've spent a lot of cash on their new security set-up.'

'What? You think they were testing out the security at Morgan Clifford? They were pretty successful at penetrating the car park. But surely you've got them on camera?'

He looks at his nails; immaculate like the rest of him. He hesitates. 'The camera at the barrier to the car park wasn't on.'

'Wow! Why not? Were they testing the system?' She doesn't wait for him to answer. 'It seems strange that just because of some young man going missing I've become the object of a terrorist gang!'

'Help me out here, Viv. Tell me what you've discovered about your young man.'

She concedes. 'Well, I haven't got much so far. He's been hanging out with a young gay crowd until recently, when he was seen with an older bloke. There appear to be drugs involved.'

'What kind of drugs?'

'From what I've seen, soft, but there could be more to it than I've uncovered so far. I was given an address in the Colonies and went to take a look. It seemed to be a kind of sleep-over place for young men. I found one guy, who wasn't very well. In fact that's why I was held up. I've just come from seeing him in the Royal. He's still not looking good.'

'What's his name?'

Reluctantly, she gives him the name. Marconi nods at one of the officers who heads for the door. Before he closes it Marconi shouts: 'Lewis, could you organise coffee for everyone?'

Viv is not hopeful, but when the coffee comes she's delighted to smell the real thing. She spoons Demerara sugar into it and wraps her hands around the cup, blowing across the top, and says, 'One of your lot is already working on the same missing person as I am.'

'And who might that be?'

'DC Nicholson. Sandra if she was telling the truth.'

He looks quizzically at the other officer who brought in the coffee but has said nothing so far, not even a thank you for his coffee. He shrugs as if to suggest he hasn't a clue then says, 'I'll check it out.'

Alone with Marconi, Viv wishes she'd held back telling him about the Colonies flat. As if he's read her thoughts he says, 'We'll tread with caution on this one until we know exactly who belongs to what.'

'The guy who owns the flat could be a prison psychologist.'

He hesitates, then, shaking his head, 'And you know this because . . .'

'I'm a bloody nosey parker.'

He smiles and sighs, 'Anything else?'

'Well, the bloke that I left in the Royal said that Sandy MacDonald's boyfriend, Robbie, is bad news. Now this could be because they don't like each other so I'd not hold out too much hope.'

'And Sandy MacDonald is?'

'The prison psychologist.'

Marconi scratches his head but doesn't take his eyes off her; she drops hers and continues, 'I'm not sure this is as big as you think. I only became involved to take a quiet look at a story about a missing person. When I looked round that flat I thought it was a bit of a vipers' nest, but only because of my prejudice. The idea of lots of young men being tempted by a warm place to sleep into having sex with old leches didn't strike me as entirely . . . moral.'

'But the fact that you were in the flat, I'm assuming uninvited, didn't cross your moral radar? Selective.' He adds. 'Amazing how selective we are.'

'There's moral and "moral". Everyone has their own compass.'

This is bull, but she can't be arsed fighting about ethics at the moment. In fact the idea of food is the only thing that might tempt her to move at all. Viv has given him more than she'd wanted to. Strangely, it feels like a weight off her mind. He has the wherewithal to find out what happens next. She scowls and wonders if now is the time to get more information about Andrew Douglas' death. Marconi notices the change in her expression and throws her a questioning look. 'Anything else?'

'Andrew Douglas, the missing boy? I was wondering if he's turned up?'

Marconi lifts a phone by his side and asks the person on the other end if there's been any development on the Andrew Douglas case, then replaces the hand set. 'He'll ring back. So what we've got is a missing boy with a penchant for other boys who has strayed into a vipers' nest of old men with access to drugs and other bad boys; bad boys who are willing to set fire to your vehicle in the car park of Edinburgh's most prestigious financier. Forgive me, Viv, but in this job you become cynical and coincidences are never usually what they first seem.'

Viv grimaces. 'I'm not keen on coincidences myself, but it does seem a bit far-fetched that a drug dealer, who finds out I'm looking for a missing friend of his, sets about blowing up a financial institution because I cut the MD's hair! Surely even you think that's crazy?'

They go over it all one more time. She's cross-eyed with boredom and no one has called back about Andrew.

'We'll keep a watch on your flat, just in case.'

'Fine. Can I go now?'

'Yes, I'll get one of the boys to drive you home.'

Too tired to protest she follows him along the corridor. He throws over his shoulder. 'I heard your dad was in the force.'

She stops as if he's slapped her. He turns and stares waiting for her to reply. She doesn't. He nods and they continue in silence downstairs to reception.

Once again she sees Sal Chapman, who emerges from the same door as before. The surprise on Sal Chapman's face almost matches Viv's.

'Hi! What are you . . .'

Marconi looks from one to the other. 'Sal. You two know each other?'

Viv interrupts, 'Well, not exactly "know", but have met. Dr Chapman is my landlady.'

Marconi, noticing their embarrassment, says. 'Right, then. PC Taylor will see you to your chariot.'

Viv starts towards the door, but turns back to Sal. 'May I ask what you are doing here?'

'I work here.'

'I gathered that.'

'I work in the profiling unit.'

'Ah! I see.'

Actually seeing nothing, Viv makes her escape, grateful not to have to go in search of a taxi. Resting her head against the cold window she looks at her driver. 'What exactly do the profiling unit do?'

'Profiles, I expect.'

'I'd never have guessed.'

For a policeman who has had an irony bypass this makes sense, and there is no further conversation until she thanks him for the lift.

Chapter Seven

The phone rings. 'Shit!' She's tempted to leave it but the incessant ring gets the better of her.

'Jules?' The last thing she wants. 'What now?'

'The news, Viv! The news! Andrew has turned up.' Viv is immediately alert. 'Well charred bits of him anyway.'

This really gets her attention.

'What the hell do you mean "charred bits of him"?'

'Never mind the echo, girl. Turn on the TV, it's all over the news.'

Sure enough, as Viv flicks to the news channel, a young female reporter looks earnestly into the camera and is rounding up with, 'This fire has been a big shock to the small community of Earlston.'

Jolted by the mention of Earlston, Viv flicks to another channel to see if she can find any more detail. She looks at another fresh-faced reporter, equally earnest, pointing to the scene of a lay-by with lots of police activity in the background. 'God!' Surely not the lay-by that Margie mentioned the other day? Jules, still on the other end of the line, barks, 'Get down there and see what you can get.'

Viv is certain of her ground. 'There's no way they'll let me near the scene. Besides, by the time I get there everyone and his wife will have covered the story. I've got another lead I'm going to follow. I'll be in touch.'

She hangs up the landline, grabs her mobile and scrolls for Pete's number, then punches 'Call'. After an eternity, it goes to answering machine. 'Hey

Pete, I'm on my way to Copa Cabana – we could have coffee?'

She's no sooner cut the call than her phone rings. It's him. There's traffic in the background. He says, 'I don't know what to do. Everyone is freaked out. I'll meet you if you like.'

'I'm on my way to Copa Cabana.'

'No! Not there. I couldn't face it. The Moon. I'll see you at the Moon in half an hour.'

After another vain attempt to find a grown-up reporter, she switches off the TV and goes in search of all that she'll need for a night of discovery. She throws her rucksack over her shoulder and pats her jacket pockets for keys, gloves and tissues.

He looks rough, eyes swollen, nose red, not a picture of someone on the pull. Viv sits down and looks straight at him across the table.

'You okay?'

'Do I look okay? It's been a bad week.'

'For me too.'

He looks surprised to discover she might have a life as well.

'What's your week been?'

'Had my car torched.'

'Wow! That's quite a big deal.'

'Yes it is, but nobody died. So what do you know that I don't? D'you want to help find Andrew's killer?'

After the slightest hesitation he says, 'Course I do. But I don't really have anything.'

In Viv's world when someone says 'really' it means, 'I have information but don't know how to use it yet.'

'Okay. Take your time. Try and recall anyone that you've seen him speaking to, arguing with, dancing with, anything, which involved him and someone else. Conversations, asides, the odd touch, anything.'

He looks bleak. Silent tears roll down his cheeks. Shaking his head he looks at the table, 'The older bloke is the only one I can think of who stands out. It just wasn't like him: Andrew loved younger guys.'

Something about this comment doesn't add up and irritates Viv, but she can't get hold of what it is.

'Describe the older guy, can you?'

He hesitates again, his eyes raised as if the answer is written on the ceiling.

'He's tall, well, taller than me. Dyes his hair. Sometimes has grey bits at the temples. Always tanned.'

'So he's known to you. You've seen him more than once?'

'Oh yes, he's always around. I had him taped as a "viewer", but it seems I was wrong.'

'What? You mean some men only watch?' She is genuinely surprised.

'God yes! The hetero-camp and the uber hets love to look. They'd love to touch as well but they're too scared of . . .'

'Of what?'

'Of disease, of being found out, of being converted, of not finding a way back to the safety of sex with women. They're actually generally pretty harmless.'

He shakes his head again as if realising this case may be the exception and says, 'Shit. You think he's the killer?'

'It's not my job to imagine. I'm looking for facts. What sort of clothes does he wear?'

'Nothing unusual. Jeans, tight tee shirts, chunky boots. It's the footwear. It says what he wants. If he's wearing chunky boots he's not come out to dance.'

'Did you ever see him driving?'

'No, only seen him indoors. Copa Cabana or the Fox. Maybe in here, but can't remember.'

'But Copa Cabana? With those big windows? Doesn't seem a place to hang out if you don't want to be discovered.'

'I know. But some of them enjoy the risk. Come to think of it, he was always at the back, by the toilets. Good viewing area I suppose.'

Viv tries to turn a sigh into something less judgmental – it's difficult and only partially effective. Pete looks at her. She pushes for more detail. 'Short hair. Long hair? Straight, curly? Dark or fair or in between? I need details. Eyes . . . any idea what colour his eyes were?'

'Short, mousey, straight hair. Receding, but not in a bad way. Always well cut. Trying to look younger.'

Viv doesn't know any man who has discovered a good way to go bald, but asks again, 'Eyes?'

A short silence. 'Blue. Yes, I'm sure they're blue.'

You have to get pretty close to someone to know the colour of their eyes, so she takes this with a pinch of salt. He's young and vulnerable. She wants to cuddle him.

'Okay, how about a jacket or coat?'

'I don't know. How would I know? He's indoors.'

'If you saw him with a coat we could work out if it was heavy or light. A heavy coat usually means you're on the hoof.'

He looks as if he's computing and Viv gives him time before saying, 'There are no rules, it's a process of elimination. If you remember anything else that could be useful let me know.'

'He . . .'

'He what?'

'He has an accent.'

She sighs. 'What sort of accent?'

'I don't know. Not Scottish.'

'Well, that narrows it down. Now we've only got the rest of the world to eliminate. European? American? Australian? South African? Any idea at all?'

'Definitely European. His English is quite good. Maybe Polish or Czech or something like that.'

She's not sure if she'd be able to distinguish between those accents either.

'Oh,' he adds, 'he always wears a gold crucifix.'

'Great. If you think of anything else, ring me.'

Gathering up her things she looks at his face and sees something she can't make out.

She closes the door of the Moon and pulls her collar up round her neck. It's as much a gesture to keep what she's discovered in as it is to keep the cold out. Since she's almost at Copa Cabana she decides to check it out. If Pete's right then maybe people's nerves will betray something. As she waits to cross at the lights at Picardy Place she spots the original barman at the door having a fag. He has his back to her and is shouting into his phone. He swings round just as she reaches the kerb. The shock on his face is a picture. He shuts off his phone without grace and she nods as she heads into the bar, wondering if he would have cut his call had he not seen her.

She's barely through the door when Liam's voice reaches her. He beckons her up the stairs and having no excuse not to she makes her way up.

'Hey, Vivian. You seem to be addicted to this place. How many times you been in here this week?'

His voice is only one of a list of unattractive things about him. She looks at him and tries not to shudder. Then says, 'Who's counting?'

'Well, since Dawn popped it you haven't been out at all. Now all of a sudden it's like every day . . .'

Viv could smack him for this, but instead turns and walks back downstairs, her body language louder than any comment. His strained laughter follows her. As she heads for the bar someone grabs her arm. She pivots and pulls free. It's Red. Neither says anything until Red shouts to the barman and orders two halves of cider. When they appear on the bar Viv pulls out her wallet, but Red slaps a tenner onto the counter. Viv can't be arsed arguing and takes a long swig, then asks, 'What now?'

'Just thought you could do with a drink. After . . .' She nods in the direction of Liam.

Viv lifts her glass again and says, 'Cheers. It would be doing a disservice to weasels to call him one. He doesn't bring out the best in me.'

'Nor me, but he's got eyes like a hawk and he's easily bought. Makes a god of money. Don't worry, guys like him always get their comeuppance. His can't be far away.'

Viv isn't stupid – she knows what Red is after. She also knows what she'll do to get it. They drink in silence for a few minutes, then Viv says, 'So what've you got on Andrew?'

'Not much. I hear you've been out talking to John Black again.'

Surprised, Viv keeps her eyes on her glass. 'So you'll know that he had nothing to say.'

'I know that you met the psych. And that he warned you off.'

'Well, you know more than me. I don't remember any warning.'

'Look, Viv, I wish you'd stop treating me as if I was the culprit. We're on the same case.'

Viv raises her eyebrows, drains her glass and walks towards the loo. When in doubt take a break.

As she enters there's a woman drying her hands. At least the machine's working tonight. Catching a glimpse of herself in the mirror it crosses her mind that perhaps it's time to go home. She looks rough. To call her hair wind-swept would be polite and her lips are chapped. Why is it that even when you know not to lick dry lips the temptation is too great? Sitting on the throne she wonders if all the aggravation is worth it. Will she end up with information that will keep Jules sweet? This story is probably already past its best. On that note she checks her phone, but can't hear the message, which is being drowned out by the din of the next loo flushing. She waits and tries again. It's Jules, hoping to persuade Viv to go to Earlston. Not a chance.

Leaving the cubicle she can't bear to look in the mirror and keeps her eyes on the dirt-engrained floor. She doesn't pay attention to the footfall. It's only when her arm is being yanked up her back and her cheek pushed against the cold mirror that she realises the attacker is a man. He whispers in her ear, 'What kind of telling will it take?' Her arm is pushed even further up her back. 'Eh? Lost your tongue, but not lost your nose. Eh?'

Even if she wanted to speak it would be difficult to make herself understood with her lips squashed against the mirror. He grabs her hair and shoves her head into the sink so she can't see his face. But she can smell expensive cologne and peppermint on his breath from newly brushed teeth.

'Now, you gonna hear this? Back off. You don't know what you're getting into.'

With this he releases her. Rubbing her wrist she turns to face him. Vague recognition.

'Why is it that people keep telling me that?'

'Because you're too stupid to listen. It should have been enough to lose your car.'

'What? . . .You . . .?'

He is well-built, good looking, but probably the wrong side of thirty. His perfume may be expensive but his manners are cheap. He wipes the heel of his palm up his nose, sniffs.

Viv, trying to think quickly, says, 'To whom do I owe the pleasure of today's warning?'

'You don't need to know who. You just need to do as you're told. Have you got that?' He jabs a thick finger at her face.

She stares at him, thinking how looks can deceive. He seems about to leave, but then wheels round and slaps her face. She kicks out just as Red appears from the doorway, leaps in and grabs him, effortlessly bouncing him off a cubicle door.

'Know this man?'

Viv, touching her stinging cheek, shakes her head.

'Robbie, say hello to Dr Fraser.'

Red wheels him round and slams him into the mirror. He groans as his cheekbone meets the glass but doesn't speak until Red releases him.

'Fuck you!'

'Original! Apologise to Dr Fraser.'

Viv has had enough of the show and starts towards the door, colliding with a young woman who is on her way in. Red shouts, 'Not now!'

The girl, looking from one to the other, backs out. At the door, Viv turns to Red.

'Nice timing. Thanks.'

'Wait! D'you want anything done with him?'

Viv hesitates. 'His name, what's his name?'

'Right, sunshine, you heard her. What's your full name?' Red thrusts his arm even further up his back and squashes him back against the mirror.

'Back off a little, he'll not be able to speak.'

Silence. Red puts more pressure on his arm.

He splutters. 'Okay, okay. Robert. Robert.'

Viv says, 'Unless you're a cocktail waitress, you must have a surname.'

'Croy.'

'Ah. That figures.'

Red obviously knows the name and Viv, running it through her brain in search of recent Roberts, remembers Robbie, Sandy MacDonald's boy. Although he isn't as youthful as the guy she saw in the hospital car park. It's the hair. He's dyed his hair. It was blond and now it's dark brown. The blond was kinder. Viv asks, 'Was it actually you who blew up the car? Or are you the puppet?'

This gets Red's attention. 'What car?'

Robbie kicks sharply back into Red's knee-cap and makes a run for it. As Red squeals and goes down Viv grabs his arm but he manages to pull free, leaping over the stair-railing, down the six steps and into the crowd below. Viv watches as he shoves people out of his way and stumbles out through the exit. The crowd look on until the door closes behind him then the noise of chatter erupts again. Viv scratches her head then turns and helps Red up, who has already pulled out a mouthpiece and is shouting into it: 'Male, late twenties, early thirties, just run onto Leith Walk. Pick him up.'

'You'll be lucky . . . How's the leg?'

Red stretches and flexes until she can put some weight on it and says, 'So which car was that? If explosions have become part of this case then there's more to consider than a lost boy.'

'Dead boy?'

'We don't know that for sure yet. There is a body but it's so badly burned that the ID is difficult.'

'Shit! Are forensics onto it? And where was it found?' The first part of this question doesn't need an answer. Viv knows some of the SOCOs. Their efficiency is legendary. Pete hadn't mentioned the burning bit.

'Lay-by on the A68. Right. We'd better go somewhere where we can talk. This has gone beyond a missing person story.'

Viv's brain is in overdrive. Surely it's too much of a coincidence that she'd heard a conversation earlier in the week about the black bags in the lay-by on the A68?

'That leg okay? Can you walk?'

'Sure, but not fast or far.'

As they make their way through the crowd Viv can feel many eyes on them. Then above the crowd the scraping tone of the weasel can be heard, 'Bye-bye, Vivian.'

This time she turns and stares at him as if she would bore a hole through him. Red whispers in her ear, 'Not worth it. Definitely not worth it.' Once outside she continues, 'My car's over in Union Street, let's start there.'

Chapter Eight

Darkness has already fallen which, coupled with a chilly wind, makes Red's suggestion more attractive than it would normally be. Red limps. 'I've got an old injury. This won't have done it any good.'

Despite her instinct, Viv supports Red's waist and tucks her arm over her shoulder, steadying her until they reach the car.

'Thanks. I didn't think you had it in you.'

'I don't. It's too cold to hang about. End of.'

Red laughs an unconvincing laugh. Viv can't help thinking Red would make a better cop if she would be herself, but some people don't care about themselves enough to do that, and rely on stereotypical crap to get them through. Red's veneer is thin. There's nothing like an injury to bring out vulnerability.

Red says, 'I think we should head for Fettes.'

Radioing ahead Red alerts HQ that they are on their way, mentioning that if Chapman happens to be in they would like to see her. Viv can't believe her ears. Chapman, her landlady? Christ, what next?

'Not Sal Chapman?'

'The very one. Know her, do you?'

'Not really.'

Red eyes her with suspicion before attempting to engage the gears, but there's no way she can drive with this leg. Viv takes over. As they approach the gates to Fettes car park she snorts, 'Before this week I'd only ever been in here once in my life and now it's twice in one day. They'll think I'm addicted.'

Red smiles, 'What else have they had you in for?'

'The explosion. My car was torched, remember?'

'I hadn't made the connection. That's Marconi's department. We'll need to bring him in as well.'

'Why? This isn't a terrorist incident.'

'Maybe not, but he heads the NTF and if we have anything out of the ordinary which could be connected to an existing case he'll want to be kept in the loop. And I'm not going to be the one who keeps him out.'

'Your call. Waste of police time if you ask me.'

'I didn't,' Red barks.

Silence. Until Red needs a hoist up the front step. In the foyer Viv looks around and feels butterflies in anticipation of seeing Sal Chapman again. One cup of tea and she's like a lusty school girl. A door opens on the right and Sal walks towards Red with her hand outstretched.

'DC Nicholson, hello.' And with her head at a questioning angle, 'And Dr Fraser! This is an unexpected pleasure.'

Viv puts out her hand. The shake lasts seconds longer than it should. Enough for Red to look at them both and say, 'I thought you didn't know each other.'

'We don't, but we've met. It seems Dr Fraser and I are destined to get to know each other.'

Viv, irritated at being caught off balance, says sharply to Sal. 'What's your role here? I thought you were an academic.'

'To be honest I'm not sure what my role is in this particular case. I work with any department where they need a profiler. It's supplementary to my real job. Let's go through to the office.'

Chapman throws this over her shoulder as she leads the way, and Red, looking intrigued, hobbles behind with Viv.

This is a privilege. The suite is quite different from any other police office that she's seen. It obviously doesn't house any criminals – too clean. Sal Chapman may be a tiny woman but her presence is substantial. People passing her in the corridor defer to her and already she's been asked if she would like coffee to be brought. Not bad for someone whose real job is elsewhere . . . or was that stuff about being an academic just a ruse?

A PC brings the coffee but doesn't hang about. They sit at a round table. Chapman has a pen and paper at the ready, prompting Viv to take out her own little pad. The three of them look at each other until Chapman says, 'Well, shall we start at the beginning? Dr Fraser?'

Viv is still irritated. 'If we are here to collaborate then I'd like us to be on first name terms.'

'That's fine with me. You okay with that, DC Nicholson?'

Viv notices how ashen Red is and softens, 'Do you need to see someone about that knee?'

'I'm fine.' Then, emphatically, 'Thanks for asking.'

Viv begins. 'I was asked to look into a young boy missing from his home. He'd been away for three nights when I started, which means it's nearly a week now. First I checked out the gay bars – the word was that he preferred young boys. On my first visit to Copa Cabana I bumped into Red.'

'The name's Sandra.'

'Okay, but Red suits you better.'

Red smiles and says, 'Whatever. People have called me much worse.'

'Anyway it turned out that she was interested in Andrew Douglas as well, probably for different reasons, but I don't know what they are.'

'Drugs,' utters Red.

'That's what I thought. Then, as a consequence of talking to some young men who know Andrew I visited an address in the Colonies and came across a guy, very ill and needing help, but he was not Andrew. I discovered that the flat belongs to Alexander MacDonald, a prison psychologist with a penchant for boys. While visiting the young man in hospital I encountered MacDonald who gave me a warning. Told me to back off and said I didn't know what I was getting into. Also, while filling up my car with petrol I was given another warning. Warnings all over the place: nice to know people are looking out for me.'

Red cuts in, 'You've missed out the minor detail of the explosion.'

'Oh, that little detail. I was working in the office of Morgan Clifford, and someone blew up my car.'

Sal's face is a picture of shock. 'When was this?'

'Yesterday. In the morning.'

'I see.'

Viv's not sure what Sal sees, but her tone suggests she's acknowledging something of their first encounter.

'Your friend DI Marconi thinks it's to do with Morgan Clifford. But I really don't think it was a terrorist attack. More, as Andrew's "friends" keep telling me, a warning for me to back off.'

Sal sighs, 'I'm with Marconi on this. If someone was prepared to blow up your car in such a prestigious location they mean business. And you need cover.'

'Whoever they are they've also paid me a home visit. I've had a note under my door.'

Shaking her head Sal snorts, 'Don't you think you're taking this all rather lightly, Dr Fraser?'

Viv raises her eyebrows at Sal's return to formality.

Sal acknowledges this with a nod, 'Okay. Viv?'

'Well, I suppose things are beginning to stack up, but I'm not sure it merits a guard.'

'If these people have access to explosives and know how to use them I'd say that they have more to hide than the odd ounce of marijuana. Don't you?'

Viv bristles at this question. It reminds her of Jean Johnston and her years of 'Don't you think?'

'I can see that there's some mileage in that, but surely anyone can put a lighted taper in a petrol tank? A better question surely is, why me? I haven't actually got anything. Well, nothing useful. But someone sees it otherwise.'

'What exactly have you got?'

'I've already told Marconi.' Then, looking at them both she sighs and says, 'All right, here we go again.'

Sal interrupts when Viv is describing the inside of the Colonies flat. 'If you can remember all the details, what was in the bathroom and the fridge?'

Viv visualises the cupboard. She recalls and smiles. 'It's really more about what wasn't there than what was, but there was a box of new toothbrushes in the bathroom. There must have been a couple of dozen in it. Now, even I call that obsessive. And loo roll, industrial packs of loo rolls. They obviously know something that we don't! The fridge had lousy food in it. Value labels, nothing nutritional. Sell by dates were current.'

Sal stops writing and lifts her head, 'Does sound like a hostel, doesn't it?' When Red and Viv don't respond, Sal continues, 'We'll do better if we actually collaborate.'

'I've already said it didn't look like a home. Apart from the oversized TV, none of the features of domesticity were there. It was functional.' Viv searches for an appropriate description. 'It hasn't got a woman's touch, which in a gay home is pretty unusual.'

Red interrupts. 'I think we should take another look.'

'Why?'

'Well, the explosion for a start.' Sal shoots Viv a look of annoyance.

Viv thinks they're all getting a bit tetchy. She continues: 'Robbie Croy, the guy who just warned us off again, is supposed to be MacDonald's special "friend". If we could find out his address it would be worth looking there, but the flat's pretty rudimentary, a stopgap at best. Come to think of it there weren't any wardrobes or chests of drawers; just one bedside cabinet, but nowhere to store clothes. A neighbour said they were a bunch of paedophiles. Said she's seen boys in school uniform going in.'

Sal doesn't rise to this. 'We must keep an open mind.'

But Red bursts out, 'Yeah sure, Sal. Open to what? What else is being kept from us?'

Viv doesn't understand this comment from Red, but the look that passes from Sal back to Red is a warning and Red backs down. Sal resumes. 'I'll check with Marconi?'

'Check what? Have I missed something?' Red is even more hostile now.

Viv, amused at the sparring of the other two, interjects, 'Well, is one of you going to fill me in on what's going on? In the interests of . . . collaboration,' she adds, with just a touch of sarcasm.

Then she remembers the state of the young man in the Royal. 'If John Black survives he'll be a useful source, but the last time I saw him it wasn't looking good. We should check how he's doing. The nurse said they thought he'd had a bad drug cocktail. That he wasn't the first with those symptoms.'

Sal lifts the phone. 'Could you find DI Marconi, please, and ask him to join us? In room three in the unit.' She listens for a minute then says, 'Okay, do what you can.'

Viv can't work out what Sal's role is. People do as she asks; her tone is respectful and she puts people at ease, but she's definitely got more power here than a profiler.

Nodding at the phone Sal says, 'They'll try to locate him, but they're not sure if he's still in the building. What else have you got, Sandra?'

'The missing boy may have been found, but that's not looking good because he hasn't been identified yet.'

Sal tilts her head.

'The body's too charred.'

'Damn. What about dentals?'

'Yep. We're waiting, and if it is Andrew it certainly ups the stakes. Explosions and drugs are one thing. Murder takes it to another level. Apart from that I've got much the same kind of info as Viv. Viv may have a bit more, though.'

This puts Viv back in the hot seat. 'I've spoken to his mates in Copa Cabana and one of them is really worried. He's been in touch with Andrew since he went AWOL, but he doesn't know if Andrew went of his own accord or if he was forced. He also said there was an older man, apparently good looking, with Andrew on the night that he went missing.'

Just as she's wondering whether to say she has the number from which Andrew made his last call, Marconi raps at the door and breezes in. He looks strained, but gets straight to business. 'What's happening, then?'

Sal answers. 'We're not sure how much more we have than Viv has already given you, but what there is seems enough to get a search warrant for the flat in the Colonies.'

'What makes you think that?'

Sal fills him in on Robbie's new attempt to put the frighteners on Viv and adds that he's injured Sandra. Red adds, 'I did send out a description to the surveillance guys, but they only tracked him as far as GHQ then lost him. Said that it was as busy as ever up there. You'd think they'd move on. They're a hardy lot considering these temperatures.'

This brings a smile to everyone's lips. Calton Hill has long been known as GHQ, Gay Head Quarters. Since the toilets at the East End closed, due to over-activity, Calton Hill has become the place to go, and it's easier to escape from, if a tad chilly. Marconi turns to Viv. 'Describe to me again what you saw in that flat?'

Viv does a rerun, jots down a floor plan and hands it to Marconi.

'As you see, it isn't the grandest of places; three or four steps take you from one room to another . . . stepping over multiple sleeping bags, mind.'

Marconi immediately lifts the phone and asks for a car to do a drive-by. 'See if there's any activity. Lights, TV on, any voices.'

Viv interrupts him before he hangs up. 'There's a nosey neighbour. The name on her buzzer is Walker. She'll give them access, and undoubtedly a bit of grief. She complained that the police don't do anything about their activities.'

Marconi passes this on and nods his thanks to Viv. Red makes to stand but collapses back into her chair, drawing air through her teeth. 'I could do with some painkillers and an ice pack.'

Viv says, 'How far is it to your place?'

Red grins. 'Thanks for asking, I'll get a PC to drive me home.'

Relieved, Viv explains, 'I don't have any more to give you and I'd really love to go home.'

Marconi nods. 'We'll be in touch if anything turns up at the flat.'

The meeting is clearly at an end. Red seeks out a PC and asks Viv if she'd like a lift. She's in two minds, wondering if Sal's doing anything when she's finished here, but accepts anyway.

Minutes later, just as she steps into the car Sal rushes out and shouts, 'Viv! One more thing!' She looks into the car and says to Red, 'I'd like a word with Viv. It's other business.'

Red raises her eyebrows. 'Sure thing, Doc.'

Viv gets out and stands avoiding eye contact until Sal says, 'It's about the flat.' Then laughs. 'Well it's not really about the flat.'

Rolling a stone under her foot, with her eyes on the ground, Viv smiles before looking up and saying, 'We could discuss it somewhere warmer.'

Sal's face lights up. 'Okay, I'll get my coat.'

'Italian do?'

'Great! Two minutes.'

Chapter Nine

They are lucky to get a table. San Marino is hotching with Italians; a good sign. The tension between them had melted away while they were walking and making chit-chat, but now they're confined the atmosphere is electric. Viv shifts the cutlery and adjusts the place mat, squaring it with Sal's. When the waiter offers them menus they both speak at the same time. It's pathetic. Viv excuses herself and heads to the loo. Taking deep breaths and looking at herself in the mirror she tries to give herself a talking to. Taking a lipstick from her inside pocket she applies it then immediately scrubs it off, leaving her lips as swollen as her cheek. She splashes cold water on her face, then dries it with the hand drier; she takes another deep breath before returning to the table.

'Phew! Needed that!'

Sal smiles and leans across the table as if she's about to move a stray hair from Viv's eyes. Viv sits back in surprise. Immediately regretting this, she says, 'Sorry. I'm a bit edgy. It must be the last couple of days catching up with me.'

They both turn their attention to the menu.

Sal says, 'I'm not that hungry. A salad will do me.'

'Me neither, but if I don't eat I'll pass out and that would be embarrassing.'

'How have you managed the last couple of days, Viv? It's not every day that someone blows up your car.'

Viv is mortified to feel tears pricking her eyes. She jogs along through life and as long as no one is too nice to her she manages. The tone of Sal's voice has made contact with part of her that she does everything possible to keep buried. Eyes firmly on the menu she says, 'I think I'll have the risotto.' She lets out a breath, looks up and meets Sal's eyes, then quickly looks away. This wasn't such a good idea.

'You don't have to be so brave you know.'

'I'm fine . . . thanks.' This comes out more defensively than she means it to and she looks again at Sal. 'This is difficult . . .'

A silence follows and is fortuitously interrupted by a jaunty waiter. He places a jug of water and some bread on the table, allowing Viv a moment to steady her thoughts. 'So how come you're an academic and a police officer?' A rich question given her own occupations.

'Oh, I'm not a police officer. I definitely see myself as an academic.'

'You seem to spend an awful lot of time in Fettes for an academic.' Sal doesn't answer. Viv continues, 'What is it you teach?' Back on safe territory, Viv sits back and lets her shoulders drop.

'I teach a few courses, but the one I'm most passionate about is the history of Freud and psychoanalysis.'

Viv raises her eyebrows. 'Wow! I love Freud, In fact I used a Freudian model for my field work. Strange guy. Even though he was a bit of a misogynist, with a reputation for gay bashing, I couldn't help myself becoming hooked.'

Sal smiles and shakes her head. 'Poor Freud. So misunderstood. He was a product of his time. I know it's a bit of a cliché but he did have homosexual friends and a view of women's psyches that reflected his time. He wasn't as bad as people have made him out to be. There's no middle ground with Freud; you either love him or hate him, and that tells us more about ourselves than about Freud, doesn't it?'

'I suppose. But surely the stuff about penis envy must cause you some . . . distress?'

'Oh sure, he made mistakes, but we ought to be careful. Everybody makes mistakes.'

Their food comes and the atmosphere lightens.

'So what have your mistakes been, Dr Chapman?'

Sal plays around with her fork in the air as if warming up for fencing, then laughs and says, 'Well, my most recent one was thinking I knew somebody quite well when I didn't know them at all. Made a bit of a fool of myself but, hey, life's short. I'll get over it. How about you? Bet you don't often make mistakes.'

Viv's reply is quick – too quick? 'I was going to say the same to you.' She adds, 'My biggest mistake so far was not telling someone how much they meant to me.' She looks down at her plate then up into Sal's face. 'Before it was too late . . . She died.'

She is unsure why this has come out. She doesn't even know this woman. Feeling the colour rushing up her neck to her cheeks she tries to lighten up again. 'But I make tons of mistakes every day. Take the car that's just been blown up. I bought it against all reason. It looked great, but that was its only virtue. So I suppose they did me a favour! Mistakes are fine though, as long as you're willing to admit them.'

'But that's rarer than you think. You know it used to be rare to find plagiarism in the university, but now almost every semester there's something.'

'Which uni?'

'Central. I used to be at Edinburgh, but Central offered me a fellowship so I took it, and I already have a lovely house in a village called Doune. It's only a ten-minute drive from work. I couldn't live without the big skies.'

Viv watches the change in Sal's demeanour as she talks about home and knows what she means about the big sky thing. Her own flat has fantastic views and that was her main reason for taking it. She hadn't imagined that Sal would be a country person.

'I didn't have you down as a country girl. I imagined you being addicted to pavements and cappuccino bars. Wrong again.'

'I'm glad to have been in your imagination.'

Viv colours again. This little woman is lovely. Power packed and lovely. Viv should be on her guard.

They both finish as much of their food as they can, then order coffee. Sal has cappuccino and Viv an Americano – although she doesn't usually drink coffee after ten unless she's on an all-nighter.

'At least I was right about the cappuccino,' she says, meekly enough.

They are interrupted by Sal's phone. She excuses herself and goes outside to take the call, returning with a smile. 'It was Mac.'

Viv gives her a quizzical look.

'DI Marconi. We were at school together, and his nickname was Mac. The local kids couldn't get their mouths round the Italian names in his family so they got called the Macs. Anyway he's had a report of activity at the flat; he's on his way there now and asked if I'd like to go with him. He's coming by.'

They pay and head outside. Marconi is already pulling up. He gets out of the car and gives Viv a look that's difficult to interpret, but seems a lot like a dismissal. He opens the passenger door and puts his hand on Sal's back. Her shrinking is entirely visible. This isn't the first time that Viv's had to compete with a man who hasn't read the signs.

She smiles at Marconi who says, 'Can I offer you a lift anywhere?'

Viv looks at Sal who says, 'Get in, you can come with us.'

Marconi starts to protest, but Sal pats his arm. He relents but not without firing Viv a look in the mirror.

The journey is short and very awkward.

Sal tries. 'So what did the uniforms report?'

Marconi is petulant. 'I didn't send uniforms . . . They saw a guy get out of a transit van and head into the building. He fits the description of Robbie Croy.'

Viv cuts in. 'Surely he's not that daft?'

'It seems he is. Anyway they watched and the lights went on in the flat and he seemed to busy himself from room to room. Just when they phoned in, another guy turned up. Older, not looking too fit. They're both still in the flat at the moment.'

'So what's next?' Sal says.

'I plan to have a chat with them. But I don't plan to have Dr Fraser with me when I do!'

Sal turns to Viv with a look that says 'this is out of my control'. Viv smiles and shakes her head. She almost rubs Sal's shoulder but instead says, 'I'll get out here.'

Her sentence is barely finished when Marconi pulls up at the kerb, about fifty metres from the car park of the flat. Viv jumps out and says to Sal, 'Speak soon?'

'Sure, I'll keep you posted.' They drive off. Viv watches as they turn into the car park. Not sure how to play this, she hovers around for a few minutes, enough time for them to get into the building. Then running over to the door, she tries it. Locked. She presses the buzzer for Walker and a woman's voice says, 'Christ! What now?'

'Police again, sorry to bother you.'

Miss Walker doesn't say any more, but buzzes her in. Viv, preparing her story, is surprised that Walker isn't on the landing. From inside the flat, Marconi's voice is recognisable, then Sandy MacDonald's, pathetic but protective. 'He was just . . .'

A harsh voice cuts in, louder than the others. 'Oh, shut it, you. What do you know?'

Then Marconi again. 'And what is it that he doesn't know?'

'Now that would be tellin'.'

'You can either tell us here or at the station.' Marconi's voice has a sharp edge to it.

'Now look what you've done!'

'I told you to shut it!'

There's a scuffle and MacDonald shouts. 'Stop!'

What the hell's happening in there? Viv approaches the door and gives it a gentle push. It opens. It creaks. The noise is enough to make her shrink back against the wall. She hears another noise, like a stifled sneeze, coming from above. Edging her way to the bottom of the next flight of stairs she looks up and sees a man's back. Not sure what to do next, Viv sidles her way back downstairs and out into the car park. She can hide behind the transit van, which won't be going anywhere if they're off to Fettes. It's freezing – Edinburgh isn't called the windy city for nothing. Viv pulls her hands up inside her sleeves, which isn't much help. Before long Marconi, Sal and Robbie come out of the building. MacDonald is clearly lurking behind one of the voiles at the window. Within moments another bloke trots out and into a separate car.

All clear. Viv makes her way back to the building and buzzes MacDonald. He doesn't answer. She buzzes again. He still doesn't answer. She tries one long and three short blasts.

'What the fuck?'

'It's Viv.'

'Who?'

'It's Viv Fraser. We met at the hospital.'

After a few seconds he shouts, 'Just fuck off. Did you get that? Fuck . . . Off.'

'I can help.'

'Yeah! You can help by pissing off!'

'I'm staying here until you let me in.'

Silence. Then the buzzer releases the door and she punches the air before running upstairs.

Pushing the door open she steps into the hall. Sandy grunts from the kitchen, 'You're an interfering shit. Why don't you back off like I told you before?'

'You know I can't do that. I'm being paid to do a job just like you.'

He raises his eyebrows then smirks. 'If only I could.' And as if demonstrating why he can't, takes out an inhaler and gasps in whatever legal poison it contains. He looks pretty awful, but his dark eyes maintain their appeal.

'So what else has Robbie been up to?'

'Why ask me? You probably know more about what Robbie does than I do. He's open – you might say boastful – about his conquests, and his economy with the truth has always been a strength. I never listen to anything he says. I was his counsellor, you know. So I have privileged access to the way he operates.'

'Would he kill someone?'

His hesitation says it all.

'How much would it take?'

He shrugs. 'I can't see it somehow.'

'How come you stay with him?'

'You women never get it, do you? Robbie's given me what I've wanted. Okay, he's a bit of a drama queen and he thinks he's got me over a barrel . . . but what he doesn't realise is that my wife knows, and she's even less interested in my hobbies than he is. It suits all of us really.'

'Who did all the sleeping bags belong to?'

'Christ, how would I know? I only own the place. Robbie runs it. But even he won't know. It's not what you think, though. It's just somewhere for young guys to doss down if they haven't got anything else . . . organized.'

'Not to mention school boys.'

'No one who stays here is under eighteen.'

Viv makes no effort to hide her scorn. 'Please! You can't believe that. The neighbours have reported seeing boys in uniform going in and out.'

'Well they must be eighteen.'

'God, MacDonald, you really have convinced yourself that that's true. You're kidding me and yourself.'

He is defiant. 'Robbie and I have a deal. Nothing unlawful under this roof.'

'So the whacky backy and poppers – and God knows what else – don't count? Spare me.'

'I don't have to spare you a fucking thing, lady. Now why don't you take your slender arse out of here before I get mad.'

This is rich coming from someone who couldn't fight his way out of a damp
tissue. He may have been fit once, but that time is long past. Viv thinks about Robbie Croy: tall, dark and handsome, with a loathsome attitude . . . not to mention time in prison for drug possession and cottaging. It must have been there he seduced Alexander MacDonald whose weakness for dark, over-sexed young men outweighed his reason.

MacDonald's first mistake was becoming involved with Robbie. Once on the outside Robbie saw Alexander, now Sandy, as a source of revenue and a free roof over his head. Viv imagines Robbie is the kind of man who has sex with anyone, but that relationships are off his radar. In fact anything related to morality wouldn't register on his internal compass: his true north is Robbie

Croy. He believes he's got Sandy where he wants him because of the wife, but he's made the mistake of underestimating Sandy, and equating compliance with ignorance. The wife must, in many ways, be no better than Robbie, also exploiting Sandy, seeing him as a source of money, an eternal roof over her head. 'She leads her life and I lead mine.' Imagine marrying a man not knowing that he was more interested in the waiter. Still, we all make choices.

'Before I take my arse out of here, have you heard anything about Andrew Douglas?'

'Only that he's dead, but you already know that. So why bother me?'

'I was hoping you might confess.'

'You're off your . . . ' He looks at her and sees that she's taking the piss. 'Time's up.' He points at the door. 'Robbie's lost the plot a bit recently, but he's not that bad.'

'Bad is relative, though. If he's been selling contaminated stuff then he's for the chop. When you see him next remember to thank him for doing my car.'

He looks at her with knitted brows. He obviously has no idea what she's on about.

It's definitely time for a shower and bed. Outside, she heads towards Dundas Street in the hope of a cab and it's not long before she flags one down. Within ten minutes she has negotiated the smokers outside the Bow Bar at the bottom of her stair and pushed her key in the outside door. On reaching her landing she can hear the phone ringing inside. She lets it ring. Today's been a marathon even for her. Then she recognises Sal Chapman's voice and runs to pick up. Too late. Yawning, she decides it will be no bad thing to sleep on today's developments, so she steps into a long, hot shower, which she follows with a cup of lesbian tea. Soothed by the fragrance of peppermint, she slips beneath the duvet.

Chapter Ten

Opening the curtains, she watches rubbish blowing around the gateway of Greyfriars graveyard, a sign that it's not as benign out there as the blue sky would have her believe. Breakfast consists of a stale oatcake and a cup of lorry driver's tea, her belly objecting to such an assault. An oat catches between her teeth and no amount of prodding with her tongue will dislodge it. Only a second brushing will do the trick so she heads back into the bathroom. The phone rings mid-excavation and she hesitates, waiting for the answering machine to kick in. Hearing Jules, she decides not to answer.

It's Friday so she makes a mental note to ring Jinty to say she's not going to manage drinks. Her clients today are good fun. The first is Ailsa, who is writing a history of an East Lothian village. The last time Viv saw her she'd uncovered all sorts of family skeletons that she wasn't sure she could include without causing a major fracas. She'll be having colour, which takes a bit of time; then it'll be on to Niall, a retired headmaster who always comes up with exciting nuggets of science.

She checks her wallet for pound coins and finds two, which will only get her an hour. After a bit of rummaging in pockets she finds another three. That should do it. Then she remembers she has no car or kit. Shit! She has some doubles – scissors, combs and brushes, even a drier – but the rest means a trip to Ogee.

She calls Ailsa: 'Hey, I have to go for supplies and could be a bit late. Is that still okay? Great! See you then.'

That takes the pressure off. To Ogee by taxi, which idles outside while she makes her purchases, then the short journey to Learmonth Terrace. She's only twenty minutes late. The daily opens the door. She smiles and points to the bedroom asking, 'How's it going, Viv?'

Viv shakes her head and says, 'Hi Sue, not bad. I've had worse. She's having colour today; we usually do that in the kitchen.'

She can hear Ailsa on the phone, and leaving Sue on the landing she goes down into the kitchen and sets up. Before she's done Ailsa comes in and lets out a huge groan. 'Pressure, the pressure. God, you'd think I was writing a new chapter for the *Encyclopaedia Britannica*, not a pamphlet about Tranent.'

'It's more than a pamphlet.'

'Don't you start! They are paying me for a pamphlet and a pamphlet is what they will get. If they want more then they have to pay me more. They're giving me peanuts as it is . . . Viv, it's great to see you. Let me get the kettle on.'

One of the really reassuring things about Ailsa is her ability to switch from rant to reality in a second.

'They should pay you more. You're worth . . . in fact you're priceless.'

'And you are an angel for saying that. I always get stressed at the end and they always want something extra. The concept of "less is more" hasn't reached them yet.'

'What shall we do with you today?'

'Just make me look like, what's her name . . .' She clicks her fingers trying to recall the name. 'Angelina Jolie. That's it.'

'So you want a dark brown tint and twelve inch extensions?'

They both laugh. Ailsa's hair is short and blonde and has had very few variations over the last decade. Viv sets to work and they continue their discussion about Ailsa's writing and her tendency to sign contracts that tie her in to producing fantastic research for below the minimum wage.

Before Viv leaves Ailsa says, 'What are you up to this weekend? Fancy coming to dinner on Saturday? We have an old friend, a journalist, coming and he'd love to meet you. I keep talking about my fab hairdresser.'

'Too bad, I've already said yes to another invitation.'

'You going to Jinty's?'

Damn. 'Yes. As a matter of fact I am.'

'I'd rather be going there than having to put up with this bore . . .'

Viv shakes her head. 'That wouldn't be the bore you were about to set me up with, would it?'

They laugh and Ailsa playfully pushes her through the kitchen towards the stairs. Viv is almost out of the main door when Ailsa shouts, 'I haven't paid you!' She runs downstairs and hands Viv a cheque. 'You're worse than me!'

The case she'd had to buy this morning looks as if it should belong to a photographer – one of those shiny, silver cases. If it hadn't been half price she'd have made do with a carrier bag. This is way too flashy. She knows that she'll walk the distance in about the same time as it would take a cab to negotiate the traffic jams, so she sets off into Stockbridge and along St Stephen Street. It's one of her favourite streets in Edinburgh. The shops have been through so many incarnations that she knows there's bound to be something different to catch her eye, and sure enough there's a new deli.

The window looks great, she thinks, but I'll give it six months. Hoping that she's wrong she opens the door and is tickled by an old-fashioned bell alerting the owner to come out. He has a pure white pinny on, an indication that there hasn't been much custom this morning. He's trying really hard to sell good food, so she orders as much as she can carry. She now seriously regrets buying the huge work case.

The rest of the walk is less comfortable than she'd like, with the case banging against one knee and the weighted bag of groceries the other. The wind has dropped and wisps of vapour trails linger across the sky. She can barely remember the last time she took a holiday abroad and next week's trip to Assynt is now a no-goer. Since Dawn died she's been pretty static. No sooner is the idea of a trip becoming possible than guilt kicks in, wiping pleasure off her radar. By the time she reaches Niall's her arms are aching and she dumps the bags at her feet while she buzzes him. No answer. She tries again, this time with a smidgen of irritation, not least because she needs the loo. Still no answer. Strange. Looking at her watch, she's about three minutes late, so he should be here. She gives her arms a good shake to relieve the tension in her shoulders. One of his cars is there but she can't see the other.

Resigned to waiting an obligatory ten minutes before heading home, she decides to check her answering service. The remote interrogator takes a minute to claim the messages and sure enough there's a garbled one from Niall to say he's stuck in the dentist's waiting room with a frozen jaw, and could he reschedule. Time to hail a cab. Walking out onto Bellevue Crescent there's no sign of one, so she decides to stay put for the moment. It takes five minutes before she spots one, and she puts her arm out. It drives straight past, as she stands with her jaw dropped. Then in a voice that should be selling fish, she shouts, 'Your light's on!'

The next taxi appears only seconds later. It stops, revealing a driver who is way too chipper for Viv's liking, so she keeps her head down as if she's looking for something. He isn't deterred. Eventually she looks up and sees his eyes staring at her in the mirror. A vague recollection touches her, but nothing tangible.

'The West Bow, please.'

'Sure, sunshine. I've lifted you before. Wasn't it from . . . now where was it? Oh yeah, it was the Royal, yeah. That's it. The Royal. You weren't havin' a good day that day either.'

Viv sighs, thinking, 'If I wanted a shrink I'd bloody well get one,' but she grins up at him and says, 'Hard times, mate. Hard times.'

'You should talk to somebody about it then.'

Is he real? He's only getting paid to drive her a mile and a half. Sighing again, this time more emphatically, 'Yeah, sure, I should.'

It's the longest mile and a half she's had in a while. As she drags her bags out onto the pavement he rushes round to help her. She snaps, 'Look, I'm fine. Here,' handing him a tenner. As he goes to get her change, she mutters, 'Forget it.'

Once inside the stair she leans briefly against the door, wondering why she's feeling quite so snippy. The thought of the eighty-six steps between her and a pee is almost too much, and there's less than no chance of doing them two at a time today.

Viv's done enough soul-searching to understand that her reaction to the taxi driver was out of proportion. He's no idea what's been happening in the last few days. Feeling guilty for the second time today she zips into the loo before unpacking the goodies from the deli and shoving the kettle on. She ignores the phone ringing, relieved when she hears Jules' voice again. So what! She can wait. There's no deadline now that the story has completely changed. Then she hears, '. . . It wasn't Andrew.'

This catches her attention. How does Jules have this information when Marconi didn't even know last night? She checks her mobile again. There's another rather cautious message from Sal saying there's been a development, with such a generalisation that she must be referring to the case. Sorry that Sal had left so few details Viv rings back, but it goes straight to answering machine. She leaves a message saying thanks for the message and she'll ring again – equally vague.

After unpacking the food she realises that she hasn't got anything for lunch apart from a bag of organic coffee; everything else is just a component part of something. Sundried tomatoes on toast? Not ideal. The freezer compartment of the fridge throws up an ancient tart, which has lost its box. She wonders what it might be. Too hungry to wait she heads back out and down the Grassmarket to Petit France, her favourite bistro, known locally as Bella's, which does excellent lunches at reasonable cost. She seizes a newspaper off the stand as she walks in, and Bella catches Viv's eye and points to a table by the window. Viv nods and gives her the thumbs up, then acknowledges Benny, an old chap who regularly sits all morning purchasing one cup of coffee but drinking many more. Bella says, 'The usual, Doc?'

'Yep, and extra bread if you've got it.'

Bella calls back over her shoulder. 'More than we know what to do with. It's been quiet.'

'Maybe they know something that we don't.'

'Well, they shouldn't be doing it on an empty stomach.'

Viv laughs and Bella shouts through the hatch for the dish of the day. Viv used to spend ages looking at the menu, and then when a waiter or waitress came she'd ask for their recommendation. She always took what they recommended and got far better food than if she chose from the menu.

Bella sidles up to the table and lowers her voice. 'Hey, Doc, do you know that you've got a guy on your tail?'

Bella's not kidding.

'What have you seen?'

Bella and Philippe spend a good deal of time out on the pavement either serving the smokers or joining them.

'The last two . . . or is it three days, every time you pass the same bloke passes a minute later. You and I don't believe in coincidence, so I watched him one day and you stopped abruptly as if you were going to come back, and he leapt into the stairwell next door.'

'What does he look like?'

'Broader than he is tall, looks fit but not athletic, always wears a suit and a headset. Short mousey hair, thinning. Looks as if he might have played rugby.'

Viv relaxes at this. He must be one of Marconi's lot. They said they'd get someone to guard her. Wondering if they report her every movement to Marconi she reminds herself to pay attention when she leaves. Either her tail is really good or she's not much of an investigator. Lanky, dark-skinned, brown-eyed, beautiful Bella. There isn't a man who comes here who doesn't mainly come to look at her. She could be on the cover of *Vogue* if she wasn't so self-effacing.

The food comes piping hot with a basket of bread. It smells amazing, but Viv waits, knowing her weakness for gobbling and burning her tongue. Bella plonks herself down. 'So why are they tailing you, Doc?'

'I think they're looking out for me. At least I hope that's what they're doing. How about you? Being quiet is only a blip, eh? Although I don't see anyone queuing at the other bistros either.'

'It's since they put the price of parking up. It's out of the box. Three quid an hour means six quid on top of lunch. Too much. And where are they going to park anyway? 'Cos I don't know about you but we can never get a space, and we've got permits!'

'I don't have that problem at the moment. MG's been blown up!'

Bella laughs then sees that Viv is serious.

'You can't be serious.'

'Yes, I'm afraid I am.'

'Shit! What happened? You weren't in the car? . . . Obviously not or you wouldn't be here telling me. Christ, Doc, what is it you said you do?'

Viv smiles and scratches her head. 'Sometimes I wonder. But don't you worry. I can look after myself.'

Even she can hear the lack of conviction in her voice.

Lunch does the trick and Viv, feeling better after her reality check with Bella, decides to nip back to the flat to do a bit of on-line research. Starting with Facebook she looks up 'Robbie Croy Scotland', and finds his profile, which is nothing if not creative. If only he'd been as selective with his photographs as he had with the info in his profile. She hadn't imagined he'd have so many friends, although Robbie seems to use the word 'friend' loosely. He looks better in the flesh than in any of his pics, in most of which he looks drunk or worse. Scrolling through this little lot is going to take hours, but there's no time like the present. Armed with the remaining chocolate digestives and a pot of tea she settles down.

It's laborious work having to enlarge each photo so that she can make out the other people in them. A few familiar faces jump out and she reminds herself to be vigilant next time she's in Copa Cabana. Eventually one photograph does make her stop. It's Liam and Robbie in an embrace. 'Yuck! What is that about?' Viv can't believe that Robbie, who is as vain as they come, would even be in the same room as Liam. The only explanation is drugs. Got to be drugs . . . or money. She doesn't know what to do with this little nugget and realises that she really has to go back to the very beginning. She types in 'Andrew Douglas Edinburgh', but the phone rings and without thinking she reaches to answer it. 'Hello?'

'Hi, it's Sal.'

This wakes her up. 'Oh, hi!'

'I rang earlier and left a message.'

'Oh, I just got in and went straight on-line. I haven't checked my messages.'

The phrase, 'Liar liar, your pants are on fire' comes to mind. 'I'm doing a bit of work on Croy. I now think he's even more dodgy than I suspected. Have you guys heard anything about John Black?'

'He's in a bad way, but hanging on. They did a blood transfusion. Waiting to see if that was successful. But there's no chance of speaking to him.'

Viv, keen to keep the conversation on business, 'Have they identified the substances?'

'I don't know. Marconi didn't say.'

She sounds petulant. Perhaps Marconi is still in the huff. As if she's noticed, Sal returns to her normal tone.

'The body – the one that we thought could have been Andrew Douglas. It isn't him. The dental records didn't match. I thought you'd like to know.'

'Wow, that's a huge blunder. How did that happen?'

'You should ask Marconi about that.'

'Yeah, thanks. That's a relief . . . Well, I'd better get on.'

'Sure.'

'Cheers.'

'Yes, cheerio.'

Viv looks at the handset. What did I do there? Picking up the phone again, she punches in Jules' number. 'Hi, Alice, Jules around?'

'My God, Viv, is she gunning for you? Are you ready for this?'

Jules, never one for social graces, bellows, 'Where the fuck have you been? Did you get my message? This isn't working. I need more contact. We should speak . . .'

Viv interrupts her, 'No, we should speak when it's necessary. It hasn't been necessary. There was nothing that either of us could report when we thought he was dead. Now what have you got that you think will help me? A decent more recent photograph of Andrew would help by the way.'

'Okay, okay. It's just so frustrating.'

'What? When you can't control everybody?'

'Don't you . . .'

'Jules! Stop! Let's just get on with the task.'

After a brief, frosty silence Jules concedes. 'I'll email a photograph. His parents are offering a reward.'

'I thought rewards were for finding killers. We don't know whether he's alive or not.'

'They're desperate. Offering it for any information.'

'Christ! They'll have every Tom, Dick and gay boy who has never known him on the phone. Whose idea . . .'

Jules doesn't answer but Viv hears her sighing – Jules has clearly had something to do with the reward. Viv also sighs and says, 'Speak later.'

Clattering the phone back into its cradle she checks her email before heading for the kitchen to refill the kettle. She needs more tea like a hole in the head but it's something to do. By the time the kettle has boiled there's an email from Jules. Opening the attachment isn't successful at first and her Mac has to change the format, but finally a vision of Andrew Douglas appears on her screen. He's bonny, no doubt about that: fresh faced, no trace of acne and managing to make his school uniform look stylish with the collar of his blazer up and his tie in a huge knot. The gel on his dark hair would last anyone else a month and the marks on his ears indicate he wears earrings, but obviously not for the school photo. He's definitely got style. He hardly looks fifteen let alone eighteen. This image of Andrew differs from the one that she'd created from the earlier photograph where he was even younger. She had him chunkier and not so beautiful. When she's had enough gazing at the screen she sits back and stretches her back, which makes a cracking sound. Kneeling on the floor she does a few back lifts until it loosens up.

In preparation for her next Copa Cabana visit, the pockets of her jacket are freighted with stuff that she'd usually put in a wallet or rucksack, but tonight she wants to be able to run. The West Bow is busy with traffic and she realises how liberated she is without the MG. Another car can wait for now. At the top of her street she turns left then immediately right onto the Royal Mile, now almost a pedestrian precinct, with only the odd taxi permitted to use it. She passes the City Chambers and the many signs advertising ghost and literary tours. Edinburgh has more than its share of ghosts, ghouls and literary giants, which has created opportunities for entrepreneurs who concoct tours round their haunts. Even on this late January day there is a smattering of people queueing.

She turns smartly onto the North Bridge, where the stench of carbon monoxide is almost enough to make her choose another route, but she tucks her chin inside her collar and fastens the button, so that she can breathe into the fabric of her jacket. This route may be grubby but it is the quickest. It's also Suicide Row. The North Bridge straddles the main railway lines from the south and has become a popular spot for people to jump. It's a long way to the ground.

Viv designed her life so that she wouldn't have to do nine to five or work for anyone else. Being freelance must have its downside but she can never think what it is. Just as the air brakes of a bus startle her with a raucous hiss, her mobile rings and she fumbles about, freeing her hands from the chest pockets of her jacket. Whoever it is, they're not hanging up. 'Jules! What now?'

'You're never going to believe this but we've just had it down the wire. It was him after all!'

'But you said the dentals weren't his.'

'No, I didn't. I just said it wasn't him. Who'd you get the dentals from?'

'You. You said . . .'

Jules loses the rag and shouts. 'No I didn't, because I didn't have any detail at that time. Viv, what are you up to?'

Viv tries to recall what Sal said; convinced that it was Jules who had mentioned it. 'What the hell does it matter? We both know it's standard procedure to do a dental check if the body is unidentifiable. But how could they get that wrong? It's so basic.'

'The father is also called Andrew Douglas and it's the same dentist. Apparently he's mortified.'

'I should think so. Look, I'm on my way back to Copa Cabana. I'll get what I can but I expect they'll have heard as well. Christ, what a disaster. The parents must be . . .'

The phone cuts out. Nice, Jules, nice.

Carrying on down Leith Street she comes to the pub and damn it, it isn't as busy as she'd hoped. It is, however, warm and she unbuttons her jacket, rooting for her wallet. The barman from her first visit is on. His glare of welcome could have been worse.

'I'll have a half of organic cider, please.'

'That's not all you'll have if you poke your nose . . .'

He looks over Viv's shoulder and she turns to see a man coming through the door. The only way to describe him is suave, not to be confused with sophisticated. His dark green, boiled wool coat didn't come from M&S and his Manolo Blahniks are testimony to vanity beyond repair. Despite his tan appearing more tartrazine than Tenerife he is very good looking. The barman seems to have lost his tongue and a little line of sweat appears above his upper lip. Viv looks from him to the man walking towards the bar, but doesn't say anything. The barman looks relieved as she strolls up the few steps that take her to the back of the bar. She slides into one of the booths, leaving the barman to attend to his new customer. She has a grandstand view of what's happening. The newcomer has a glass of wine in his hand and is surveying the premises as if he owns them. Perhaps he does?

Liam appears from behind the bar. Her skin crawls, but she keeps her eyes fixed on him for his reaction to the good-looking new customer. Judging by Good Looking's face, his own skin is beginning to crawl. As she expected, Liam is fawning. Liam catches her eye, but quickly looks past her. Interesting. He's been determined the last couple of times he's seen her to make a point of irritating her. GL must have power beyond his brown eyes. GL is wiping something from his coat with a look of disgust on his face. Liam takes a step closer as if to assist but, if GL's reaction is anything to go by, is told in no uncertain terms to back off. For a millisecond she feels pity, remembering that Liam spits when he speaks.

The next move is pathetic. Liam backs away – she could swear he's almost genuflecting. Who is this guy? Draining her glass she approaches the bar, but the barman gives a tiny shake of his head. GL turns to see who the gesture is aimed at. Viv keeps moving and hands her glass back, 'Stick another in there, would you?'

'Sure!' Too enthusiastic. He keeps his eyes on the glass as he pours another half. GL turns away as if he's lost interest. Leaving her money on the bar she walks back to the booth, retreating from the tension pumping out of the barman. Liam has disappeared back through the door he emerged from and GL is leaning on the rail in front of the bar questioning the barman, who is shaking his head nervously. If only Viv could hear what is being said. She decides against moving closer. She sips her cider. Is she imagining it or is the bar quieter than when he came in? He surely can't be the owner? He has money, he's ostentatious, and Liam and the barman are afraid of him. What does he do that makes them nervous? Or what do they not have that he needs? Are they in his pay?

Suddenly he stands to his full height and gripping the rail leans back and says, 'You'd better.' This threat is the only thing that he's said loudly enough for her to catch. His back is impressively broad, and as he reaches the exit he turns back and makes a shooting gesture at the barman, whose face pales as he nods. After a few minutes she approaches the bar. The barman, clearly terrified, says, 'Don't!'

'Don't what?'

'Ask me anything.'

'Doing coffee?'

He sighs, and reluctantly hands her a slim menu.

'An Americano, please.'

While his back is turned the two guys from her first visit walk in. No sign of their football colours tonight. She is surprised when they approach her. 'Hi!'

She returns the greeting.

The taller of the two asks, 'You get anything interesting on Andrew yet?'

'What? Apart from his being . . .'

They don't look as if they've heard that he is dead. They just look hopeful. Viv manages, 'Apart from still being AWOL, you mean?'

It sounds lame, and looking confused the stocky one turns to his pal, 'What does that mean, then, Thomas?'

Thomas is irritated. 'It means they still haven't found him . . .'

Viv senses that he was about to say 'stupid'. 'You guys have probably got more than me.'

'We've got nothing. Otherwise, we'd have told the cops, after that scare. What a relief that it wasn't him.'

They do look young. And they're trying so hard to be grown up. Her Americano arrives and the barman quickly turns his best smile on his new customers.

'What can I get you, my beauties?'

Thomas turns on the camp charm, but Stocky looks embarrassed.

'Whisky and coke for me, luvvy. How about you, Johnny?'

'I'll have something soft. I'm driving.'

Sensible chap. He looks at Viv's coffee and says: 'I'll have a cappuccino.'

He pays for both of their drinks. Thomas doesn't even offer.

The barman says, 'Len's just been in.'

This wipes the smile off Thomas' face. 'Shit! What did he want?'

The barman gives Viv the evil eye and says, 'I'll tell you later.'

Shaking her head, Viv lifts her coffee and goes back to the booth, hoping that eventually they'll want to ask her more questions. They must have heard what happened at the flat with John Black.

The place is starting to fill up and she doesn't have the booth to herself for very long. Two guys move into the other side and proceed to pass an iphone back and forth, laughing and cooing as if they're looking at something illicit. Viv could be wallpaper. Being the only female here isn't that comfortable. She slips out again, knowing that she'll lose her seat, then ventures over to Andrew's pals and asks if she can buy them a drink. Thomas' eyes narrow. 'What'll it cost us? Look what happened last time we spoke to you.'

His chum interrupts, 'You speak for yourself. I said nothing.'

'Aren't we all on the same side?' Viv tries.

Thomas sneers, 'Look around you, dear, haven't you missed something?'

'No, I haven't missed something. I still think we're on the same team where Andrew's concerned.'

'You don't get it, do you?'

'No. What am I supposed to get?'

'He doesn't want to be found.'

'How would you know that? . . . Who did he leave here with the last night you saw him?'

Johnny is just about to say something when Thomas says, 'Shut it.'

But Johnny, pissed off, says, 'And Tommy, when did you become the communication police? He's got to be found. How scared were you when you thought he'd been torched? Shit scared, that's what. Just like me and everyone else. So give up on the tough guy routine.'

Viv would like to punch the air but instead ventures, 'Did you see him?'

'Yes, he left with Len.'

'And does Len have another name?'

'Not that I know, but he's around here often enough. We've seen him since Andrew went missing. He says he left him outside. I don't know if I believe him, but . . .' He looks at Tommy.

Viv looks from one to the other and says, 'But what, Johnny?'

Tommy shakes his head. 'That's enough. Don't say any more.'

'Christ! What are you all so scared of? If Andrew was dead would you talk?'

'Of course, we'd have to. It'd be a murder enquiry. But we wouldn't have to talk to you. You're only after a story.'

Viv, thinking it's worth the risk, says, 'He is dead.'

The look of horror on their faces is real. Thomas croaks, 'You're making that up. You bitch. How could you say that?'

He turns and walks toward the door without looking back.

Johnny is wide-eyed, 'You're not kidding, are you?'

'No, I'm not. I wouldn't lie about something as serious as that.'

She didn't even cross her fingers behind her back. Johnny swallows, his face sheet white. Viv thinks she's been pretty mean, but what choice did she have? Not to tell them when they'd find out anyway wouldn't be right. Now that she's got Johnny on his own she suggests another drink.

'No. I'd better go.'

'I suppose I'll head home too. Where are you heading?'

'The Grange.'

'We could share a taxi?'

She knows he's driving. Well brought-up boy that he is, he offers her a lift.

Chapter Eleven

Outside, Viv as usual pulls her jacket up round her chin. The temperature can't have got above zero today and the wind chill, whatever that is, means the cold bites her hard. Johnny motions towards Royal Terrace. He walks quickly and although her legs are longer than his she has to run a step, walk a step to keep up with him. In the small car the smell of its newness is overwhelming. She's glad that he's sensible and wasn't tempted to have 'just one'. The car starts first time.

'Thanks, by the way. It's good of you to give me a lift.'

'I'm so shocked about Andrew. Are you absolutely sure? It couldn't be another mistake?'

'No. I heard it through official channels.'

'What? Are you working with the cops?'

'Well, not officially. But they have asked me for the information I've got on what's going on at that flat. Have you any idea? Have you ever been there?'

'I've been once. Wasn't my scene. The old guy who owns it is a good bloke.'

This is a surprise to her. 'Sandy?'

'Yeah. He looks after people. There are tons of guys who make their way to Edinburgh thinking it's the gay capital – and you'd think it was if you believed the pink mags. But the reality can be bleak. Accommodation is expensive, booze is expensive – everything is really. So they end up having to get work, and what could be easier than renting?'

Viv takes a second to get his meaning. 'Rent boys?'

'Yeah. Renting your arse isn't that different to just giving it away night after night, which is what they end up doing. At least they've got a chance of a bed for the night. Maybe even breakfast if they're lucky.'

Viv can't help herself and interrupts. 'You're a bit jaded, aren't you?' She waits, tempted to add 'for one so young', but that'll not win her any favours. 'You're an intelligent bloke. What's Len's part in this?'

'I'm not sure. But he's rich and rough and straight.'

Viv turns in her seat. 'Christ!' This is getting beyond curious. 'Straight? Are you sure?'

'Yeah, he runs the boys.'

'He's their pimp?'

'Don't know if that's what he'd call himself. But he gets them set up. I've never done it, so I don't really know. But Andrew . . .'

'What – he sold himself? I wouldn't have thought with his looks he'd have had to. I mean sugar daddies an' all that.'

'He's got a habit . . . had a habit. And doesn't . . . didn't like older men. Not as straightforward as you think.' They sit in traffic at the top of Leith Walk waiting for the lights to change.

'Oh, I don't think there's much about this case that's straightforward, but you're right, I have made assumptions. So, Len? You sure he doesn't have a last name?'

'No idea. Always just known him as Len. I've never spoken to him or anything. Tommy has, but he wouldn't do it for him. There's so many who will. Len doesn't need to push anyone into it. They all do it by choice.'

How naïve.

'Where will I drop you?'

On their way up South Bridge she says, 'Anywhere around here. The end of Chambers Street's fine.'

He pulls over and she tries to open the door but they are too close to the railing.

'You'll have to pull forward a bit.' He does and she jumps out. 'Thanks.'

He nods and drives off.

With a good deal to think about she jogs along Chambers Street, past courts, museums and libraries, until she reaches the West Bow. Home.

She feels slightly nauseous. Bad idea to combine coffee with cider. She flicks on the TV and tucks her feet under her bum. The news channel has nothing about Andrew, which is strange. She looks for another news programme, but at five fifteen she's between bulletins. Her eye is drawn again to the iron mark on the carpet. The sculpture that used to cover that mark was moved to accommodate her ex's music stand and her double bass. The gap hardly seems big enough now. Dvorak's *Serenade for Strings* floats through her head. Viv visualises Dawn perched on her high stool balancing her bass. Viv's knowledge of classical music was all gleaned from Dawn. Wiping her wet cheeks on her sleeve she flicks through more channels.

Why she's so emotional is anyone's guess since they weren't exactly the ideal couple. At best their relationship would have been described as volatile, but love is a weird anaesthetic. While her laptop boots up on the desk in the corner she decides to move the furniture to cover the mark. The Chesterfield weighs a ton, and as she edges it round bit by bit, a fingerless woollen mitt is exposed. Viv gently lifts it, idly picking at the fluff that's gathered on it. It's unmistakably Dawn's. She was paranoid about her hands being cold, too cold to play. Get a grip, Viv. She's been dead for nearly two years. Startled by the phone; she pockets the mitt and lifts the handset.

'Hi, Viv, it's Marcus here. We've got Robbie Croy in with us. Tried to be brave to begin with but he's beginning to squeal a bit now. Mentioned a guy named Leonard Whiteman. Have you heard of him?'

'Funny you should ask, but this very evening I didn't quite meet someone called Len; suave chap. Been almost barbecued under a sun lamp. Saw him in Copa Cabana.'

'And you were there because . . .?'

'I was looking for those young guys, the friends of Andrew.'

'And? Any luck?'

'Yep. One of them told me about a Len – no idea what his second name is, but it's bound to be him. There can't be two unsavoury Lens hanging about the gay scene. This one is apparently straight.'

'Yeah, that must be him. We thought it was weird, but money is money whatever way you look at it. Young gay men are as vulnerable as young women and just as easily exploited.'

'He was scary. Had the barman and another guy licking his boots.'

Viv reflects on Liam's reaction. It makes her skin crawl again.

'Viv?'

'Still here. The guy that's supposed to be the manager is not a nice man. Liam Doyle.'

'We've just had a look at his file. Dirty Doyle.'

She sniggers at this. 'You bet. He's totally unscrupulous. I don't know what he's had to do to get the job. In fact it could be a partnership.'

'Yes, it looks as if he has an "interest", shall we say, in Copa Cabana.'

'Red, I mean Sandra Nicholson, shouldn't rely on anything he says. He's never known the difference between fact and fiction.'

'You seem to know him quite well. I take it you had met before this investigation?'

'Yes. Liam and I worked together. He was caught thieving. My money as it happened. You could say there's no love lost between us.' Is he really as ugly as she's painting him? Recalling his voice, that pernicious whine, she decides he is. 'Although he's unscrupulous I'm not sure he'd have the brains to set anything up, but I've no doubt he'd want to play if there was money to be had. By the way Len, whatever his name is, treated him as if he was a bit of shit on his shoe. If I know Liam he'll hold a grudge against him for that.'

Marconi is a good listener, not prone to interrupting unless he really does need clarification. He says, 'Worth having a chat with him them?'

'I'd say so.'

'Anything to add on Mr Croy? We can keep him for a bit; he had a quarter ounce in his possession.'

Playing for time she says, 'I'll go over my notes and if there's anything, I'll ring you back. By the way could we lose the tail? It's unnecessary.'

He doesn't answer immediately then says. 'Okay.'

They end the call and Viv looks around for her notebook, not expecting to find any major revelations. If this guy Len is a pimp what's the difference between buying young boys from eastern Europe or young boys from round Scotland? It's surely still trafficking? No one has mentioned the T word, which is unusual since it's the buzz word that ticks the most funding boxes.

She finds the notebook beneath the tartan rug on her bed. Curious. She can't remember leaving it there. As she flicks through it the skeleton of something begins to emerge, but it'll take a few more bones before its identity is known. When she returns to the sitting room the Chesterfield is still out of place. She drifts into thinking again about Dawn. They had been moving in the direction of breaking up. Viv, a devoted monogamist, couldn't cope with Dawn having other ideas of what that meant. Dawn died before they had an opportunity to talk. Her things lay in the flat for weeks before her sister picked them up. It was messy. The sister, an Episcopalian priest, hadn't known the truth about her sis and was less than polite when having to confront the reality. Not too chuffed about the eighty-six stairs either. Thank God that's all in the past.

The light on her answering machine is flashing. She presses the button and the voice of Sal Chapman says, 'Hi, Viv, it's Sal here. It was just to let you know that Mac, I mean Marconi, is going to ring you. He's looking for anything you've got on Robbie Croy. Hope you're okay. I expect the shock of the blast is catching up with you. My mobile number is . . .' Viv rakes around for a pen, grabbing one only to find its ink has dried up. By the time she's found another, the number has gone from her head and she has to play the message again. A tingling sensation runs through her. It's warming, but scary, to hear concern in Sal's voice. Others have worried about Viv, but she hasn't been able to handle their concern, and even her few years of therapy didn't resolve that. Although having therapy did make her clear about the difference between hearing and receiving, it's like the difference between hearing the rain and being out in the rain. Neither is going to harm you, but the effects of being under rain are immediate.

Her notes aren't very comprehensive, and there are one or two anomalies that she'd like to follow up. The description from his crying friend of the guy who Andrew left Copa Cabana with, sits uneasily. He could have been describing Len. Still, that can wait. She also needs to see John Black again, which will have to wait too. Time for bed.

115

After a night of unbroken sleep and with no hair clients to see today she relaxes, knowing she can spend her day with the duvet. After coffee and toast she settles in on-line. Nothing shows for Leonard Whiteman in the UK. Leo Whiteman comes up on Facebook, but he's only about sixteen. Too young for the Whiteman she's looking for. After endless scrolling down, she finds a number of newspaper articles and the first she opens is about her Whiteman's wedding. A grand affair. He's described as a 'philanthropist', which is stretching it by anyone's standards. Married a beauty – with no brain? – a model. Viv wonders if Mrs Whiteman knows what her husband's sidelines are. Feeling stiff, and realising she's been at this for hours, she refuels with tea and biscuits before returning to see if she can find more on the wife. Just as her hand is hovering on the mouse pad she hears a noise in the hall. On opening the sitting room door she can see a hand holding the letterbox open and a pair of eyes staring back at her.

'Who is it?'

A faint voice. 'It's me.'

She doesn't recognise it and feels the hairs on the back of her neck rising.

'Yeah, and?'

'It's John.'

It takes a few seconds for this to sink in before she rushes to the door. 'John Black?'

'Yours truly. How many John Blacks do you know?'

'For God's sake. I told you to ring before you came.'

By the look of him he must have discharged himself; there's no way they would let him out looking like this.

'How did you get here? And how did you know where to come?'

His breathing is laboured, and sweat's trickling down his waxy brow.

'As you see, it wasn't a picnic trying to find you, but I remembered Robbie saying something about 'that bird from the West Bow', and gathered that he meant you. I've been up and down the street looking at every name, and narrowed it down. Because there are surprisingly few flats with no name, I guessed that one of these was likely to be yours and this is my third try. Could do with a seat after that climb.'

All this time he's been leaning against the wall in the hallway.

'Shit! Sorry. Come through. You look hellish!'

'Thanks, you're all heart!'

Once she's got him into the sitting room she heads back to the kitchen to put the kettle on before returning to ask what he'd like.

'You couldn't get closer to God, could you? I counted eight-nine steps.'

'Three too many – there's only eighty-six.'

'Pardon me for exaggerating.'

It's nice to hear him raising his game, but the cost sounds too high if his breathing is anything to go by.

'Tea? Or something stronger?'

'I could start with something stronger.'

Viv's drinks cabinet isn't exactly overflowing, but there's a bottle of malt whisky she got from a client one Christmas, which hasn't been opened. Reading the box it says 70 per cent proof. Firewater; it'll kill or cure. She's not much of a drinker and rarely drinks alone, but pours them each two fingers. They both sip and he looks at her with respect.

'You make this yourself?'

'Got the "still" out back.'

He smiles. If he wasn't so ill he'd be nice to look at.

'So, John, how come you're here?'

'They kept pushing me for information.'

'Who did, you mean Robbie and Sandy?'

'No, the nursing staff. Wanting to know about family. But the family didn't want to know about me when I was well, so why would they now?'

'Families are weird things, John. Any hint of losing one of the brood and they come clucking.'

'Trust me, there'd be no clucking from my family. My mother's terrified of my dad. I'm their only son. Big disappointment, not having a son to carry on the line. We farm. Well "we" don't, which is the problem. Dad's the fourth generation of cattle farmers in Aberdeenshire. They don't have gay sons, although *Grindr* would tell them otherwise.'

She knows how difficult families can be when things don't go as hoped.

They see everything as a reflection of themselves. She guesses John's father is embarrassed by his son, and wonders when he'll realise his loss. She sometimes tries to imagine how her own dad would have been with her choices, her mum has always been fine with her varied 'friendships', at least on the surface. She did hear her mother once saying to someone, 'Oh, Vivian's a career girl.' That over-worked euphemism is at least better than 'spinster'.

'I'm not sure I get your meaning entirely. So, who is Grinder?'

He smiles, 'An app for gay men. My dad has got no idea just how many of my school pals were gay. Never heard of the one-in-four statistic. My school had more like one-in-two.' He laughs, which morphs into a racking cough. As he calms down Viv thinks about her own school chums. Not many of them were gay, but how would she have known if they were? She'd been clueless about such things then. The bruisers in the hockey team that she thought were certs were churning out babies before they got their exam results. Not that that means anything.

'So, Viv, how come you're in on a Saturday night?'

'Shit!'

She leaps up and checks the time on her laptop. Six-fifteen. She'll make it if she rushes. If only she'd phoned Jinty when she said she would. She'd forgotten and really needs to show her face – she owes it to Jinty – and one drink will cover her duty.

'I have to go out for an hour but you can make yourself at home and I'll sort out the bed when I get back.'

'You said I'd be on the couch.'

'Yeah, that thing you're sitting on is a bed settee. Even has springs. All mod cons here. It'll be too heavy for you to pull out on your own. I really will only be an hour. It's a duty call.'

He's not in any state to argue or ask any more questions so he unzips his jacket, and with a bit of effort, manages to get it off and swing it over the back of the couch.

'Thanks for this, Viv. You don't even know me.'

'The silver's in the second cupboard on the left; help yourself! But if my guess is right you can barely lift your eyebrows so my silver is the least of my worries.'

Viv puts another whisky in front of him. 'Go easy.'

In a few minutes, she emerges from her bedroom in a little black dress and pumps. She pinches her cheeks and asks, 'Will that do?'

'Christ! Women are amazing. How could you look like the most normal dyke one second and as if you'd be at ease on the cover of a magazine the next? You look great . . . not my type, but glam.'

She takes that as an okay and heads for the door. Running back she fishes about down the side of the couch and hands him the remote.

'See you in an hour.'

Chapter Twelve

When the taxi pulls up outside Jinty's, the front door is open and a couple are having their coats taken. She slips past them – she's no intention of leaving her jacket – and bumps into Jinty with a bottle of champagne in her hand.

'Viv! You came. Excellent. I'm thrilled to the tits. Come through and I'll get you a glass.'

The inner hall, usually a gallery of oddities, is now obscured by many bodies, each holding a glass of bubbly. The bust of Flavia – a loved family pet – can just be made out behind the legs of a very glamorous blonde, who has glazed over at whatever her companion is saying. The woman's lack of interest is so obvious that she bends to the side to look beyond his head, and following her gaze both he and Viv see Jinty's husband Rod holding court; nothing unusual in that. The group, just inside the dining room door, are hanging on his every word; there are two blondes of a certain age and a couple of men, one of whom is Max Scott. Spotting Viv, Max excuses himself and squeezes through the crowd towards her. He's wearing that public school uniform of mustard corduroy trousers and a raspberry V-neck, no doubt cashmere, with a shirt and tie underneath. Why does he need to pull the sweater so far down? It makes him look out of proportion; as if his legs are too short. He's getting on for six foot four so there's nothing short about his legs.

'How are you? Didn't expect to see you here. Although I'm delighted that you are.'

'Thought you were going to China?'

'Yes, well . . .'

Taking hold of her arm he steers her into the dining room, just as Jinty marches over with a drink.

'I see you already know Max.' Then she looks up at his hair, 'That explains it. I've always thought he looked rather well groomed for an Edinburgh financier.'

'Yes, Jinty, my secret's out. Viv cuts it at the office.'

'Bet he doesn't serve good coffee?' she says, turning to Viv.

'No, he doesn't, and his iron maiden receptionist is never likely to offer. It's been . . . what is it Max, how many years?'

'At least a decade in the property we're in at the moment. It wouldn't have crossed my mind to offer you a coffee.'

Jinty smiles and licks her finger, marking one up for her, then slides off through the crowd. If Max steers her any closer to the window they'll be on the outside sill.

'Max, what the heck are you up to?'

He looks round furtively to see if anyone is within earshot, then whispers, 'You haven't told anyone about the explosion, have you?'

'What do you think?' Viv is aware the papers had run a story about a suggested gas leak, as a cover, but there had been no mention about her car being blown up. 'Of course I haven't mentioned it. Juliet Muir would have me drawn and quartered.' Jules didn't get to hear anything about it. Everyone knows who she is – in fact it'll be a first if she's not here. She manages to get invited to everything that Edinburgh has to offer, public or private.

Max is running his fingertip round the top of his glass, making a squeaking noise, which is beginning to irritate Viv. She eyeballs him and nods at his gesture. He stops and whispers, 'Have the police had you in again for questioning?'

'Yes, Max, they have. They've been very thorough. How about you?'

She's surprised when he says yes.

'More than once. That guy Marconi seems to think there's a connection with something else he's working on.'

'Did he say what?'

She guesses correctly this time.

'When I asked, he gave me the runaround. National security kind of stuff. Didn't convince me or the woman who was with us.'

Viv wonders if it was Sal, but erases the thought. No reason for a profiler to be in an interview about a city blast. Come to think of it there's been no need for a profiler on anything that Sal's involved in so far. 'What did she look like?'

This is out before she realises. She flushes as he describes Sal Chapman as, 'Small, good looking, feisty. Got the impression she was a country girl. Don't know why, but she didn't strike me as one of you city slickers.'

Viv can hardly believe that Max uses words like 'feisty' and 'slickers'. He's been watching too many old movies. Men only think women are feisty when they disagree with them. The next step up for such a woman in Hollywood terms would be 'ball breaker'. She doesn't imagine Sal has any notion of being either of those, but it comes with the territory of being female and good at your job. Max keeps looking round, nervous; there's got to be more to it than just whether Viv has mentioned the incident. He stands in front of Viv as if he's trying to block her from view. Or is it viewing? Viv, definitely tetchy now, tries to sidle along the wall, but an ancient tapestry prevents her progress.

'Right, Max, what's going on?'

'Nothing, as long as no one knows about the blast.'

He's trying for 'confident' but ends up with comic. Eventually Viv puts her hand on his broad chest and pushes him out of her space.

'It's getting too hot in here. I'm going to get some air.'

She can feel his eyes on her back as she heads towards the back door. The smokers are clustered around the fountain just a few steps outside. They needn't be. Jinty isn't anti-smoking in the least – in fact she's likely to come and herd them in so that she can get a nicotine fix without the earache she receives when having a fag herself.

Leaning on the doorframe Viv wonders how long she has to stay before it's not rude to leave. She doesn't think ten minutes counts. Then, feeling someone's breath near her ear, she ducks and turns to see the blonde she spotted earlier standing as close to her as she can. The perfume she's wearing is musky and likely to give Viv a headache if she gets too much of it. Viv moves outside to let the woman pass, but she doesn't appear to want to. There's something familiar about her. Her tan, real or otherwise, looks perfect. Her clavicles stand proud beneath shoestring straps, and remind Viv of the hind end of a cow that's past its birthing years.

'We haven't met. Zoe Whiteman.'

She offers a boney, long fingered hand that isn't as youthful as the face, and Viv reluctantly shakes it.

' Viv, Viv Fraser.'

'Oh, I know who you are. We thought you might be here. Max and Sonia are great chums of ours.'

Viv puts two and two together and tries to move into the garden, but the woman has a discreet hold of the back of her dress. Viv turns abruptly, hearing fabric tear.

'Back off, lady, before we embarrass our hostess.'

Viv says this through tight lips, but is aware that the blonde has taken hold of her dress again. Viv turns again, this time throwing her champagne at the woman. She leaves her standing and barges back through the crowd. On reaching the front hall she spots Jinty and waves. Jinty shouts, 'Viv, don't go!'

There's something in her tone that makes Viv halt. Jinty's eyes tell her all she needs to know. The crowd parts to let them through. Viv can't have been the only one to catch her panic. All eyes are on them. Jinty whispers something and Viv thinks she hears 'Whiteman'. 'In here.' Jinty pulls Viv by the arm into a tiny cloakroom, which is also home to the washing machine and a glass case containing two eccentric stuffed stoats dressed in little girls' frocks. Jinty is breathing heavily and Viv touches her arm. 'It's okay. Everything is okay.'

'That's what you think. Rod is going mad out there. Max and Sonia Scott rang up and asked if they could bring a friend along. I said no problem, but apparently she's married to one of Edinburgh's richest dirty men, Leonard Whiteman. Rod can't be seen to have anything to do with him. We can't have her in the house. What did she say to you? I saw her cornering you.'

'Well, she didn't really say anything. She just grabbed my dress and it ripped when I tried to break free.'

Jinty turns Viv round to look at the damage.

'It's only the seam. By the way, it's the first time I've seen you in a dress; it suits you. But what would she want with you?'

'God knows, but she's pushing her luck if she thinks she's found a shrinking violet. I had to throw my drink at her before she'd let me go.'

'My God. I bet you think . . .'

'Whatever I think it has nothing to do with your hospitality. You've never given me any cause to doubt you. But Whiteman is another story. What do you think is going on with Max and Sonia if they've become friends with those unsavouries? And why did they want to bring her here? I need to speak to Max again. Are you okay?'

'Yes. I'll be fine. D'you think she'll head off now that her frock is wet?'

'I don't imagine she'll want to hang around, but it depends on her mission. Let's go and find Max.'

The crowd has thinned a little and their movement is easy until a red-faced Rod shouts, 'Jinty, where the hell have you been?'

Realising that he's captured the attention of almost everyone, he tries to lighten up, but as soon as he's up next to Jinty he whispers through gritted teeth, 'Get her out of here.'

Jinty looks at him, aghast.

'What . . . Viv ?'

'No, the skeleton in silver sequins. Get her out!'

This is going to be difficult for Jinty so, in an attempt to aid her friend, Viv reaches for another glass of bubbly, saunters towards Mrs Whiteman and feigns a trip. This time Mrs Whiteman lets rip in an accent that is definitely more Mordun than Morningside, 'You fucking bitch!' Too loud. The room has fallen silent. She puts her head down and makes toward the front door, throwing over her shoulder, 'You'll regret this!'

Viv's no doubt she will. She looks round and catches Jinty's eye, who mouths, ' I - O - U, thank you.'

Viv blows her a kiss and puts her hand up in a phone sign. They both nod and Viv moves into the outer hall, battling to get through a knot of people trying to identify their coats. They've obviously had enough entertainment for one evening. Max and Sonia are among them. Viv looks at him, her expression indicating unfinished business. He gives the slightest shake of his head and looks at the back of his wife's head. Viv's beyond caring. 'Later Max. We'll speak later.'

The chill hits her as the wind funnels along the street from the east. Her short jacket barely covers the tear in her dress. A taxi pulls up and she gives him the address.

'Cold night!'

'Sure is. It sure is.'

She takes a deep breath and lets it out slowly with control. Holy Moly. What was all that about? What could Zoe Whiteman's errand have been?

Home can't come soon enough. As she turns the key she remembers she's got company. Sighing, she plods up the stairs thinking through the possible connection between Max and Leonard Whiteman and hopes that it is as simple as the two wives meeting at the gym or the beauty salon. When she walks into the sitting room John is asleep. From the cupboard in the hall she fetches a spare duvet and a pillow. He stirs when she lifts his legs onto the couch, but soon settles back to sleep.

She changes into tartan winceyette pyjamas, bedsocks and a sweater and sets about finding out more info on Whiteman. Her laptop stirs into life as soon as she handles the keyboard. Deciding to type Max and Whiteman in the same search she's a little surprised when a list comes up. She doesn't scroll for long when, 'Bingo!' They both play golf at the Balfour, an exclusive club out on the west side of Edinburgh.

Viv has been there a couple of times, once to a funeral and the other time, invited at the last minute, to make up the numbers at a dinner. It was a memorable night not least because the female players had nowhere to change; only a tiny, but beautifully decorated toilet – the rest of the building was unquestionably designed by males for males.

She is staring at a photograph of Max, Whiteman and two other men grinning into the camera with their hands on a cup. Max must know him fairly well if they play in foursomes together, and surely can't have avoided the rumours. He must know what Whiteman is. Is he choosing to ignore it? Or has he something to hide himself? They say there's more business agreed on the course than off it, but what kind of business would they need to do so far out of earshot of anyone else? The club has a complete 'no mobile phone' policy, in the clubhouse or on the course.

The date on the golf article is five years ago, so they are not just recent acquaintances. Another article is on the Whiteman wedding, with a photograph of the family group. Zoe looks fresh and glamorous. Her father looks a lot like Whiteman: tall, broad and dark, though the father has a boxer's nose. She and Whiteman have been married for a decade. Zoe was definitely in better shape then. Ten years of starvation hasn't done her looks any favours; sure she's still glamorous, but up close, the scraggy skin and brown spots tell a different story.

John stirs, mumbling. Viv glances over the back of the couch; he looks as if he's dreaming. He can't be more than twenty-five and yet his body has taken such a thrashing. Drugs both legal and illegal have taken their toll. This gives her something else to look up. Googling 'Rehab near Edinburgh', there are four possibilities. The first two, one in Ayrshire, the other north-west of Glasgow, are too far away, but one in West Lothian looks possible. The website is extensive but gives nothing away. By the time she's read it she's no more informed about what they actually do or what it costs than when she started. The last one is in East Lothian. The website would lead readers to believe they were going to a health spa. Maybe it is a health spa. Scrolling down, it ticks all the right boxes, but must cost a fortune.

John stirs again, this time waking and looking around him.

'Hi. I didn't want to wake you. The light in my bedroom isn't great at night so I thought I'd do this here.'

'I must have been out for the count. The whisky. Must have been the whisky.'

She smiles. 'Must have been. Can I get you anything?' Then, remembering just how limited the contents of her fridge are, she adds, 'I'll nip down to the shop and grab some bits and pieces. Anything you fancy?'

'Could murder a bacon roll. Crispy bacon, not that barely cooked, slippery wet stuff they give you in hospital.'

'You must be feeling better. When I saw you last you could hardly speak, never mind comment on the cuisine.'

Tucking her pyjamas into boots and pulling on a long raincoat she grabs her wallet and heads for the door. Before she gets there he shouts, 'I'd love a razor. The hospital only had electric razors. Makes you feel manky.'

'I've already got some. Check the bathroom cupboard. Help yourself to a shower if you can manage.'

'Sure.'

On her return he's in the shower. It feels nice to come home to someone else in the house. Even if he is a stranger. Viv hates living alone and yet the vibes she's given to previous partners haven't exactly made them feel wanted.

She turns the control of the oven and wonders if it will actually work tonight. When she sticks her hand in she can feel there's nothing doing. Good old frying pan will have to do. By the time John has finished in the bathroom the smell of bacon is wafting round the flat.

He lifts his head and draws in a breath. 'Smells like proper bacon. Even my poor gut is getting excited about it.'

The kitchen is small with a table intended for two Lilliputians, so she takes their rolls through to the sitting room on a tray where two 'eco' wall heaters are blasting out mega watts. She kneels on the floor in front of the empty fire surround, sorry that the smokeless zone prevents her from having a real fire. She hands him a plate.

He looks at her and says, 'I don't know why you're doing this for me, but I'm really grateful. I've got money you know. Just don't have access to it until I pick up the rest of my gear from the flat.' Then, seeing the look on Viv's face, he hastily adds, 'No, not that flat. My sister's flat. Don't look at me like that.'

Viv, with eyebrows knitting, is about to ask why he's here if he has a sister in town, when he interrupts her thoughts. 'My dad has said if he ever finds out that I've been there she'll be in the bad books as well. He has some idea that she'll be contaminated by my behaviour. So that's why I can't go there. I've got her into enough trouble. My building society book is there. He hasn't stopped my allowance yet, which is a miracle – it's probably my mum who has managed to keep it going. If I phone my sis she'll bring my stuff round.'

Viv doesn't ask what trouble there was. There'll be time for interrogations later. But she's not sure about having a family reunion in her flat. 'Good rolls!'

He nods his agreement. 'Haven't felt like food for a while. They kept me on a drip after the blood transfusion. I suppose they know what they're about. But they're not exactly promoting health with the food they serve. Everything's processed. I've been brought up on Aberdeen Angus and veg from the garden. My mum always makes her own bread.'

'Well, you'll have to put up with what I could get. The gourmet section was closed.'

He looks at her and seeing that she's taking the piss, smiles and apologises.

'Beggars and all that,' mutters Viv as she unpacks a few treats from a carrier bag.

'This is great. No complaints.'

'Just as well.' She grins.

'How was your drinks party?'

'Eventful!' She shakes her head and through puffed cheeks lets go of a lungful of air.

'How come?'

'Have you come across a guy called Leonard Whiteman?' She stands poised, pointing the rolled up carrier at him as he leans back on the couch.

His face says it all. 'You don't want to get involved with him . . . Baaad news.'

'Tell me about him. In what way is he bad news? Does he own Copa Cabana?'

'Yes, he does, along with everything else that's . . . I was going to say "gay" but I think he owns a couple of snooker halls as well. Tanning salons, nail bars. He even has a gym.'

'So, plenty of opportunity for shuffling money and staff around?' Viv makes the sign of inverted commas round 'staff'.

'I guess. I've never been involved with him. He hates Sandy.'

This gets Viv's attention.

'Why would he hate Sandy?'

'Despite what you think, Sandy's a good guy. He looks after young guys. Okay the flat's a bit of a shambles, but it's a lot safer than . . .'

'Than what? Come on, John. There's something really dodgy going on, and now that I'm in this far I'm going to find out whether you tell me or not.'

'But if I tell you what I've heard I'll be implicated.'

'Implicated? Sounds heavy. In what?'

'That would be telling now, wouldn't it?'

'Am I missing something here? Am I wrong, or are you close to death because of something that Robbie provided? Robbie who could be tampering with supplies that are coming from . . . You fill in the gaps, would you?' She sits herself down at his side.

'I don't know for sure. But Robbie is definitely linked to Whiteman.'

'Good, carry on.'

'You know as well as I do that Robbie's been inside. He's got connections and Whiteman is one of them.' Viv pulls her knees up, and hooks her arms round them.

He sounds tired, and Viv thinks it might be better to have this conversation over breakfast. 'Why don't you give it some thought and maybe the two of us can make some sense of the whole Andrew Douglas, Robbie Croy, Leonard Whiteman and whoever the hell else is involved, thing. If you move your butt I'll make up the bed properly.'

With a bit of effort he moves over to the chair while she pulls out the bed settee. It weighs a ton and she scratches her arm on one of the springs in the process.

'Let me help.'

'No, it's okay, it's done. There. All you have to do is climb in and sleep. See you in the morning.'

Chapter Thirteen

Sunday has never been her favourite day. An expanse of nothingness isn't anything to look forward to. This morning, beyond the chink in the curtains, she can see it's raining. Much less cold than it was last night, but a lowering sky reaches as far as she can see. Dropping the edge of the curtain she huddles down under the duvet and thinks about John Black next door. After all he's been through this week he's still willing to withhold whatever it is he knows. Fear – it's our greatest motivator. She's experienced extreme fear herself, always in relation to things beyond her control, like being driven too fast, or hanging off a rope on the In Pin in Skye with adrenaline pumping round her body so hard that she couldn't get back on the rock. Just thinking about it makes her mouth dry up.

Forcing her mind back to the present, she visualises Max in that photograph with Whiteman, both looking like pillars of middle-class Edinburgh. Wobbly pillars. Yep. Wobbly pillars. No empire is secure, and certainly not if you're fraternising with a modern-day Caligula. A vision of Whiteman in a Roman toga and a laurel crown makes her smile. It won't be long before someone sticks the knife in. With her brain in full gear she throws the duvet back. She pads through to the kitchen and pushes the switch on the kettle. On the loo it comes to her that Robbie Croy is cocky enough to think of himself as an alpha male. Liam is too weak. A shiver runs over her at the very thought of the little weasel. He must have a part in this drama, otherwise he wouldn't have given her the time of day. He's snubbed her since she shopped him. So she won't be surprised if he's told someone that he knows her, trying to be a big shot. He also knows where she lives. The note through the door – delivered by him? No way. He's just an information peddlar.

There's nothing she can do until John rouses so she faffs about in the kitchen. She even reads the ingredients on the packet of cereal, and knowing that ingredients are in order of how much is in the product, she baulks that the second on the list is sugar. So much for the healthy option; she might as well have picked up another packet of chocolate biscuits – at least they're not pretending to be healthy. After her second cup of tea she hears movement from next door. A sleepy John sticks his head into the kitchen and yawns a, 'Good morning.'

'Are you sure it is?'

'Ooh! Who's an unhappy bunny this morning, then?'

She smiles, surprised that she had sounded so jaded.

'Not unhappy, frustrated. I'm sure things will start coming together today.'

'Why do you think that you have to solve this?'

Good question. 'Well I was asked to do a job, to find out about Andrew Douglas and the story has, let's say, developed. I can't start something and not finish it. Especially when they blew up my car.'

'No way. When did that happen?'

She's forgotten that he doesn't know anything that has happened beyond her finding him in Sandy's flat.

'Let's get a tray together and I'll fill you in.'

He actually looks much better. Must have been the bacon rolls.

When he returns from his ablutions he says, 'God, what a relief it is to be away from hospital smells. The very thought of that makes me quiver in my boots.' She looks at him quizzically, and he explains, 'Had surgery as a young boy. All those memories of being forced to eat. It was bad enough this time round, but back then, I was sure they were trying to kill me.'

'Well, let's see how you improve in my care.' She can't believe she's just said this, so qualifies it with, 'For today, anyway. You'll soon realise I'm no competition for Florence Nightingale.'

He is open-mouthed when she tells him about the blast and about the drinks party last night, but the state of her dress is all the proof he needs.

'I'm going to find out a bit more about Leonard Whiteman. So Google and I will be on intimate terms today. What do you need? I imagine you'll not be going far either? So do we need any ground rules?' Viv cocks her head.

'I could do with some things from my sister. I'm sure she'd drop them off if that's okay with you?'

Now that this is posed as a question, she's not in the slightest concerned.

'That's fine. As long as we don't have the rest of the family tapping on the door.'

'There's no chance of that. I'll give her a ring.'

While he does this, she boots up. Outside the window the cloud is so low she can't even see the Pentland Hills; a good day to batten down the hatches. Only once since the car incident has she regretted postponing her holiday, but that bleak sky is a reminder of what she might have faced if she had gone north. Besides, Assynt's not going anywhere.

Once Viv gets on-line she's consumed. There is so much information available it's almost criminal. She smirks as she clicks on another article. Max and Whiteman, it turns out, were at school together. Edinburgh's impressive old school network is alive and kicking. The photograph makes all four men look much the same, the golf uniform doing its job, unifying them. Viv's vision of Whiteman is so different from that of Max, who is the epitome of Edinburgh establishment. She imagines Max thinking that Manolo Blahnik is a composer or a chef, unless of course Manolo were floated on the stock market. Whiteman went into the family firm and diversified. 'He sure did,' Viv mutters.

'What was that?' John stirs from his slumber on the couch.

'Oh, nothing. It's just that parents have no idea how their hard-earned school fees are going to pay off. I've got one guy allegedly a pillar of Edinburgh society, and the other from the same school – Whiteman. You sure you don't know anything more about him? I'm surprised he shows himself in Copa Cabana. Confident, he's confident.'

'I've only seen him a couple of times, both of them in Copa Cabana. And then Robbie . . . well he's always showing off about something, so he's mentioned him a couple of times.' He leans on his elbow and turns to look Viv.

'Can you remember what context?'

'I can't stand Robbie, as you've probably gathered; he doesn't think too highly of me either. He plays the big man, but I'm not sure how much is bluff. He's fucking horrible to Sandy, excuse the French, and I hate that. He threatens him with blackmail then says he was only kidding. I don't know why Sandy doesn't dump him.'

'Sandy, if I'm not mistaken, is an adult. He can look after himself. But what about all those sleeping bags lying around the flat? Who do they belong to? It didn't look . . .' She recalls the state of the flat and grimaces. John notices.

'It's not what you think. Sandy really is a rescuer. There are so many young guys turning up at the club who, if they're not careful, are gonna end up in the hands of creeps like . . .'

'Like?'

'Like Whiteman. He is one of the worst.'

'One of the worst what?'

He raises his eyes to the ceiling. 'I'm sure you can guess.'

'Humour me.'

He sighs. 'I've heard that he can organise any boy you want. Any age, colour, shape or size. You name it, he's got it or can get it.'

She presses. 'All under age?'

'Not always, but if you like it that way, yes. He has them trawling Calton Hill. They wear specific things if they belong to Whiteman.'

'What sort of things?'

'Say, white jeans and a bag worn on the left shoulder.'

Viv remembers that, at one time, guys who wore an earring in a particular ear or had a set of keys attached to a particular side of their belt, or even before that, parted their hair on the 'wrong side' did so to indicate their orientation. Nothing changes. She runs her hands over her face. 'Christ, Whiteman is a total creep. Sandy and he must be enemies?'

'Well they're certainly not mates.'

This is what she'd imagined, but hearing it makes the hairs on the back of her neck rise. What could Zoe Whiteman have had in mind for her? Whatever it was, it sure wasn't an invitation to drinks.

'When did you last see Sandy?'

'Thursday, yeah, I'm sure it was Thursday. He brought Robbie, but the nurse gave them an earful and Robbie had a fit. Honestly, when he's with Sandy, he acts like a naughty toddler.'

'Only he's not. He's a full-grown man keen to throw his weight about. Look, I might need to go out, when is your sister coming round?'

'She's on her way.' He swings his watch round, a huge heavy thing, which makes his wrist look even frailer than it is. 'She'll be here any minute.'

Viv goes back to the screen and scrolls down looking for anything else on Max and Whiteman, but the rest are doubles of the ones she's already looked at.

Opening her email she's taken aback to see one from Max. She's never given him her email address. He wants to meet her at the office.

'Yeah, do I look daft?' She hadn't meant to say this out loud. 'Sorry. It's this email.'

'What is it?'

The buzzer interrupts and Viv says, 'That'll be your sis.'

She nips into her bedroom and changes into jeans and a sweatshirt, before throwing her swimming kit into a bag. Showing John her sports bag she says cheerfully, 'I'll be back in about an hour. Have fun.'

Viv passes a sturdy young girl on the stairs. There's definitely a family resemblance, but John is more finely built. Viv nods and says, 'Your brother awaits.'

The girl looks surprised, but replies with an automatic thank you.

As Viv jogs up Candlemaker Row and along Chambers Street, the grey sky threatens to dump its next load, but for now it's only a threat. Infirmary Street baths has a swimming pool as well as real baths, built by Victorians to cater for the many not privileged enough to have a bath of their own. The heat is wonderful after the cold dampness outside. The smell of decades of carbolic soap still permeates every wooden surface. Somewhere in this building there must be the biggest hot water tank and boiler known to man. Viv has on more than one occasion been known to stand beneath the shower for over ten minutes and the steam hasn't faltered. It's one of the rewards for doing her fifty lengths. As she walks to a cubicle the one woman in the pool says, 'Great once you're in, hen. But dinny hesitate whitever you dae!'

The water is even more inviting because there's only one person in it. Viv suddenly regrets not shaving her legs, but it's too late now and she takes the plunge. After thrashing up and down a few times she slows into a rhythm, leaving a wake that's kinder to her fellow swimmer.

When Viv pulls herself up and out of the pool she looks at the woman, who must be in her seventies, swimming at a pace that befits her rubber floral cap, and admires the fact that she hasn't stopped and will probably do as much exercise as Viv has, only in less of a rush. Now for her prize. With towel and shampoo in hand she heads toward the showers. Under the cascade of hot water, she closes her eyes to allow the shampoo to run off. She is startled when a familiar, but out-of-context voice says, 'Just when you're ready, Viv.'

'Didn't expect to meet you here, Max. Given up your membership at One Spa?'

She continues to rinse her hair; the heat of the water is too good to relinquish. She asks, 'What's eating you? You were tetchy last night and your email this morning was less than friendly. What's going on?'

'You going to stand there all day?'

'Will my being dressed make any difference to your story? How did you know where to find me, anyway?'

'Never mind that.'

'I damn well do mind.' Hoisting her towel from the hook she says, 'I'll be five minutes,' and marches off. In the changing room it strikes her that whatever is going on, he must be terrified to go to this trouble. Although she loves swimming she hates the getting dressed bit; not quite dry skin refusing the advances of socks and tee-shirts increases her already significant frustration. Max is waiting in the entrance and points to his car outside, 'Let's get some coffee.'

This is a whole different man from the one she's been preening for the last decade. His hands are shaking as he opens the door for her.

'Let's go to the Elephant House,' Viv suggests. 'It'll be quiet and they serve decent coffee.'

He nods, attempting a u-turn in the narrow street, but catches his one hundred and fifty quid a pop tyres on the pavement opposite.

George IV Bridge has God-botherers out in force and parking is tricky. He pulls onto a double yellow, and they join the short queue inside the coffee house. He keeps looking round him.

'Max, for God's sake, who are you expecting?'

'You've no idea, Viv. No idea.'

'No, but I'm hoping that you're just about to tell me.'

They end up sitting next to the loo door, so that no one will be tempted to join them.

'Viv, I'm sorry about your car.'

She didn't expect this and gives him a quizzical look. 'Fill me in, Max, I must have missed something.'

'They were trying to scare me.'

Viv is astonished. 'What? . . . Wait a minute. Are you saying that someone trying to get to *you* blew up my car, huh . . .' She catches her breath. This is getting less laughable by the minute.

The look on his face is so serious. Viv feels her suspicion rising and snorts, 'Who are they? And does this have anything to do with Whiteman?' He drops his eyes, so she doesn't have to ask again if Whiteman is involved but goes on, 'Okay, what have you done to incur his wrath? Or should I just say how much do you owe him? 'Cause it's bound to be about money, am I right?'

She can't imagine how Max, on his six-figure salary, plus, plus, plus could be in debt to anyone. Max doesn't answer, but sits staring into his coffee. Viv isn't getting it. The face that she's used to isn't the one that's opposite her at the moment. Then suddenly an ugly possibility strikes her. 'Max, it isn't boys? Tell me it isn't boys.'

His face turns beetroot. She wants to jump up and leave, but forces her butt to stay put.

'Nothing happened. I swear. Nothing happened.'

When anyone says, 'I swear' she knows they're lying. So starting with this premise she nods in the hope that he'll continue without her goading him.

'It was . . .' He struggles to find the word and she struggles to listen to whatever crap he's making up as he goes along. 'It was just a bit of fun . . . for a laugh. I should have known not to trust him.'

'Trust who? Whiteman?'

He nods. 'Oh God, what a mess. He's got photographs.'

Viv shakes her head, 'For fuck's sake, Max. How stupid are you? He's one of the dirtiest pockets in Edinburgh from what I've gathered, and you've known him long enough to know what he's capable of.'

He interrupts her. 'I had no idea what he gets up to.'

'Bullshit. You must have known if you asked him to organise a young boy for your . . . entertainment.' She shakes her head. 'If you're not going to be straight with me we're not having this conversation.'

Questions are racing round Viv's mind, but she can hardly bear to be in the same space as him.

'When he turned up . . . the young man I mean, I freaked out.'

'Why?'

The look on his face is one of self-disgust. 'Because he turned out to be the son of one of my clients. That's why. The boy was completely stoned and I don't think he recognised me, but I sure as hell recognised him. Nothing happened. You've got to believe me.'

'Why, Max? Why the hell should I believe you and why are you telling me all this?'

'Because the boy was Andrew Douglas.'

She draws in her breath and counts to ten as she releases it. 'Oh, God. Tell me you had nothing to do with his death.'

He's silent.

Seizing her swimming bag off the floor she says, 'Tell this to Marconi.'

He grabs her arm. The place is busy now and she shrugs him off, but he grabs her again.

'Don't, Viv. It's too big.'

'Keep walking.'

Outside she heads right, along George IV Bridge and he trots at her side.

'Whiteman says he's got photographs with the date on them. I don't know if that's true or not. If he has there's nothing compromising in them apart from the fact that the boy was already reported missing by that date. It had already been in the paper. I had no idea who he'd send and freaked out when I saw Andrew . . . I told him to get rid of him . . . I didn't mean literally. Just to get him out of my flat.'

The fine drizzle is soaking them both but it's a small price to pay to find out who was behind Andrew's death. Not to mention the demise of her car. Viv halts abruptly and spins round. 'You must know if there are photographs. Did Andrew have a camera with him? Was there a third person? Someone hiding in the stairwell as you opened the door? Think Max. You'll have to think. This is serious. You need to go to Marconi. Now! I'll come with you.'

'You think I don't know how serious this looks? . . . You're mad if you think I'm going to tell Marconi about this. There's no way. They'll hang me out to dry for that young bloke. When he left me he left on his own two feet. I had nothing to do with his death.'

She thinks he's protesting way too much but pushes him for more detail. 'Okay. Let's go back to the photographs. How likely is it that they managed to get photographs? And what would you like me to do?'

'I don't know yet, but Whiteman wants you and . . .' He looks away.

'And you said you could get to me? Is that right? Have you told Sonia?'

At the mention of her name his eyes almost pop out. 'You're kidding. Her father would kill me.'

'I'm not asking about her father. What the fuck has he got to do with anything?'

'She's Sonia Morgan. That's what.'

'So all you're worried about is your reputation and your job. And a young boy is dead. Max, you've lost it. Totally lost it.'

The door to her flat is about twenty paces away and she says, 'Go away, Max. Think about this again. I'm going through that door and I'll speak to Marconi. I don't give a shit about Mr Morgan – or Mr Whiteman for that matter.'

'Don't, Viv. I said I'd talk you round. That we'd be able to come to some agreement.'

'You thought you could buy me off to save your arse. You don't know me. Or such crap would never have crossed your mind. Whiteman isn't stupid even if you are. Where is he?'

Her key is in the door and she can see him glancing round. The gods are on her side – her neighbour Ronnie comes round the corner huddled up against the rain with his papers tucked inside his coat.

'Hi Ronnie, what a horrible day.'

Glaring at Max she closes the door and chats at Ronnie on the way up stairs.

Chapter Fourteen

Ronnie has a calming effect on Viv, so by the time they reach their landing her breathing has slowed and she's much less irritated. Bidding him good day brings a smile to her face. What an all but invisible neighbour Ronnie is.

Once she's inside her own flat, the smile drops from her face. John looks bigger today, taking up more space in her sitting room than he had even this morning. His sister wasn't exactly laden with things as Viv passed her on the stairs, but whatever it was has expanded. Her face gives her away and John says, 'Don't worry, I'll tidy up. I couldn't find my account book and had to empty everything out.' He holds up a red book, grinning as if he's won the Lottery. 'This little baby is the only thing standing between me and abject poverty. I can now buy you dinner tomorrow.'

It's her turn to grin. She likes him. Likes the fact that he notices things and he isn't a freeloader – although she was willing to put up with that if he had been. He looks up at her from the couch and asks, 'How was the swim?'

'Interesting.' Viv hesitates, not sure how much to tell him, but decides he's not on the side of the bad guys. As her tale unfolds his face becomes a picture of disbelief.

'So, you're a hairdresser? . . . and a journalist?'

She is quickly on the defensive. 'Look, John, you're not exactly in a position to make judgments, are you? But for now let's say, yes I am a hairdresser, and yes I happen to write for our national broadsheet.'

Her tone has a warning and his response is, 'Well you have to admit it is unusual.'

She retorts, 'Yes, it's unusual, but only because people have fixed ideas of what hairdressers do. Avoid stereotyping and you'll get fewer surprises. I've never spoken to a single person who has said that their hairdresser was thick. Quite the contrary. I met a guy recently who is writing a book about his hairdresser, and he's having her edit it. I have a theory about hairdressers . . .'

Seeing the look on his face and losing interest in her own rant she decides it can wait. 'Okay, I'll save the lecture for another day. I need to make contact with the police.'

'You're turning him in? This Maxwell Scott guy?'

'I don't see it as turning him in. It's damage limitation. If Max keeps quiet much longer Whiteman will have more to blackmail him with. Then Max will really be up to his neck in it.'

'Don't you think . . .?'

Viv, as quick as a flash, turns on him, 'No, I don't think. You can probably tell that I never think about anything. I'm the type to jump straight into every situation without giving it the slightest thought.'

John comes back equally quickly. 'Okay, okay. I get it. You know that there's no way he'll go to the police, and if he doesn't he's in even more . . .'

'He's already lied and withheld information as it is, but he could still get off with a warning.'

She notices that as they speak his colour drains. 'Look, let's get you a cup of tea. Then I'll ring someone I know at Fettes.'

'What's Fettes?'

She's forgotten that he's not from Edinburgh, and it's oddly reassuring that he isn't familiar with Edinburgh's main cop shop.

'Fettes is police headquarters.'

She must be careful; he's still pretty frail.

Once they've had tea and digestives, Viv checks her email, reading an earlier one from Max. He does sound scared, but there are worse things in life than offending the in-laws. There's one from Jules saying she's just heard about the shenanigans at the drinks party last night. Viv wonders who Jules' source was, and rattles off a quick reply that she'll fill her in later. Then she picks up the phone and dials Marconi. It rings and rings before going to voicemail. Not sure who else to try, Sal Chapman comes to mind, but she decides against – nervous that Sal interprets such a call as a curved ball to something else. What now?

The phone rings. It's Marconi.

'Hi, Viv, Marcus here.' First name terms, a good start. He sounds breathless.

'Thanks for ringing back. I think it would be useful for us to meet.'

'Why, what have you got?'

'I'd rather we met. So that I can go over the whole thing.'

'What have you been keeping from us?'

'No it's not that, it's . . .'

'Okay Viv, we can meet. I'm out running at the moment, but I could be back at the office in fifteen minutes. If you give me half an hour you won't have to put up with me in running kit.'

'Fine. See you in half an hour.'

The idea of him in running kit isn't as off-putting as he thinks. He's in good shape and not bad looking. Something stirs in Viv that hasn't been awake for a while and she quickly shakes it off. A feeling of anxious excitement is the last thing she needs.

'John!' She calls from the bedroom. 'If you're up for a DVD you'll find every possibility in that cupboard at the bottom of the bookcases. Or if you fancy reading, as you see there's no shortage.'

It was one of the things that made Viv want the flat. In fact she was almost desperate to get it when she saw that bookcases took up the length of the hall, still containing a smattering of titles she recognised as 'progressive'. Her own books now take up 70 per cent of what's here. Now that she knows that Sal is the owner it seems weird, having made all sorts of presuppositions about what kind of person the collection must belong to. Radclyffe Hall and Kate Millet were a bit of a give-away.

Viv changes into warmer clothes. With a rucksack thrown over her shoulder she goes through the ritual of checking her pockets for keys, mobile, tissues and gloves.

'I'm off. I should be back . . .' the clock reads midday, '. . . two, two-thirty.'

'It's fine, Viv, I'm not your mum.'

'Thank God for that!'

They both laugh and she trots downstairs hoping that a taxi will be around. There isn't one. She finds one waiting at the lights on the High Street and runs over before the lights change. The driver gives her a disapproving look. 'You'll get me shot, hen. Where to?'

'Fettes, please.' She adds, ' HQ' before he asks if she's going to the school.

It's never been quiet on any of her visits. Criminals never sleep. Marconi looks fresh, with his hair still wet and skin that looks shaved to within an inch of its life. The office smells faintly of lemon, a nice change from testosterone. The PC who has shown her in leaves them and suddenly there's an awkwardness that has never been there before. Perhaps they've never been alone before. Viv pulls out a chair and it clunks against the legs of the one next to it. The sound is amplified in the large, empty room. Last time she was in here Sal and another couple of officers were in and out. She could be wrong about Sundays; criminals might have a long lie. The only time Viv wants a long lie is during the week, but it's sod's law that at weekends the lights come on the instant her eyes open.

Marconi twirls his pen, and even the noise of that sounds too loud. She must be hypersensitive after her swim. 'How was your run?'

'Not bad. You're not a runner, are you?'

'Occasionally. Not keen on pounding pavements, though. Prefer natural terrain. Had a swim this morning . . . Not much that's natural about chlorine, I suppose.'

She's justifying herself without cause. She takes a deep breath and launches, 'This morning I had a surprise visit from Mr Maxwell Scott. He wanted a chat, but also to get me to back off. But the thing is I'm not sure what exactly he'd like me to back off from. Last night I went to a drinks party . . .'

Marconi interrupts. 'Whoa! Slower please.'

Viv takes a breath and continues. 'Max was there and unbeknown to me had brought along a friend, who, it turns out, is the wife of Leonard Whiteman.'

Marconi nods and raises his eyebrows.

'This Mrs Whiteman, according to the hostess, had asked if she could come along. Now what's interesting to me is why did she want to come? She sidled up to me at one point and whispered in my ear, and it wasn't sweet nothings. But when I didn't respond in the way that she expected she grabbed me, tearing my dress in the process. I only managed to get away from her by throwing a drink at her and throwing myself on the mercy of my hostess. Whiteman's language was choice. But what I want to know is, did she ask to be invited just on the off-chance that I'd be there? Jinty was fuming.'

Marconi shoots her a questioning look. Viv clarifies. 'Jinty Stewart was giving one of her famous drinks parties. I usually have a good enough excuse not to go but this time I didn't.'

Again he raises his eyebrows. 'Jinty Stewart, as in wife of Rodney Stewart, as in Lord and Lady Glencalder? Don't look so surprised. Jinty is a client of mine. I know that you're not keen on coincidences, and I'm not getting a good feeling about the coincidences that have happened this week. I get involved in a story about a young boy who subsequently turns up dead. My car is blown to smithereens in the office car park of a man who is at drinks with a friend who happens to be an arch-hood's wife. Then he turns up again as I am washing my hair at the swimming pool.' It's her turn to raise her eyebrows, inviting a response from Marconi.

'I can see your point,' Marconi admits. 'What else did Max want?'

'He confessed to me that Whiteman had arranged for him, Max, to have a taste of youth in the form of Andrew Douglas.'

She was never in doubt about his attention, but Marconi now leans forward over the table and nods, his hunger for information definitely fuelled. 'Go on.'

'Max didn't know who or what to expect and was horrified, at least this is his story, when he saw Andrew. He recognised him from the TV and the newspapers, but he also knows Andrew's father, who is a client of his. Messy or what? I don't condone what Max was doing, even though Andrew is, or rather was eighteen. So in legal if not moral terms there isn't anything that could be done about Max's encounter with Andrew, which he swears wasn't an encounter at all. Max apparently freaked. The difficulty is that Andrew has since died, so I'm guessing that Max was one of the last people to see him alive. It doesn't look good for Mr Scott, but he sounded genuinely scared of what Whiteman might do. I've always seen the tough, cutting edge financier, but this morning he was quaking in his boots. So perhaps there's more to his part in this than he is saying, or Whiteman is even dirtier than I had imagined.'

Marconi hasn't spoken in a while, and almost whispering he says, 'We've got to get him in here before Whiteman gets to him.' He's up and across to the phone in three strides. 'Viv, you don't have an address for him, do you?'

'I do. He lives in Royal Terrace. I always see him at the office. After this morning I wonder if he'd feel safer at the office. It might be worth . . .'

Marconi pre-empts her and asks the constable to find out the number at Royal Terrace and get someone to both addresses.

'Well, Viv,' he smiles, 'I must say you look pretty good on drama. You want a coffee or something?'

'Actually, I'd love a cup of tea if there's one going.'

He looks pleased. 'Sure. We could run to that.' Then he continues, 'We've got nothing on Whiteman. He's clever. Manages to keep whatever he's washing rotating. Got nothing on the wife either, apart from the fact that her father did time in the nineteen seventies for fraud. How convenient is that? Having pa-in-law a seasoned fraudster!'

Viv says, 'I heard that Whiteman's involved in "arranging" young boys for a price. If they work for him they wear a specific outfit. At the moment it's white jeans with a bag over the left shoulder. Just like in the old days, when a pierced ear or a dangling set of keys could get you a kicking. They still hang out on Calton Hill; you'd think they'd find a new location.'

'Where did you get that information?'

'Don't remember. One of Andrew's school chums maybe? I think they're scared now. At the beginning it was intriguing, a bit of a novelty, but not now. There's nothing intriguing about burning to death. By the way I've got a visitor for a couple of days. He said the flat in the Colonies really is a safe haven. I think it was Robbie who sold him the stuff that put him in hospital.'

'What's he doing with you? You didn't know him before you found him?'

'No, but he had nowhere to go. And I offered.'

He looks a mixture of impressed and suspicious. No mean feat. Viv, once again feeling the need to justify herself, adds, 'He's just a boy, well, young man. He's looking better now than he did in the hospital. Besides he did give me information. Not much, but I only need a little to get things moving. Sometimes less actually is more. What did you do with Croy?'

Marconi shrugs. 'His lawyer came and arranged bail, and we couldn't keep him. He's been charged with possession. Would your young man testify that he'd been sold stuff by Robbie?'

'I doubt it, but it's worth a try. He's . . . shall we say disenchanted with Mr Croy at the moment. Sees him as a very bad lot. You might be lucky. Look, I'd rather not be around when Max comes in, but John Black isn't going anywhere soon, so you could come to the flat later and speak to him.'

He nods. 'Thanks, I'd like to do that.'

As she heads toward the door he remarks, 'Your flat made a bit of an impression on Sal Chapman. She thought it was pretty eccentric. I'll see for myself later.'

Outside Fettes, there's no chance of a passing cab so Viv starts the trudge towards Stockbridge. It's still a surprise to her that shops are open on a Sunday and she takes the opportunity to browse in the charity bookstores. The difficult thing is leaving them without more than one's own bodyweight in books. Today she's in luck. They have the *Shorter Oxford English*, both volumes. They weigh a ton, and any notion of a brisk walk home is dismissed before she's reached Stockbridge, where she does manage to hail a taxi. Once seated she turns to look out of the back window. She could be wrong, but she could swear she recognises a bloke frantically hailing another cab. Annoyed at herself for feeling paranoid she nonetheless checks the rear view mirror to see if they are being followed. They are. She is. The man following is the nicer of the two barmen from Copa Cabana and definitely not one of Marconi's men. Maybe another 'coincidence'.

The other cab is still tailing them when they reach the top of Victoria Street. If it turns down here she'll assume that he's on her tail. She gets her key out, ready to leap from the taxi and straight up stairs. The two vehicles turn into her street. She jumps out and aims the keys towards the street entrance, but drops them and, laden with the books, makes a clumsy retrieval. She manages to make it inside and closes the heavy outer door behind her. She pauses inside, breathing too heavily for one so fit. She can hear footsteps, then someone trying the door. For a second she thinks she hasn't secured it properly, and it gives slightly when he pushes it, but it holds and she lets out a huge sigh. Wondering what he'll do, she hovers with her back against the wall watching the shadow of his feet moving back and forth outside. Eventually, with nothing to be gained by staying where she is, she makes her way to the top.

When she walks into the hall she's struck by the unreality of her life as the sound of Julie Andrews' voice reaches her from the sitting room, and grins. She dumps the books and fills the kettle. She imagines how nice it would be to veg in front of *The Sound of Music* and forget everything for a couple of hours. So she changes into baggy bottoms and cosy socks.

John tries to jump up from the sofa when she opens the sitting room door.

'Stay where you are. I think I'll join you. What could be better than an afternoon with the von Trapps? You warm enough?' She shudders. Let's have a bit more heat. We could get this place up to a bikini state in no time.'

After she's turned up the heater she's about to settle down, but then she remembers the kettle. 'Tea?'

'Yes, please, if it's no bother.'

Within minutes she's back with a tray. Complete with tea and a bucket of Maltesers.

John laughs and shifts onto his elbow. 'You're quite a hostess, Viv. By the way I had another bacon roll. I'll see you all right tomorrow when I can get some cash.'

'I'm not worried – well, at least not about that. Malteser?'

With a grin he says, 'I'm beginning to think I've died and gone to heaven.'

For the next couple of hours they sit like old companions, who don't feel the need to fill in gaps. Neither of them is inhibited about singing along, which makes them both giggle. There's something very nice about being with a man without having to worry if he's going to make a move on you. Perhaps he feels the same about her. Viv is aware that relationships – whatever they are – never go in a straight line. One swallow doesn't make a summer and all that. Viv's relationship with Dawn was the first serious one she'd had with a woman.

Although they make a significant dent in the Maltesers, they are grown-up enough not to finish them, so as the von Trapps disappear over the mountains she takes the tray back to the kitchen. There's another note under the door.

After dumping the tray she retrieves it and reads out loud, 'He'd like to see you. Ring this number to organise a time.' Whoever it happens to be, she doesn't want to see 'him'. She supposes it's Whiteman and she takes the note through, collapsing into an armchair and handing it to John.

'For Christ's sake. What next? Stalkers at the swimming pool; now stalkers at the door. Viv, you're not going to meet him? I take it this is Whiteman?'

She nods. 'I think it must be. Who else would be so cloak and dagger about a meeting? Anyone else would just ring my bell. Glad he didn't, he'd have spoiled the film. Marconi's coming round here later. I'll ask him what he thinks I should do. I have to say I'm no longer driven by getting a story.'

John's face has paled, 'Why's Marconi coming here?'

'To speak to you.'

'Me? I've got nothing to say to the cops.' His voice has lost its strength again.

'Well he's heard about the stuff that Croy's been selling.'

'Did you tell him about that?'

Viv can't actually remember the details of what she's said about John, but says, 'Probably, but I can't remember. All the stories have become one. I'm sorry. I really can't remember. Marconi's a good guy.'

'But Viv, I'll get done for using. You must be nuts if you think I'll tell him anything.'

She sighs and lies back in the chair staring up at the ceiling. As the silence stretches out, neither of them fills it. Suddenly the buzzer makes them both jump.

Chapter Fifteen

'Marcus. Come up. Top floor. It's a hike.'

He arrives puffing and rests his hands on his knees. 'It's higher than it looks.'

Viv smiles, 'I'm used to it. Come through. John's in the sitting room.' She shrugs and shakes her head, unsure about John's reaction.

John stands up as Marconi enters, introducing himself as they shake hands, which Viv thinks is a good sign.

Marconi takes the lead. 'I expect you're reluctant to talk to me, but if we agree to do it off the record, would that help?'

John looks at Viv, then back at Marconi. 'If you're serious. It would have to be so far off the record that I'm not sure it would be any use.'

'If you could let me be the judge of that it would be a start.'

'How do I know that you're not wired?'

Marconi laughs. 'Sometimes I could kill TV producers. The whole world thinks we're *Miami Vice*.' He slips off his jacket and puts his arms in the air. 'Go ahead, check.'

John hesitates and looks as if he won't bother, then runs his hands all over Marconi. Satisfied, he nods. Viv flushes and smiles thinking she wouldn't mind feeling a bit of that muscle definition either. 'Okay. Shall I put the kettle on?'

They both say yes and she pads along to the kitchen to refill the kettle. When she returns with the tea they are already chatting. Marconi didn't get his job by being a poor communicator.

'Shall I leave you to it?'

John shakes his head. 'No, Viv, stick around. You should hear it all. Robbie Croy is a bad bastard, but you know that already. He's had a morality bypass and seems happy to sell contaminated drugs to unsuspecting idiots like me. God knows who else he's duped. I can't be the only one.' Then thoughtfully he pauses. 'You know it could actually just be me. He hates it that Sandy and I get on, but would he go as far as trying to kill me? Shit! Maybe Sandy's had a warning from him, and that's why he was determined that I couldn't doss down at the flat any more. God, he's such a creep. I'm not even sure that he's gay. I think he's one of those people who'll do anything if it gives him a sense of power.'

Viv agrees. She's met people like Croy before – Liam for one – and Croy strikes her as equally cut off from his emotions. That said he does anger pretty well. Putting her hand to her cheek she has a flash of him flattening her against the mirror. John's voice interrupts the thought. 'I bought stuff from him and it turned out to be rotten. After four days in the Royal Infirmary, one blood transfusion and too much bad food, I'm hopeful of survival. If it wasn't for Mother Teresa here I'm not sure where I'd have ended up.'

Marconi gives Viv a look that she can't work out – could have been respect. Then he nods at John, hoping he'll continue, and in the following silence says, 'Did you part with money and receive goods directly from him?'

'Yes.'

'Was anyone else present?'

'Nope. Just him and me.'

'Where did this take place?'

Hesitating, John turns to look at Viv. She shrugs. He has to make his own decisions.

'I don't want to make it difficult for Sandy. The flat really is a refuge. Sandy's warned Robbie about doing anything illegal there. But that's where I bought it.'

'Look, John, for now we're really only interested in Croy, and we're interested in him because he could be involved in something bigger. Drugs are bad enough, and what he did to you could put him back inside, but there's more. And it's the "more" that we're trying to pin down.'

Viv spots a huge scratch on Marconi's hand and is transfixed. He stops speaking and looks at her, then at his hand. 'One of my cats. She doesn't like having a manicure. This,' he raises his hand, 'is the consequence. She won.'

Viv, amazed that he's the kind of man who has cats says, 'She's quite a fighter!'

'Enough about the cats. Let's get back to business. How long have you known Alexander MacDonald?'

'About four, no five years. I came here to university and met up with a few guys from out of town who Sandy put up in the flat. Then when I graduated I went back to Turriff, supposedly to work on the farm, but that was always a non-starter. So, recently, like ten days ago, I came back, and was on his floor until your chum here rang for the ambulance.'

'Okay. And how often have you encountered Robbie in the last ten days?'

John has to think about this. 'A couple of times in the flat, the last when I bought the stuff from him, then again in the hospital. Luckily an Irish nurse with a bad temper asked him and Sandy to leave. It was then that Robbie mentioned you, "the bitch from the West Bow".' He nods at Viv.

Marconi looks at her but doesn't ask her anything. He turns back to John. 'What exactly did you think you were buying?'

'E. But it was obviously more creative than that. As you see I'm still a touch on the khaki side.'

Viv has just been thinking how much better he looks, even since this morning. Thanks to Julie Andrews and bacon rolls.

Darkness has fallen, and Viv is sure that they're almost done when Marconi's mobile goes. He retreats to the hall while she and John fall back in their respective seats. She feels knackered, but imagines John must be completely spent. She's relieved when Marconi comes back and says, 'I think that'll do for now.'

She holds back from asking how it went with Max. As if reading her mind Marconi remarks, 'Max was whistling. He must be more afraid of Whiteman than I thought. You both look pretty tired. Time I went. Cheers, John.'

Once Viv and he are out of John's earshot he says, 'Well done. If Croy thinks we've got something on him we'll have more leverage. Whiteman is the one we'd like. Croy is small fry in comparison.'

Viv looks shocked. 'But he can't get away with selling drugs. Surely you can get him on that alone?'

'It's not as simple as that and you know it. We might have to let a little fish go if it means we get Whiteman. I expect that if we do get Whiteman, Croy's supplies will soon dry up.'

Viv nods and sighs.

He looks around. 'I can see what Sal meant about the flat. It is lovely.'

'Thanks, but it was . . .'

He interrupts her. 'It's okay to take a compliment, Viv. It's a sign of evolution.'

This makes her smile. She stands against the closed door with an unidentifiable sensation in her belly. The kernel of emotion stirring is alien to her these days.

John is dozing when she pushes the sitting room door, but with its creak he opens his eyes. 'Well,' he says wearily, 'that's me done for now. If Whiteman gets a sniff of who shopped Robbie, he'll take it personally.'

Viv had thought of this and says, 'That makes two of us then. If he traces it to you, he'll then trace you to me and I'll be the one for the chop.'

'From what I hear it'll more likely be barbecue.'

They both snigger.

'That's an appalling thing to say.'

'I know, but it's true. I bet Marconi will trace Andrew's death to Whiteman. Or at least to Whiteman's back door – he's clever.'

'Even the cleverest make mistakes, John. Perhaps setting Max up with Andrew will turn out to be his biggest yet.'

'We can only hope.' His mobile rings, 'Do you mind if I take this? It's my sis.'

Viv waves her hands and nods.

In the kitchen she pulls out some chicken and spinach from the fridge, wondering if she could do something interesting with them. Viv's the first to admit her cooking skills leave a lot to be desired, but practice makes perfect and all that. Taking a copy of *The Naked Chef* off the shelf she scans the index for chicken, then for spinach. Nothing listed that combines them. She'll have to ad lib. As she peels some garlic and crushes it beneath a knife she thinks about where she might have been eating tonight if she'd gone north. The Summer Isles Hotel, or the Inverlodge; either would have been a treat – both have views to die for. She switches on Classic FM, and quickly switches it off again. The sound of Elgar's cello concerto, one of Dawn's favourite pieces, isn't what she needs right now.

Dawn's face inveigles itself into Viv's mind. She wonders what would have happened if the RSNO hadn't been struggling to find a double bassist. Dawn hadn't wanted to commit to a Scottish job, but they eventually persuaded her. Once she got on the road she loved it, but she rapidly grew into someone that Viv no longer knew: drinking too much and not turning up when she'd arranged to. Viv soon wondered if there was someone else. When it became clear that there were several, she was so angry with herself. Hurt didn't even begin to describe what she felt. Viv put the betrayal down to the artistic temperament. A lie that she was willing to put up with every time Dawn came back filled with promises and remorse. Bad times. What would have happened if she'd lived? A drunken car crash – no one knew whether it was an accident or deliberate. Dawn had always ridden an emotional merry-go-round, self-doubt exacerbated by self-loathing. Viv can admit now that she is relieved it is all finally over. But nothing is ever completely straightforward. Dawn left everything she owned to Viv: her small flat and various 'assets'. Viv hasn't been able to face lawyers for details, but knows she'll have to sometime.

John comes into the kitchen to see Viv poised with the knife in mid- air. 'You okay?'

She's startled. 'Yes, fine. Trying to create dinner.'

'You sure you don't mind? I feel like a complete free loader, Viv, and I'm really not like that.'

'It doesn't feel like that to me. Besides I'm enjoying the company to be honest. No, delete that last bit. I hate when people say, "to be honest" –

usually means they're lying and I'm not. It's nice to have someone around for a change. I spend too much time on my own. It's unnatural.'

John picks up the peeler and sets to on a few unsuspecting tatties.

'Don't do too many. They're my big downfall. It must be my Irish roots. I love tatties, in fact my hips love them so much they never part with them. D'you know what? When I was at school there was a girl, Catherine Rider, she used to sing, 'There'll be hips, hips as big as battleships in the store, in the store . . .' I'll never forgive her for drawing attention to them. It doesn't matter that the rest of me looks okay; having saddlebags is my great imperfection. Well, one of them.'

'It's one of the bonuses of being a man. No saddle bags!'

'Don't rub it in or there'll be no dinner for you.'

Her proximity to him in this tiny kitchen should be claustrophobic, but isn't. They manage to skirt around each other until their tasks are complete and all they have to do is wait.

John's mobile vibrates in his pocket and he dries his hands and moves into the hall to see who the caller is. He mouths, 'It's Sandy!' Then, 'Hello. Hello. Sandy, are you there? Hello! No one there. Sandy! Are you okay? Shit! I'll ring him back. What if he's unwell? He's asthmatic, I've seen him collapse, it was horrible. God what shall I do?' He says this as he redials the number. 'It's gone to answerphone. I don't know what to do, Viv. I'm not in any fit state to get myself down there. Would you go?'

Viv lets out a huge sigh, and with knife still in hand puts her hands on her hips. 'You really think he'll be at the flat? He could be anywhere.'

'We've got to try something. I can't not do anything!' His voice reaches a pitch that she hasn't heard before.

'Let's think this through. When was the last time you saw Sandy? Was it with Robbie at the hospital? Did he say where they were heading? You see I'm not sure if I were him, that I'd be hanging out at the flat, knowing that the police are interested in Robbie – even in you, come to think of it.'

His face drains and she knows she's not going to get out of this. She sighs and negotiates past him into the hall. 'All right, I'll go and see if he's at the flat. But if he isn't there I'll be coming straight back.'

With the smell of chicken and garlic flickering round her nostrils she peevishly grabs her jacket and wallet and heads for the door.

She's onto the street before John has time to suggest an alternative. It's still damp and drizzly, definitely a night to be tucked up in doors. Not even the smokers are out. Before she reaches the top of the road her hair is clamped to her head. This kind of drizzle is more damaging to a good blow-dry than a downpour; it's more sneaky. She spots an orange light.

The cabbie is chatty and Viv can't imagine it's been a quiet day for him with weather like this. On nearing the Colonies she's alerted by a spinning blue light in the car park and she asks to be dropped at the main road, which allows her to approach unnoticed. She sidles into the car park and crouches behind a four by four. Two paramedics bring out a stretcher from Sandy's building. She can't make out who they are carrying, so she moves onto the next car and crouches down, which is fine but not exactly inconspicuous. The woman she met – Sandy's next-door neighbour – is at the entrance to the building and has her hand up to her mouth. Viv thinks the woman might have spotted her so she raises her own hand in the slightest wave, but there's too much commotion for her to notice. Surprised that an ambulance is still cause for a crowd to gather, Viv checks out the other people standing in the rain. It wouldn't be the first time an accomplice has hung around to watch the playing out of events – if indeed there's been an accomplice.

Another blue light arrives along with an Audi. Marconi steps out of the Audi and Viv ducks down. Not sure why she has done this, she straightens up and looks over the bonnet. Marconi is met by a tall guy in black jeans and a leather jacket – the unofficial uniform of CID – who leads him straight to the neighbour. Marconi guides her back inside holding her arm. Viv makes her way across the car park and asks a middle-aged bloke in a fawn anorak, just about to get into his car, who's in the ambulance. He confirms that it's MacDonald. Viv says to one of the paramedics, 'Is anyone going with him?'

'Not that I've heard and not that he'll care. He's unconscious.'

She rejects the idea of getting into the ambulance, and instead tries briefly to think of ways she might justify being here to Marconi – she'll worry about that when the time comes. In the hubbub, she slips into the building unnoticed, and makes her way to the neighbour's flat. A young PC opens the door in response to her tap and recognises her from a meeting at Fettes. He lets her in without any questions. Marconi does a double-take when she walks into the sitting room, and the neighbour remarks, 'I thought you said you weren't police.'

Marconi is standing with his hands on his hips. Viv stutters a reply, 'I . . . I'm not, but I do help them with their enquiries when I can.'

Marconi stares in disbelief then asks, 'What brings you here, Dr Fraser?'

'We might speak outside.' She gestures to the landing, and Marconi moves after a microsecond's hesitation.

'What exactly are you doing here, Viv? Haven't we talked enough about "coincidence"?'

'He rang.'

'Who rang?'

'Sandy rang John on his mobile, but couldn't speak. Since John isn't well enough to come gallivanting out here he persuaded me to come in order to put his mind at ease.'

'What time was the call?'

'Twenty, twenty-five minutes ago. Half an hour tops. We could find out exactly from John. What happened? John says that he's asthmatic and has collapsed before.'

'It could be that, we'll have to wait and see. Now you head home and I'll get back to my interview.' His tone is way too patronising for her liking.

As he turns his back she blurts out, 'She hates him.'

Screwing up his eyes and shaking his head he turns round again and enquires, 'And how would you know that?'

'I spoke to her the day that I found John. We had a kind of chat.'

'What kind of chat?'

'Actually she offered her opinions and her sightings and I listened. Remember I was keen to find Andrew at that point. She claims they're a bunch of paedophiles. So no bias there.'

'Tonight she's just claimed that MacDonald was arguing with a woman. Definitely a woman's voice.'

'He's married. Apparently the wife lives in the prison houses out at Saughton. Could have been her.'

'I'll have her checked out. Anything else you haven't told me?'

'Oh, no doubt, but whatever I've got you're welcome to it. If I think of anything I'll ring you.'

'You've said that before.'

'But . . .'

No point in speaking to a retreating back. Viv turns and heads out into the cold.

Chapter Sixteen

It's great to see the relief on John's face when she tells him that Sandy is now in safe hands, although it disappears at the mention of his being unconscious.

'No point in worrying over something that you've got no control over.' Rich, coming from someone who once wondered if she could market worry. She continues, 'Besides, Marconi will keep us informed.' Hearing the lack of conviction in her voice she shrugs. 'Not much we can do tonight. Let's eat, then get some shut-eye.'

'There were a couple of calls. Only one left a message. Sounded like a very posh hair client confirming his appointment. I let the machine take it.'

'I'll deal with it in the morning.'

He rescues the chicken and they eat in silence before they head to their beds.

Viv is restless, thinking about why Sandy's wife would turn up at the flat and what they might have argued about. It could have been anything from the electricity bill to divorce, and it's unlikely that she'll ever find out. She's assuming it was his wife, but there are other women in the world. Too soon to make such leaps. Better to sleep on it, but sleep isn't on the horizon. Seduced by a new copy of McDermid's *Trick of the Dark* sitting on her bedside cabinet, she bolsters the pillows, anticipating a literary feast.

Later, waking from a dream where she was being chased by Marconi through some kind of collegiate setting, legs of lead as usual, unable to cover ground, she panics, wondering how loud a dream scream is, and lies panting, waiting to hear movement from the sitting room. Nothing.

Monday morning. Her diary is clear but she checks the message from last night. She smiles when she hears the voice of Lord Kinardoch, Teddy to her. A High Court judge, who rings to confirm his appointments because there have been times when his court has been sitting in another county and he's forgotten to let her know. To give him his due he has been mortified and paid her for double sessions so there was no great hardship for her. He's definitely going to be in Edinburgh next week. He's great company and, ironically for someone in his profession, an avid reader of crime fiction – for years now they've exchanged books. She doesn't need to ring him back but, determined to address the car issue today, she lists everything else that she has to do. First Marconi, then perhaps Max. No, not Max, he'll be dealing with the family fall-out after yesterday's exposure. As she pours Gold Top milk onto her cereal John appears at the kitchen door, stretching to reveal an impressive Jacob's ladder.

She raises her eyebrows and he says, 'Sorry. I obviously feel too relaxed with you already. D'you sleep okay?'

'Not a chance. But I made great inroads with a new book. You a reader?'

'Yes. Started a Hollingworth yesterday. Bit slow, good cure for insomnia, but I'll persevere since he's one of us.'

The phone rings and Viv goes into the sitting room to retrieve the handset. It's Sal Chapman. 'Hi. I thought it might be Marconi.'

'No. Just me. Marconi is at the hospital questioning Mr MacDonald.'

'Good, that's a relief.' Putting her hand over the mouthpiece she says to John, 'I think Sandy's okay.'

Sal has heard what she said, 'I'm not sure how "okay", Viv, but conscious. Mac – Marconi decided it was worth trying to question him. I'm phoning to say we have a description of a woman leaving the flat last night and it wasn't Mrs MacDonald. This woman was tall, blonde and skinny as a rake apparently. Marconi thought you might know her.'

Before she's had time to think it through, Viv says, 'It could be Mrs

Whiteman. But what could she want with Sandy? . . . Maybe she was looking for Robbie and got Sandy instead?'

'So that description fits Mrs Whiteman, then?'

'Yes, and a thousand other anorexics in Edinburgh. But not all of them know the flat.'

Viv, hearing how guarded she sounds, makes an effort to lighten her tone. 'How are you anyway? I suppose Marconi has filled you in on the last couple of days. Barely a dull moment.'

'I'm fine, thanks. I wondered whether you'd mind if a friend of mine came round to look at the cooker and measure up for pipes and things.'

The thought of disruption in her haven fills Viv with dread and she hesitates. 'Well. I'm actually on holiday this week and had planned to be away. I've also got someone staying who isn't too well.'

Sal interrupts her list of excuses. 'That's okay, maybe you can let me know when it would be convenient.'

'The flat is actually perfect for me. You don't need to go to the bother of upgrading. Not on my behalf. Couldn't you leave it until I move out, and the next tenant comes in?'

'Oh! Are you planning to leave?'

'No. No. I was speaking about the future. I'm not going anywhere . . .'

Her words aren't coming out right and John is standing in the doorway making faces.

'Sal, would you mind if we speak later, I'm in the middle . . .'

'Sure. They've brought Maxwell Scott in again. I expect Mac, I mean Marconi will ring you later.'

'Okay, thanks.'

Viv throws a pillow from the couch at John's head. Then when she sees him ducking and landing awkwardly on the couch she exclaims, 'Oh God, I'm so sorry. I forgot. I forgot. Are you okay?'

He smiles up at her from his foetal position and says, 'I'm not feeling nearly as bad as I was. You sounded as if you were digging a hole. Who was it?'

'My landlady.'

His eyebrows meet, confusion all over his face.

'Sal Chapman is my landlady, but she also happens to work with DI Marconi. Incestuous, I know. I don't think she's officially on this case, but she seems to know what's going on. Come to think of it I'm still not sure why Marconi is on this case either. He's supposed to be heading up the new NTF, Northern Task Force, for those who don't know. Actually I didn't know myself until he told me last week. When my car was blown up he became involved, and I suppose he's sticking with it. Let's get some coffee before I die of caffeine deprivation.'

Viv rings the DVLA and explains to a monosyllabic moron that the bits of her MG are going to be in police custody for the foreseeable future. Eventually, the moron agrees to send her the forms for a refund on her road tax. The next task is to find a car. She fleetingly thinks of Dawn's little VW sitting in a lock-up off Broughton Street, but still can't face going there. The fact that she'll eventually have to sort out Dawn's estate is like having a piece of grit in her sock.

The Yellow Pages, with endless adverts for car outlets all over Edinburgh, proves too daunting, and she decides it would be wiser to check out e-bay. It's extraordinary that with a few taps on the keys, a selection of cars all within ten miles of her postcode comes to life. Knowing that she'll probably never have another sports car, and that the time for careless purchases has passed, she spots an old Toyota for sale in Corstorphine. It says 'Top condition, one lady owner'. Maybe. But it's not far and worth a look.

The sky looks much the same as yesterday: dark grey and heavy with the promise of another good dunking. The notion of lying under a car looking for rust or worse fills her with dread, but needs must. She emails the owner to find out if she can have a look at it this morning. As she waits for a reply she uses the time to tidy her desk. Beneath the piles of bank correspondence, insurance statements and junk mail, she comes across a letter from Dawn's solicitor asking her to make an appointment at her earliest convenience. The letter is dated almost a year ago. On impulse, she picks up the phone and asks to speak to Mr McGrath. Before she knows it, she's made an arrangement to see him, four-thirty p.m. today.

Her belly reacts immediately, making necessary an emergency visit to the loo. On her return the car owner has replied and yes she can see it this morning, if she can make it at ten-thirty. She glances at the clock and still has time to ring Marconi and find out what's happening with Sandy. Only his answering service responds to her call. Viv drums her fingers on the desk and stares out of the window at the gloomy sky: a deceptively busy space with all those unseen air lanes, radio waves and wifi of one sort or another.

Her thoughts are interrupted by John's voice. 'Hey, where have you gone? You're on another planet.'

'I wish. I've got stuff to do today that I hadn't anticipated. Feels awkward.'

'Don't do it then.'

This is the voice of a different generation where responsibilities haven't yet built up.

'I've already put it off for almost a year. The time is now.' The sooner it's done the better. Reminding herself that it'll be over by five o'clock, she wraps up warm, then says goodbye to John.

Corstorphine is easy to get to; almost every bus from Shandwick Place runs through it. Caroline Gardens was named after Queen Caroline, but bears no relation to anything regal or stately – the houses have only been there since the nineteen thirties and the best thing about them is their view. They face to the south and west of Edinburgh with a 180-degree panorama of the Pentland Hills, which probably makes it worth living in one of them.

She rings the bell, taking in the manicured planting on both sides of the drive. There isn't much that'll show its face at this time of year, but the display of snowdrops here would make anyone optimistic.

A small man opens the door, with a smaller woman right behind him. Viv nods and gestures back to the snowdrops. 'Lovely to see something growing. I'm here about the car.'

They stand awkwardly on the doorstep for a moment, until the woman gives her husband a little nudge, and he says, 'Come on in and I'll get the key to the garage.' The house is as immaculate as the garden and more tasteful than she'd expected. 'Come away through this way and I'll show you the car.'

'I don't remember what the mileage was on the advert.'

'Oh. Did I not say? Silly me. It's got twenty-four thousand on the clock.'

If this is the one lady owner, maybe Viv was being too sceptical about the advert.

The woman says, 'I'm selling it because I've retired and we only really need one car now.'

The garage is massive and contains two shiny silver Rav 4s, one behind the other. Viv feels like a child in a sweetie shop. You really could eat your dinner off the floor in here, and both cars are in showroom condition. The man's hands are shaking and Viv wonders if he still drives. She ventures, 'Goodness me, they both look great. Which one is it?'

'The three-door. We'll hang onto the bigger one; need it for the hillwalkers.'

Surprised by this, Viv pays more attention. Both of them look pretty fit. Neither of them carries any extra weight and their skin is weather-beaten. That'll teach her for making assumptions. Viv walks round the car, pretending she knows what she's doing, then sits inside. He hands her the key. 'Switch her on. You'll not get a better drive. It's smooth and more economical than the five-door.'

Viv isn't getting the arithmetic: she can only see two doors but is embarrassed to ask. She can also see how proud he is; the way he runs his hands gently over the bonnet, then takes out his handkerchief and rubs at a tiny fleck. Viv raises her eyebrows and the woman notices. 'They're his pride and joy. We can't justify having them both when one or other is always in here.'

'Would you mind if I had an AA check? I don't know a lot about cars and . . .'

'We've had one done, I'll get it.'

Viv tries to imagine herself nipping confidently around Edinburgh in a car that actually works. She could definitely get used to the idea. But this is too pristine, and her car is her office, not to mention her dining room. Then there's the parking. She certainly wouldn't be bumping this out of a parking space. It's too good for her — but then she checks her attitude — she deserves a proper car. The little man hands her a report. It is dated the previous Friday, and unless they've been rallying or off-roading with it over the weekend it's in mint condition. Tentatively, Viv says, 'I'd like to drive it if that's okay.'

'We'll get our coats and shoes on.'

When they come back it's no surprise to Viv that they are wearing matching Goretex jackets and woollen hats.

He manoeuvres it out onto the road and then lets Viv take over. It is gorgeous. She knows within fifty yards that she's going to have it, but she gets as far as South Gyle before she says so. As they return to Caroline Terrace Viv tries to think of ways to negotiate with them on the price but once back inside the house she's too embarrassed to barter, so says she'll ring and organise a banker's draft. They shake on it, and she almost skips back down to the main road. It's the first time she's had anything this grown-up, but telling herself that it'll last a lifetime helps ease her conscience.

As she turns the corner at the bottom of Clermiston Road she sprints to catch a 26 bus just pulling away from the lights. Thankfully an elderly couple at the bus stop struggle to board and in the end, huffing and puffing, she has plenty of time. Fumbling about in her bag for change she budges over on the step of the bus to let someone else on. They're even more out of breath than she is. Once she's seated she pulls out her mobile and flicks it open, but is suddenly aware that the person behind is too close to her ear for comfort. It's barely a whisper, but it's definitely a threat. 'You've had your fun, Fraser. Now it's my turn.'

Viv tries to turn, to see if she's correct in her identification, but there's something sharp like a nail touching her neck and the whisperer says, 'I wouldn't if I were you. I bought this little baby for filing crystal.'

The sickly smell of musk leaves Viv in no doubt about who it is. Zoe Whiteman is obviously a woman of habit.

Still whispering Mrs W says, 'You ruined that dress. A Sonia Rykel. But that's not all you're trying to ruin. Is it?'

'What are you on? I was doing my job.'

'Don't give me that. You're an interfering cow. Can't leave things alone. I bet you're a curtain twitcher. How many warnings does a girl need? Notes, telephone calls, fire-bombs and you didn't even listen to Sandy. Which bit of "back off" did you fail to grasp?'

The bus is getting busier and Mrs Whiteman has to make a decision.

'At the next stop you and I will take a walk. Don't even try to run. This little implement could prove fatal.'

This woman is being so ridiculous Viv can hardly believe it's happening – although the tiny pricking sensation next to her carotid artery certainly keeps her attention. She hasn't yet set eyes on her assailant and feels a giggle rising, but manages to hold back. They leave the bus at Roseburn, and Whiteman, slightly taller, prods Viv in the direction of Wester Coates. Once they round the corner off the main road she pushes Viv towards the old railway line.

Viv used to run along this line and is familiar with the time it takes to get from here to Stockbridge, providing the dog walkers don't have their beloveds on extending leashes. Spinning round, Viv hits out with her elbow high and knocks Whiteman off balance, then sprints away from a torrent of abuse towards the Water of Leith walkway. It's almost midday and there isn't a soul about. She glances back to see that Whiteman wasn't off balance for long, and looking lithe in head to toe black lycra, including a tight fitting hat that covers her hair completely, she is making up on her. About a quarter of a mile on there's a bend in the path. Viv vaults over the fence onto the river-bank, and stands flat against the wall. Grateful that the river isn't in spate and there aren't any nettles at this time of year, she prays that her heavy breathing won't give her away. Footsteps race by and she immediately climbs back onto the path and scrambles up the steep embankment on the other side. This is a tricky operation, as mud and leaf-mould keep shifting beneath her feet. She manages to dig her toes in but not before a lengthy slide back downhill. She retraces her slither, grasping at a low branch of a tree. Once her foot is jammed in behind the trunk she pushes herself up towards another fence, which runs along the crest of the banking protecting some private gardens. Finally she reaches out and grips the iron railings.

While she's getting her breath back she hears voices below and spots a couple of elderly female dog walkers chatting. They lean over the fence, looking into the water. One of the dogs starts sniffing about on the slope, moving in her direction, but to her relief it returns when its owner calls it to heel. Now Viv takes the opportunity to look around and get her bearings, but can't work out if she's on Ainslie or Moray Place. She squints, trying to identify her exact position from the buildings, which she knows, on the other side of the river. If she's correct she's on Moray Place and will be able to follow this fence along to Doune Terrace. She's edging her way along when she spots Mrs W with her hands on her hips panting and walking back and forth on the path below. A screen of gnarled elder trees should be enough cover but taking no chances Viv hunkers down and grips the railing even tighter. The elders do the trick and Mrs W trots back up the river in the direction they had come. Viv remains still. But her eye catches a movement two gardens further on. The sight of a black spaniel makes her grin, and she continues with enthusiasm along the fence. Unable to believe her luck she calls, 'Beetle, come on boy.' And sure enough the dog trots up to the fence and licks her hand. Moray Place. Thank God.

With less agility than she'd like, she levers herself over the fence, hearing her jacket tear as it catches the spike on the top of the railings. Once she's in the garden the dog jumps up and down barking, and within minutes Carol, one of Viv's hair girls, comes to the kitchen window. Viv waves and smiles as Carol opens the door and shakes her head at the mess that Viv is in. 'What . . .?'

'Don't ask.'

Carol, a polite woman, doesn't ask, and invites Viv in.

'You can leave those,' she points at Viv's boots, caked with mud, 'in the utility room! Shall I put the kettle on?'

Not waiting for a reply she does just that, and over her shoulder says, 'Nice of you to drop in. Unorthodox route, but nice.'

'Okay, okay. You'll never believe me but I was being chased by a nut case.'

Carol's eyebrows shoot towards her hairline and Viv says, 'Told you. Can hardly believe it myself. Trust me, I was being chased by a not very nice woman, and managed to shake her off down on the walkway.'

'Now, Viv, we all know that you've had . . . shall we say, alternative relationships, but this is taking it a bit far, even for you!'

They both chuckle and take a seat at the kitchen table. Viv has never been in this kitchen. Carol always has her hair done in one of the spare bedrooms. Clients seem to fall into two categories, bedrooms and kitchens. Those who need a mirror, that is, those who are less trusting or less secure, choose the bedroom because there's always a mirror. The kitchen is for those who both trust and can't bear to look at themselves. Viv prefers the kitchen. The power points are usually more accessible and the hair doesn't stick to the carpet. This is the kind of kitchen she'd have imagined Carol in: eclectic, always smelling of something nourishing, today with jars of marmalade sitting on a tray awaiting their labels, the aroma of hot sugar and fruit still heavy in the air. Carol is an artist and Viv has had some of her deepest conversations with her. When they first met Viv got the impression she was snooty and aloof, but it turned out she was just shy . . . and had a wicked sense of humour.

Once they've chatted about Beetle not winning any prizes for being the ideal guard dog, and about when Carol's hair is due for its next cut, Viv stands to leave, brushing earth off the wooden chair and apologising for the intrusion. She also thanks her for the coffee, but Carol says, 'Wait, I'll get my keys and give you a lift. You can't walk about looking like that, even if you are a feminist.'

The glint in her eye makes Viv hold off protesting. Instead she says calmly, 'Fair enough. The chair will need a proper wipe. I landed on my tush and slid down in the mud.'

'I can see that. Come on, it'll only take ten minutes.'

Chapter Seventeen

When Viv puts her key in the door a strange sensation runs through her. After taking her grubby boots off in the hall she dumps her jacket on the floor by the kitchen door, ready for it to go into the washing machine. She calls out, 'John!' No answer. She shudders as someone walks over her grave.

When she enters the sitting room the place is empty of both John and his things. The bed linen is folded on the couch. No sign of a note, which is odd, since he hadn't mentioned going out. The light on the answering machine catches her attention and she distractedly hits the play button then spins back to look at the machine as John's voice says, 'It's weird sitting here on your couch hearing my own voice recording onto your machine. I couldn't do it any more . . . trespass on your hospitality. I'm sure you've guessed by now who has been passing on your movements to the "Mafia". If you knew . . . Never mind. Maybe you'll understand anyway.'

She is shocked. Then shock turns to disappointment; she'd enjoyed his company. Unlike many men she found him easy to have around. The place feels empty. She runs over the events of the past week and it all fits. John was letting 'them' know when she'd been in to see him at the hospital, and when and where she'd gone swimming. 'Yuck! What a shit.'

How stupid to think that she could do someone like that a good turn. But, stopping to think it through – what must they have on him? No wonder he was in such a state about Marconi's visit. At least John had the decency to say thank you, which is something. The next message is from Marconi, asking her to ring him back. She can't be arsed. The morning is catching up with her and she feels drained, and in need of a quick duvet session she heads for the bedroom, strips off and slides in.

When she wakes she feels better until she remembers what John has done. She sits on the edge of the bed wondering what it can be that the 'Mafia' do have on him. Must be drugs. Why did he tell her . . . actually he didn't tell her, he mainly listened and fed her little snippets, but he gave her nothing of consequence, nothing that would compromise his relationship, whatever it is, with the Whitemans. She shakes her head – my, my, you really have been taken for a ride, Viv, that'll teach you. In the hall she takes a clean towel from the linen cupboard and buries her face in its warmth, trying to recall what else she talked to him about. He was so easygoing. What kind of guy is he? Desperate?

The pulse of the hot shower works wonders for her anger management, and by the time she's rubbing her hair dry John has been transformed from a knuckle-dragging troglodyte into a simple lesser mortal. She must phone Fettes.

'Hi, can I speak to DI Marconi please? It's Viv Fraser.'

After a short pause, she hears, ' Viv, what have you been up to? I've tried a few times this morning. Thought you must be having a long lie.'

'Yeah sure, no such luck. I've had quite an adventure with Mrs Whiteman. Listen to this. She tried to stick some sharp file thing into my neck on the upper deck of a bus in Corstorphine.'

'What were you doing in Corstorphine?'

She looks at the phone in disbelief, 'What's it to you? Surely you should be asking why Mrs fucking Whiteman was threatening me on a 26 bus.' The pitch of her voice is extremely unattractive, so she takes a deep breath and says calmly, 'What can we do about the Whitemans?'

'Your Mr Black didn't give me anything we didn't already know. Our surveillance team have already got the current uniform of Whiteman's boys. You could hardly miss them. GHQ on Saturday night looks like a high street in Ibiza.'

'By the way. He's not my Mr Black. He's moved out leaving a confession.

Get this. He has been keeping the Mafia, I'm guessing the Whitemans et al, up to speed about my movements. So much for Mother Teresa; Fagin more like . . . What did you ring for anyway? I've got nothing for you until you bring in the unhinged Mrs W. Looking forward to the streets being safer without her.'

'I rang to ask if you'd like to have lunch sometime.'

This comes completely out of left field.

She clears her throat. 'Did I hear you . . . did you say lunch as in a lunch lunch?'

He laughs and says, 'Yes. Lunch. Forks and knives. You'll have heard of it. We could start with lunch.'

'Whoa!'

'No, I didn't mean that. Lunch just seemed more polite than dinner.'

She really is flummoxed. Dawn's words come back to her. 'Once you've had a woman, you'll never want a man again.' At the time Viv thought she was right, but now she's not so sure.

'Yes, okay, lunch would be fine.'

'Fine! Easy on the enthusiasm.'

'No, no, lunch would be lovely.' Feeling herself colour she puts her hand to her forehead. Hot.

'When?' persists Marconi.

'I'm off work this week. In fact I should have been touring the Highlands, but all this stuff, and the car and the threats . . . sorry, how about Wednesday?'

'Wednesday is good. I'll speak to you before then. I don't know if we're going to wrap Mr Whiteman up, but it will be one helluva ding dong if we do. If there's any development I'll let you know. And by the way call me Mac. My friends call me Mac.'

'Thanks, I'll do that.'

Well, well, how about that? She flicks on the TV, not sure what to do with herself. Surely she can have lunch with him without it becoming a 'thing'. Then she spots the time. 'Shit! Oh, my God!' She's to be in Stafford Street in ten minutes. Can she do it? Stupid question. She's done it before.

As she enters the offices of McGrath and McGrath she looks at the old clock on the wall. Three minutes late. Miraculous. The room smells established. The receptionist says, 'He'll be with you shortly.'

Viv responds breathlessly, 'Does that mean he's somewhere busily sawing off a couple of inches of leg?' The receptionist, already nonplussed, catches Viv's expression, and scowls like a demon. What is it with receptionists? Aren't they supposed to be the face of the company? Yet they always seem to be grumpy sods, and it doesn't matter how beautiful they are. This one is instantly cat-like when she frowns. Viv entertains herself with these musings until a dapper man with dark slicked-back hair, younger than she'd expected, comes out of a polished wood door, and stretches out his hand. 'Dr Fraser? Thank you for responding to my letter.' Not a hint of sarcasm in his voice.

'Thank you for seeing me at such short notice.'

As he closes the door to his equally polished office, he looks round at Viv and says, 'I wondered how long it would take. You've had the family on tenterhooks. They're desperate to find out what's in the will.' He smiles, then gestures to a large leather chair and she sits down opposite him. The distance across this tidy desk makes him seem completely inaccessible. So what? It's not his job to be her chum.

'I hadn't thought of the family. She, Dawn, had a . . . turbulent relationship with them.'

He nods, 'Yes. She put her will together quite a few months before she died. As you'll have guessed, I am the executor. Have you any idea what might be in it, Dr Fraser?'

The sound of her formal title again grates on her so she says, 'Viv. Call me Viv.' He nods again and waits until she continues. 'Well I know about the mews. I was relieved that you managed to get a tenant for it.' Nodding her appreciation she continues, 'I know about the lock-up with the VW in it, but I don't know if she rented that or owned it. I hope she rented it, but I imagine you would have heard from her landlord if they hadn't had their money.'

'The lock-up is owned by her father's estate. But let me take you through Miss Rhodes' assets.'

By the time he's through Viv's mind is reeling. Dawn was up to something leaving all of this to her. No wonder the family are keen to hear about the will.

His voice floats back into her consciousness. 'Miss Rhodes, in her letter of wishes, states categorically that the family must gain nothing from her estate. I did say that this would make life difficult for the recipient of the assets, but she was adamant.'

So even in death Dawn's giving her more than grief. Viv looks directly at him and asks, 'Do the family know that I'm here today?'

'No, why would they? And I am under no obligation to let them know.' He gives a hint of satisfaction as if his pleasure in saying this is too much to hold back. 'They've been . . . shall we say . . . difficult. Yes, difficult.' He lifts his hand and is about to run it through his hair but stops, remembering that it's full of wax.

'I don't know what to say. It's all too much. Can we go over again the bit about land in Doune. I had no idea about her . . . ancestors.'

'She was left an area of land, with a farm which has a long-term tenant, a couple of cottages also with tenants and a ruined keep. She looked into restoring it, but never did anything about it. Now it's over to you.'

'I'll need time for this lot to sink in. How is the flat in London doing? I mean are the tenants okay, or . . .' She recalls Sal Chapman and her keenness to make improvements for Viv. 'I mean is the heating and everything up to speed?'

'I'll send all of this out in writing to you, but for now let's just say you are a wealthy young woman.'

This irks her. 'I'm wealthy already. Only I don't measure it in bricks, mortar or land rights for that matter. Dawn may have had assets, but they're not much good to her where she is.'

McGrath sits quite still.

Silently, she looks at her hands, struck by how different they are from Dawn's. After a few moments, she stands up to leave and says, 'What next? Am I supposed to do anything? Should I write to the family?'

He raises his eyebrows and pulls himself up out of his chair, expelling a long slow breath, 'I don't advise it. They're prepared to contest her wishes.

They'll never do it, but greed's a funny animal. If you need any help or clarification feel free to ring. Or if you have your own solicitors I can communicate with them if that suits you better.'

The handshake is generous from both of them.

Outside, she turns right and walks, in a daze, to the top of Stafford Street where excessively bright lights return her to the present. It feels Christmassy, too Christmassy for February. She sinks her hands into her pockets, puts her head down into the incessant wind and heads right onto Shandwick Place. It's heaving with bodies just finished work. People bump and side-step, rushing for their buses, and at one point she's pushed off the pavement into the path of an oncoming bus, but someone pulls her sleeve and shouts: 'Mind out!'

At the junction with Lothian Road she decides to nip over to the pavement adjacent to Princes Street Gardens. It's not much quieter, and unfortunately she can't walk through the gardens as they close at dusk, so she has no choice but to elbow her way to the Mound before heading up across the High Street and down onto the West Bow. She turns anxiously as she hears steps behind her, but it's only another pedestrian with his head down and his shoulders hunched like her own, hurrying to get home.

The flat is cosy, and before she thinks about her messages she flops onto the couch, letting go of a huge sigh. She is not sure whether to be relieved or not and she tells herself that nothing needs to be done at the moment. She glances round the room wondering if it's her imagination or can she smell John's cologne. It is empty in here without him, but at least it's warm and homely. Wondering where he's gone, she absentmindedly presses the TV remote to catch the six o'clock news. Hopping through channels she stops when she spots a familiar Edinburgh skyline, showing 'Breaking news' with Calton Hill as the backdrop. The reporter looks frozen and her hair is being blown across her face and into her mouth. She keeps pushing it back but the wind is the winner in this contest. The poor girl manages to say, 'The police have four young men in custody after a raid on Calton Hill this evening. They are alleged to have been caught "loitering with intent" and are being questioned . . .'

Viv says, 'What! Intent indeed.' She looks over her shoulder at the answering machine, and stretches out her arm to press 'Play'. She's heartened to hear Marconi's voice, 'Thought you'd like to know that we've taken action. Give me a ring. I'd rather you heard the details from me than from STV.'

She rings him back anyway. His voice is distant, as if he's holding the phone away from his mouth. 'Marconi here. Oh, hi! Let me just move somewhere more private.'

She can hear his footsteps and a door opening then closing behind him.

'Glad you got the message. We've brought Whiteman in.'

'Mr or Mrs?'

'Mr. You are never going to believe this, Viv.'

'Try me.'

'Well, a call came in to report an attempted robbery at the Whiteman property but that's not how it turned out.'

'What? I don't get it.'

'It's not difficult. Someone phoned in and reported that they saw a young man acting suspiciously on the Whiteman property. How they saw this with defences greater than Barlinnie is a mystery, but I don't have to tell you how diligent the public can be.'

She is getting the picture, but can't quite see where he's going with this.

'When we responded to the call we found Mrs Whiteman recovering from a beating. No sign of a burglar, only hubby doing lengths in the pool, and her nursing a black eye and a bloody nose.'

'That'll have been some door she walked into.'

'You got it.'

'No! He didn't say that! Tell me he didn't really say that!'

'He might be creative with young men and drugs, but not so with explanations about the state of his wife. Anyway, while PC Aitken checked the rest of the house for evidence of a break-in, I questioned Whiteman on his wife's injuries. PC Aitken asked me to come and listen to something he'd just heard being recorded on Whiteman's answering machine. Get this. The call, to a private line, was from a bloke calling to "order" boys. Couldn't believe my ears. When I challenged Whiteman on this, cool as they come, he slid underwater and continued doing laps. You see, the caller gave an "account number" and thanked him in advance for four blond boys at "the usual place" on the hill at four p.m.'

Viv can't believe it, Whiteman can't be that stupid. This stinks of a set-up.

'Was he set up?'

'What! By us? Not on your life. You don't know me if you think I'd entertain that kind of crap. No, it was a gift. I wasn't meant to be there but luckily it was a good copper who knew about our interest in Whiteman and radioed in that's where he was headed. We were able to get there as he arrived so he didn't have to deal with a pro like Whiteman on his own . . . although not quite the pro that he might have been. We've got the lads as well. Loitering with intent.'

Viv continues to be amazed. 'Will you actually get him?'

'We've got the recording of the bloke "ordering" the boys along with his bank details – no name as yet though. We caught the end of the registration plate of a Lexus leaving the hill in a hurry. Must have been suspicious of our unmarked vehicles at the entrance. If we can tie the owner to the account we'll be onto a winner. Besides, Whiteman's human, might speak if he thinks he's the only one taking the rap. Although, if I had to guess, I'd say he'll not be as brave as he looks on paper.'

Viv sighs and runs her hand through her hair, seeing where this could lead.

'It's good news if you get a result.'

'Don't worry, Viv. This is just the beginning of the fall. Mrs Whiteman won't speak, but we're thinking if her father sees the state of her face, he'll be more than happy for Mr Whiteman and his little empire to crumble.'

'Unless the father-in-law is one of the "pillars".' Viv recalls the photographs of them together. Both smiling directly into the camera, each with an arm draped over the other. The euphoria of their win or what?

'Viv, do you know something that I don't, but should?'

'Only that when I was researching – don't you love that word? It covers so many possibilities. Anyway when I was researching I found quite a bit on-line about Whiteman. He and his father-in-law were in a number of photographs together, they play golf on the same team, and are members of the same club, so I got the impression they're quite thick. I wouldn't be too sure that seeing his daughter's bruises will push his buttons as much as you think. But take a look at their Facebook pages – you'll be amazed . . . There's one other thing. I wonder if Whiteman has a stash of photographs somewhere. It's just a hunch but could be worth checking his computer.'

'I'll get someone onto that now. We've got some material from the web already, which shows the father-in-law's antagonism towards Whiteman, but we'll look at that other stuff before deciding which angle to take. Thanks. If anything else comes to mind you know what to do.'

'Yep. Thanks for keeping me in the loop.'

'No problem. You feel like one of the team. Cheers.'

Sinking back onto the couch Viv can see that if Zoe's father has too much to lose by squealing on Leonard, he'll find another way to punish him. What can she do now, since the Whitemans appear to be taken care of?

She changes into comfort kit and immediately feels less out of sorts. Her brain is now more interested in how to prioritise it all. She goes through a list of people she still would like to speak to. The small matter of Andrew's death hasn't yet been cleared, unless they've got Whiteman primed for that as well. There are the three Harpies. It wouldn't do any harm to speak to them again. Copa Cabana will be a different place without Whiteman around. The temptation to go along there tonight is strong but she's had enough for today, and needs to curl up with a book. Copa Cabana will still be there tomorrow. *Trick of the Dark* wins and she settles down on the couch wrapped in her duvet. When she wakes a couple of hours later with a crick in her neck, she staggers through to bed pulling the duvet behind her.

Chapter Eighteen

When morning comes after another turbulent night she's glad to see a slash of blue through the gap in her curtains. It's late and she's starving. Having missed dinner last night the idea of going out for breakfast strikes her as appealing. She justifies it by telling herself she would have been in a B&B somewhere in the north having a full fry up, had it not been for the shenanigans of the last week. Slipping into clean clothes she looks toward the graveyard – her window on the weather – and is heartened that there's no evidence of yesterday's wind.

The bistro has only two tables left and she settles as close as she can get to her regular one, which is occupied by two teenage girls in white shirts and green skirts. Their green blazers hanging on the backs of their chairs confirm that they're from St Jude's but one jacket has the yellow piping of a prefect round its edges. Before Viv can speak to them Bella greets her, wearing a white tea towel over her shoulder and a long clean apron that looks spanking new, 'The usual, Doc?'

'Yep.' Viv's distracted. 'You don't have the *Guardian*, do you?'

'It's through the back. Jacques is having a go at the sudoku.'

'He can keep the sudoku. I just need the main section. Feeling out of touch.' She keeps an eye on the girls but soon her food arrives, and as she makes a start on breakfast they prepare to leave. As they slip on their blazers Viv scrapes her chair back and steps towards them. 'Excuse me, I notice you're from St Jude's . . .'

She doesn't get the chance to finish her sentence as the prefect interrupts her, 'So? What of it?'

'I just wondered if you knew a friend of mine.'

The girl softens, realising that Viv isn't on the look-out for truants.

'And who might that be? It's a big school.'

'Pete, he hangs out with Tommy and Johnny.'

The girls look at each other. The prefect's eyes widen and she imperceptibly shakes her head when her chum looks as if she might speak. A warning.

She looks defiantly at Viv, 'Even if we did know him we're not permitted to discuss school matters . . .' She falters, her cockiness failing, and pulls her friend towards the door. The friend objects, 'Don't Ruthie.'

Viv blurts out, 'Wait!' But there's no question of them doing that. She turns to look at her rapidly cooling croissants and sighs, returning to the table. Their uniform reminds her that Colin, a 'friend' stroke pain in the arse from university, worked at St Jude's. Wondering if he's still there she takes out her phone and scrolls down her contacts. She obviously never had a mobile number from him, so it'll have to wait until she gets back. They stayed in touch largely because the woman he married is worth the effort. Last time they met up he had some spurious reason for being none too pleased with Viv. What the hell – her pride will have to take a back seat. Colin was employed to teach physics, but spends most of his time on the rugby field. He should have a view on what's been going on.

Before anyone else can take the table by the window she moves. Now she can relax and enjoy her industrial strength coffee and basket of not so hot croissants. There's another teenage girl at a table beyond, no uniform though, listening to her iPod – too much matt make-up isn't doing anything to disguise her spots. She's nodding to the beat of God knows what while doing her homework. When she catches Viv looking at her she instinctively curls an arm around her page. Viv smiles at the idea of being able to read anything from this distance.

Viv shoogles her shoulders and rotates her neck then looks down at her breakfast and selects an almond croissant – this is just what she needs. A few minutes of normal activity without interruption to make her feel grounded again. She turns to the review section of the paper and immerses herself for the next half an hour.

On her way home her phone vibrates and checking it she doesn't recognise the number. The message reads: 'U r safe now x.' Interesting. The temptation to press 'Reply' is strong, but she reaches the stair door and while she's opening it tucks her phone away. Maybe it's from Marconi. He'd surely have signed it. Not his style anyway.

Once inside the flat she checks the number against Marconi's, then scrolls through her other numbers. Definitely not Marconi or anyone else she rings regularly. She presses 'Reply', but it goes straight to an answering service. She doesn't leave a message, but texts Colin instead. She wonders if he's forgiven her. He accused her of using him. Unable now to remember the details, she just recalls his face turning red with fury and him stomping off. He was a total 'yes' boy at uni so she's not got much hope that he'll risk getting into trouble, but he might give something away.

With the sun streaming into the flat for the first time in too long, the place looks grubby. A good opportunity for displacement activity. She dons her Marigolds and sets to.

She's been at the cleaning malarkey for an hour before she stands back and looks round at the improvement. Presbyterianism has its pay-offs and she's had a work-out into the bargain.

She checks her phone and to her surprise Col has left a message saying, 'Coffee at midday, free period. Petit France.'

'Wow. Good on ya, Col.' She always forgets that Bella's actually has a name. If she's quick she can do it.

Bella greets her as if it's been years instead of a couple of hours since she was in. Viv's table is free, so all is well with the world.

Colin is one of those people who disturbs the air whenever he arrives and today is no exception. He rushes in, leaving a wake of scraped chairs and quivering tables, wearing undistinguished joggers and a towelling scarf, which he proceeds to unwrap from round his neck as he plonks himself down opposite her.

'Well, Viv, it's been a while.' He doesn't make eye contact, but shifts the table mat into a central position, then does the same with the salt and pepper. Then he looks up at her. 'I'm guessing this is about Andrew?'

'That transparent, eh?'

''Fraid so! The last time we met you were looking for tickets for one of our rugby matches. I don't for the life of me remember why. But, hey, what are friends for?'

She ignores his sarcasm and fires him an endearing smile. Colin is younger than Viv. At uni. she was regarded as a 'mature' student, a laugh in itself, since she is only three or four years older than him.

He hasn't worn well, for all his jogging and rugby. It's that pale blue skin that lots of Scots revert to in the winter. She thanks the Lord for her own tinted moisturiser. Both Colin and Ann-Marie, his wife, teach at St Jude's. She's in the infant school and is one of life's angels.

'How's Ann-Marie?'

'She's great. Loves the job. No sign of any offspring for us yet.'

Viv reads his disappointment. Not sure what to say she looks away and is relieved when Bella comes to take his order. Col knows that Viv writes but he's never been able to get over the fact that beneath it all she's 'just' a hairdresser. She glances back at him, noting that his hair is thinner, which is saying something because he didn't have much to begin with. He's tight with his cash and his hair has never been a priority. He has no idea that the less you have the more you need a good cut. Consequently he's on his way to becoming more Bobby Charlton than Bobby Dazzler.

Even a tiny white lie is hard with friends, but she does it anyway.

'I've been doing a story about young people who have gone missing, and yes, Andrew Douglas was one of them. D'you know much about him?'

'I'm not supposed to speak about him . . .'

She keeps looking at him until he breaks eye contact but continues. 'I do know that he was rapidly going off the rails. Drugs mainly. I expect you've spoken to his boyfriend?'

'No, is he at the school?'

He looks at her as if she's not done her homework – which she clearly hasn't if Andrew had a steady boyfriend all this time and she didn't know.

'Well. That's surprised you. He and a guy called Pete Brendan were inseparable. From third year until . . . well now. In fact another bloke, Thomas Clancy, used to hang around with them as well but he seemed to have fallen by the wayside last term.'

Feigning ignorance, she says, 'Has this Pete Brendan been at school through all this?'

'I think so. I didn't teach either him or Andrew. They, not surprisingly, opted for cross-country running. Wouldn't look at a rugby ball.'

His sarcasm isn't lost on her, and this time her response is defensive. 'Sound like wise young men to me. At least they'll . . . I was going to say keep their looks, but Andrew won't.'

'Sad, and a bit curious if you ask me. He and Pete were joined at the hip; even applied to the same universities. I got the sense Andrew was the one doing the chasing.'

Viv can't believe her ears. 'Really, how'd you make that out?'

'Well, Pete was popular with the girls as well. He teased them as if he'd change his batting order any minute. Not a chance. But actually, when I think of them together

. . . I can hardly bring myself to say this, but they did look as if they were besotted. Apart from the usual school rules, there was nothing we could do to stop them . . .'

'Stop them what? Being in love?'

Viv stares out the window, dismayed at herself for being taken in by Pete. She should have seen it coming. That one time when she saw something cross his face. She couldn't make it out at the time, but it didn't match his words. Thinking of it now it could have been disgust. But she's getting ahead of herself. 'How's the rugby going? St Jude's seem to be up there with the best.'

'Yeah, but up there isn't good enough, is it, Viv? The top's the only place to be.'

She shakes her head. How could she have forgotten how obsessive he is about the game? His competitiveness knows no bounds and he lives his life by proxy. God help his poor pupils.

As if he can tell that she's got what she wanted, he stands. 'Well. Sorry not to be of help, Viv. I'll have to get back. I'm on monitor duty for lunch.'

Viv stands and awkwardly they manage to hug, barely touching. Watching him jog back across the Grassmarket and up the steps to Keir Street, she imagines his route past the Eye Pavilion, down onto the Meadows, across the Links. He'll be back in school in no time. What now? Taking out her phone she texts Pete.

Bella asks if she'd like a top-up, but Viv declines, and sits leaning on her elbow, staring out the window. Does Pete know more than he's said? He must do. Lies are like mice; there's never only one. But why?

A small round woman with bowed legs walking her dog catches Viv's attention and distracts her. The dog is interested in every smell, and even when the owner tugs at the lead, the dog, determined to get that last sniff, digs its heels in. We are only their custodians. Viv had a Beardie once, and when Mollie died she vowed never to go through that pain again, but seeing this tenacious little cross-breed, wagging its tail at nothing that we know about, makes her wonder if she could have another one. Out of the question in her top-floor flat, but maybe one day. Dogs never lie about love. Dogs never lie about anything. But why did Pete? Maybe he was embarrassed to say that Andrew was keen on him, or perhaps Colin has got it wrong and Pete wanted Andrew more than Andrew wanted him. But killing him?

At a bit of a loss, she remembers that she still has to organise the finance for the Rav. This perks her up. As she strides back towards the flat, she passes the woman with the dog, who turns and grins toothlessly at Viv saying, 'I'm no' sure who's walkin' who.' Not looking for an answer the woman chuckles as she tugs on the lead. Spring must be in the air.

Viv whispers, 'What now?' as she steps on a sheet of A5 paper lying on the carpet when she opens the door to her flat. The note is handwritten in an unfamiliar, slightly feminine script, in green ink with a proper fountain pen, and says, 'Will be around for a bit longer – changed my mind about selling. Ronnie.' She smiles and wonders if her comment to him about missing the Bow had made a difference – still, that's one less thing for her to think about.

The woman at her bank arranges everything for the new car without any hassle. She suggests a bank transfer and Viv rings up the owners of the Rav and gets the okay from them. As soon as that's done she can pick up the car this afternoon. It's such a great day and a walk would help get her thoughts in order. If she starts off for Corstorphine now it will give the car owners time to have lunch, and no doubt their afternoon zizz.

She has no intention of re-enacting the journey of her last visit. Just thinking of Mrs W's perfumed breath on the bus makes Viv shudder. After Haymarket, the walk is quite pleasant. The road is busy but it's wide and in places opens onto huge green spaces; the playing fields at Donaldson's; the pitches at Murrayfield and mature gardens. It takes her longer than she thought it would and the final hike up Clermiston Hill takes its toll on her thighs.

The look on their faces when they open the door is one of remorse. Strange the relationship we have with inanimate objects. They are sad to let their car go, although complimentary about her, and hopeful that she'll take good care of it. She vows that she will.

She stalls as she inches out of their drive and makes the mistake of looking in the rear-view mirror, catching sight of him flinching and covering his mouth with his hand. Wishing they'd go indoors and stop making her nervous, she indicates right and heads out west towards the by-pass, planning to get to know the car better on the open road. It's luxurious. She'd got a faint smell of cigarette smoke off him, but you'd never know it from the car. It smells of newness. As soon as she touches the accelerator it responds smoothly, unlike the MG, which needed much petrol pumped through it before it would get her up to speed.

To begin with she is too heavy on the pedals, but soon she gets the hang of it and sits back smiling from ear to ear. Doesn't get any better than this. What's really good is the height. In the MG she felt as if her butt was being dragged along the ground; in this she feels as if she can see for miles. She takes the by-pass as far as the Hillend junction, then slips off down the road towards Peebles. They were generous enough to leave it with half a tank of petrol, which means it'll be a while before she has to fill up. Viv presses a button and the radio springs to life. Classic FM without crackles sounds amazing.

She gets all the way to Peebles before she thinks about turning back, but first she needs a pee break. When she parks she looks at the car and understands why the couple were sad to lose it. She's already in love.

The public conveniences in this charming little market town are cleaner than most. They have their own attendant which means there's scented loo roll, remarkable plastic flowers and enough air freshener to test the healthiest lungs. On her return to the car she passes one of those rare independent boutiques, and seeing an interesting shirt in the window decides to go in search of her size. The assistant is really astute and Viv is soon armed with two large bags.

Back on home territory, she reflects on having bought a car and a complete outfit all in one day. Profligate or what, Fraser? Before guilt gets a chance to take hold she checks her emails, reading one from Jules: 'If you can salvage anything from your "researches" we could use a feature on "Entertainment on the gay scene in Edinburgh".' Good old Jules; not one to waste an opportunity. There's one from her sister, just back from skiing and wondering how their mum has been while she's been away. This nudges Viv into action. Lifting the phone she dials her mother's number, which rings and rings. She hates it when her mum doesn't pick up quickly – all sorts of fantasies start flitting into her mind. Is she lying dead on the floor? Then an out of breath voice pipes up. 'Yes?' The irritation is obvious.

'Hi, Mum, it's Viv.'

'I know who it is. D'you think I've lost my marbles?'

Viv would like to say yes but holds back. 'Just wondering how you're doing.'

'Aye, but not wondering enough to come round for your tea.'

Here we go again.

'I could come now if you like.'

'No. Don't bother. You'll be busy and I'm about to watch a film.'

Her mother is the most devoted fan of movies of any kind. In fact anything that takes her out of her own shrunken world. In the background Viv can hear the familiar drum roll of a Twentieth Century Fox opening title, so isn't surprised when her mum says. 'I'll let you get back to your work, hen, and I'll see you for lunch tomorrow if you like.'

'Okay, Mum. I'll see you then.'

Before the phone has hit the cradle she remembers she's having lunch with Marconi. She presses 'Redial', not sure if she's more nervous of changing the time with her mum or seeing Marconi. Hearing her mobile vibrating, she bangs the receiver down and searches around for its counterpart in her rucksack. It's Pete.

'Hi, Pete, just wondered how you're doing. Thought you might like a drink.'

'What? With you?'

She's taken aback by the vehemence of his tone.

'Yes, me. Why is that so strange? It's not as if I haven't bought you a drink before.'

'Yeah, but that was before I heard they had someone for it.'

'"It" being Andrew's death, I assume?'

'Yeah. If they have someone you don't need my help in finding his killer.' His voice has a hard edge that she's never heard before. In fact, if she didn't know better she'd think she was speaking to someone else, someone possessed.

'Okay. I see what you mean. Thanks for ringing back.'

She hangs up before he does, and says out loud. 'Confront your demons, Pete, before they consume you completely.' Wondering if he'll be in Copa Cabana she decides to have one last try. If this fails she'll at least be able to gather some details of the menus and the clientele for Jules' feature.

The car starts first time and she goes the long way to Picardy Place. It hardly seems possible that it's only a week since all this drama began. Now a young boy is dead, and a number of people have been exposed as being other than who they seemed to be. She wonders about Max and what Sonia and her father might have done since he was questioned. Marconi must've been kicking himself after he had cow-towed to Max in his office, only to have to pull him in to Fettes a few days later.

Viv has sweltered on the journey, and now understands why people with decent cars don't wear heavy coats. She'll soon get out of the habit, but for now, she pulls her collar up and wanders round the corner to Copa Cabana. Early evening drinkers, still in their suits, perch on the stools, chatting and laughing now that they're released from the shackles of their day. At the bar she orders a half of her usual organic cider, and takes it to one of the booths at the back where there's a view of the door and the front of house. Slinging her coat over the back, she settles in to read a *Scotsman* that's been left lying. An article on whether people who commit knife crimes should be banned from drinking alcohol catches her attention. She's so engrossed that she barely looks up when someone slips in opposite her. When he speaks, however, he has her full attention.

'I can't imagine what brings you here again, Viv.'

His menacing tone doesn't tally with the young, distraught boy that she'd sat watching when he rubbed the tears from his face.

She looks at him unflinching. 'Can't you?' This catches him. 'I had a chat with a chum of mine who happens to be one of your teachers. He mentioned that you were pals with Andrew.'

'Yeah, so nothing you didn't already know.'

'He said that you were really close.' She tilts her head. 'You know, in the biblical sense.'

He looks at her as if his head will burst with hatred. She shudders as she remembers how tempted she'd been to hug him. He notices. 'Disappointed, are you?' He stretches out his words in a singsong manner. Christ, another one who thinks he's the lead on an American soap.

'No, disappointment only happens when you don't know how to manage your expectations. I'm quite impressed. You must be in the school drama society?'

'Witty. But you won't be for long.'

'That wasn't a threat, was it, Pete?' Her anger rising at his audacity, she rubs her hands through her hair, looking around at the punters then letting out a sigh.

'So what happened? What did you do?'

His expression doesn't look quite so cocky now. She hasn't lowered her voice and he looks round in case she's been overheard.

'You think I killed him?' His tone has gained an edge.

'Yep. I do.'

Shaking his head and smiling he says, 'You're off your head, missus.'

If he hadn't said missus she wouldn't have minded so much. 'If I'm off my head then your level of insanity isn't even on the scale.'

Now he sits forward aggressively, almost touching her with his head. 'I'll show you threat . . .'

This makes her want to laugh. He's also been watching too much *Taggart*.

'You'll eventually come round.' She says this with a lightness that she doesn't feel. Then whispers, 'Confess, Pete. Confess before you really blow it.'

'You think I want this life?' He gestures round the room.

She stands, lifting her coat and shrugging herself into it. Looking down on him she says, 'There's still time.'

As she turns to leave, he grabs her coat, 'You think you know something and you know nothing!'

'We'll see.'

Nodding to an unfamiliar barman, she heads for the door. Viv's life at the moment seems to be one big 'what now?'

She smiles as she approaches her new baby. But in an instant, before she has time to register the steps approaching, she's thrown against the bonnet of the car, and seeing some kind of bat swinging towards her head she ducks, drops to the ground and manages to roll under the car. He kicks and kicks, frenzied, trying to reach her. Her phone is in her bag now lying a few feet away, and she can't reach it. The chances of him moving seem remote. He stops kicking, and leans panting against the car. Her new car! The cheek of him. He says, 'I'll wait as long as it takes.'

She lies there with the adrenaline pumping; grateful that the ground is dry, but at the same time thinking how ironic it is she should see the underside of the car in these circumstances. 'I'm not in any rush, Pete.'

What else could he try? She gets a flashback of the guy who dropped the lighted taper into her petrol tank and feels bile rising in her throat. This is different. This wasn't premeditated. Pete didn't plan to hurt her tonight, or did he? His mobile rings and she hears him saying, in something close to a whine, 'You said . . . But I thought you said . . . Okay.'

'Your mummy giving you grief, Pete?'

He kneels on the ground and tries to swing the bat at her from his side. She succeeds in rolling out of reach just in time. He runs to the other side of the car and tries again. This farce could go on all night. From up on Calton Terrace she can hear voices getting louder. Then relief floods through her as she spots two pairs of legs, one pair limping. The legs slow down as they approach the car. Then a familiar woman's voice says, 'Everything all right?'

At this Viv rolls out from beneath the car, and Pete takes off like a bullet up the hill. Viv looks at Red and her companion and shouts, 'Quick, Red, radio in, he needs to be stopped!'

Red's colleague bolts after Pete, as Red stands with her hands on her hips, looking just like a proper cop, with her long auburn locks tied neatly into a ponytail.

'Never a dull moment eh, Doc? How come you were trapped under this car with Master Peter Brendan hanging over you?'

Viv reaches down to retrieve her bag. 'Long story. But my God! Your timing just gets better and better – I owe you twice now. How's the leg?'

'On the mend, thanks. What happened?'

'Let's get in the car and at least keep warm.'

'I'm all for cosying up, Doc.'

She smiles at Viv. But they stay on the pavement in the cold waiting to see if the other officer gets a result.

Viv smiles back. 'You're a trier. I'll give you that.'

Chapter Nineteen

Red's colleague returns with the bat, but without Pete Brendan.

'I'll call it in. You up for another trip to HQ, Viv?'

'Do I have a choice?'

'Yup. You can come with me now, or pitch up in the morning.'

Viv had planned a long lie, so she agrees to go now. 'Let's get it over with.'

She rakes around for her keys and presses the fob. The car blinks and she opens the door. 'Miracle!' Shaking her head she repeats, 'Miracle. It's a bloody miracle.'

'What exactly are you on about? Or is this a moment I should treasure?' Red's smile lights up her dimpled face. Viv hasn't noticed this before.

'It's new,' Viv says, grinning at the car.

Red looks with a mixture of astonishment and glee.

'It's the first time I've had a car that works, let alone one that unlocks its own doors.'

Red nods and says, 'Aye, anything you say, dear.'

Viv gives Red a friendly shove, 'Jump in.'

Red is about to protest but Viv 's enthusiasm for her new toy is infectious, and she throws her car keys to her colleague who trots off up the hill.

'You're my first passenger. Sit back and enjoy the ride.' Red makes all the right noises and Viv acknowledges them with appreciation.

Once they are inside Fettes the business is more serious. Red is the senior officer. She's obviously learned some of her technique from Marconi. There's no bluster and she teases out information skilfully. She already knows some of what Viv has to say, about the lies that Pete has told them both, but is interested when Viv tells her what Colin revealed about Pete and Andrew's relationship. Pete had led the investigation to believe that he was the one with the hots for Andrew, and was devastated by his being missing and then dead. One lie is all it takes, though.

'We've had our suspicions about Pete. The night Andrew was killed Pete was meant to be staying over with a friend. Only he forgot to tell the family that he claimed he'd been with to cover for him. Small lies become big deals. We're also going back out to the petrol station beyond Dalkeith. I got to thinking that Pete and Andrew look quite similar and it could be that the woman who saw Andrew actually saw Pete. Let's say Pete and Andrew went for a drive. Pete could have hitched back. It's a shot in the dark. Many young men could have been mistaken for Andrew. Speculation at the moment, Viv, but the fact that he attacked you just now isn't making him look any more innocent.'

'I know. It's pretty extreme, though, to kill someone, set fire to a car with someone in it. I mean what's been going on in his head?'

'We'll need to bring him in as soon as, and then we'll find out.'

'I wouldn't be surprised if he's gone home. I'm sure when I was under the car his mother phoned him. It sounded as if he was being reminded of his curfew.'

Red gives a nod to the other officer who leaves the room, then continues with her questions.

'What else did this teacher say? You said he never taught either of them, and yet he noticed their relationship in detail.'

'Red, have you ever been to St Jude's? They're as stuffy as they can get away with and it sounds as if Andrew and Pete knew exactly what the boundaries were. But listen, being a liar doesn't mean he's a killer, it just means he has something to hide.'

'Speculation again. No point in any of this until we have him here . . . But what about you, Viv. How are you doing? It's been some week. Or is every week like this for you?'

Viv snorts. 'No, only some. But look, before I start to draw a salary here can I go home?'

Red reads over her notes and says, 'I think between us we've got enough to raise some serious questions. I'll keep you posted.'

When Viv leaves the building it's surprisingly quiet. Tuesday night. Maybe there's a match on. She visualises a local pub full to bursting with cops watching the game. It reminds her that they're all human. She grins at having thought otherwise.

At home, she checks her messages. 'Hi, Viv, hope we're still all right for tomorrow. I've taken the liberty of booking lunch at the Outsider. Twelve-thirty. If I don't hear to the contrary I'll see you then.'

With her insides churning, she changes into fleecy PJs, fills a hot water bottle and flicks through the channels, looking for something escapist. Nothing. But then the drum roll of a film reminds her that she didn't manage to speak to her mum again. She checks the time. Too late to ring her now. She picks up her book. There's nothing like a good book to aid the task of letting go of the day.

She wakes during the night with moonlight flooding her bedroom. It strikes her that crime is tricky with such a moon; fewer places to hide, distorted shadows – even as she hoists herself up to look at the clock her own shadow looks like a monster against the wall. What a great night for the imagination. Snuggling back under the duvet, sad at the kind of twists that a life can take, she wonders if they've found Pete. We're all the architects of our own lives. We each make choices that change who we are, and what we become. Why would Pete kill someone he cared for? Jealousy? It's always a contender. She starts counting sheep.

On the second bright day in a row Viv springs out of bed and strips it, stuffs the sheets into the basket and fetches clean linen from the cupboard in the hall. It's half nine and she has much to do before lunch. Smoothing out the clean duvet cover gives her a sense of satisfaction too great for the task. But as she does it she recalls a fragment of a dream from last night: a ruddy-faced man with frizzy red hair was questioning her, trying to catch her out, but he couldn't. He smiled and said, 'Perhaps I've met my intellectual equal.' Weird.

She takes out the kit she bought in Peebles and holds this piece up to that piece, trying to decide what to wear. She doesn't really need to decide yet, because there's skin to be exfoliated and legs to be shaved before she dresses. Then she remembers that she still has to ring her mum. As she dials the number she prepares for a tirade and t+

2he usual hang up but her mum's answering machine kicks in and Viv punches the air. She leaves a message saying she has to work. It's the only thing that will pacify her mother, albeit in small measure.

She doesn't feel like breakfast but knows if she doesn't eat something she'll feel sick at lunchtime, so she sticks a slice of bread in the toaster, and puts the kettle on. As she waits the phone rings. It's Red with an update on Pete. 'You were right – he had gone home. He won't talk but his mother is in a complete panic, making up all sorts of crap. His father is apparently on business in the Middle East. We caught a pair of Pete's trainers just about to go through a boil wash, but a gallus PC spotted them in the machine and managed to get them out before the water came in.'

Viv imagines, if she were a mother, she might go to similar lengths to save the skin of her child.

'Get this, there was goat shit on the soles of the trainers which matches some found in the lay-by in Earlston. Only one organic goat herd north of the Border. The mother is saying that they're her shoes, only there's a discrepancy of five sizes.'

Sounds like a huge pair of trainers, and visions of possible owners race through Viv's mind. 'But Red, the goat shit only proves that the shoes were in the lay-by. It doesn't have him torching the car.'

Red sounds slightly irritated. 'I know that, but at least we're now sure he was there and he'll have to talk sooner or later.'

Frustrated, Viv says, 'No, that's my point, you only have the person who was wearing the trainers at the scene. You don't know for certain they belong to Pete or that he was the one wearing them, do you?'

'Well no, but I'm guessing they're his or otherwise his mother wouldn't be in such a state . . . Relax, we won't take anything for granted.'

'Have you spoken to his mates Thomas and Johnny recently?'

'No, but we've been keeping an eye on them. Don't worry, Viv, we're not as incompetent as you think.'

'I do not think that. You should get your money back on that crystal ball. It's not working.'

'Ha bloody ha. Speak to you later.'

When Viv hangs up her earlier high spirits have evaporated. She switches on the news. Nothing. Maybe he's a minor after all. She can't imagine them not having something about this development, but if he's under eighteen they won't risk jeopardising the case by reporting it. Too many cases get thrown out on a 'technicality', which is often code for media blabbing. Viv sits staring at the mute TV screen. What the hell has Pete done, and did he do it alone? Who else could be involved? Talking about technical, it's time to check up on Johnny and Thomas again. She boots up her laptop and types Pete Brendan into Facebook. There's been activity from him in the last twelve hours, although nothing of consequence. She scrolls through his Wall and discovers no activity on the night of Andrew's death. Could be coincidence; he does have long spells with no postings.

She finds Thomas and Johnny on his list of friends. Viv is astounded at what she finds on people's Walls. Talk about lots of words but no information. Thomas is obviously addicted because there's barely half an hour goes by when he doesn't leave a posting. She scrolls back to look at what he was writing on the night that Andrew was found. Nothing. 'No way. He couldn't stand to be away from his iPhone, not for a whole night. So what were you up to, Thomas my boy?'

Viv notes the names he has most contact with and his pattern of activity. He's also as camp as frilly knickers, so obviously 'out'. Johnny's page is entirely different. He doesn't communicate as if he's 'out', and his friends are mainly sporty. He also has long periods without posting anything at all, including the night of Andrew's death. Doubting her own observations she scrolls through them all again. Shit! All three of them out of communication on one night. What are the chances of that not being suspicious? Viv chastises herself for not thinking to ask Colin about these two but it didn't occur to her at the time. She rings Red back but her mobile goes to answering machine, and Viv has to settle for leaving a message. 'Red, been taking a look at the Facebook pages of the three Harpies, and I'd say it's worth you lot asking them some questions about it. None of them have any postings on the night of Andrew's death – a really glaring absence of activity if you ask me. Give me a call.'

Viv kneels on the floor, scouring a pile of CDs. She uncovers the *Mamas and the Papas Greatest Hits*, slips it into the machine and turns up the volume. Within a few moments she's singing her heart out. The first shave of the season takes longer than she's planned, but once performed she is at liberty to select what to wear. After several false starts, she's in a 'that'll have to do' mood. Her hair won't behave and should have been cut over a week ago. Still, it is shiny. Everyone comments on how glossy it is. It's a complete fluke. The telephone ringing gives her an excuse to abandon her titivation. It's Red.

'Hi, I hoped it'd be you. Did you get my message about the boy's Facebook pages?'

'Yeah, good call, Viv.'

'Any chance I could come in and ...'

'Oi, Doc, stop right there. I'm the one who'd get her head in a sling.'

'C'mon, Red, I've just handed them to you on a plate. There's got to be a way.'

Viv can hear the cogs in Red's brain clicking, searching for a solution.

'Leave it with me.'

She hangs up and Viv stares at the receiver convinced that Red will work something out. Just as she's about to have another go at her hair, the phone rings. It's Red again.

'If you're really quick I can let you into the observation gallery. We're talking within the next twenty minutes. Sal's just left for another meeting . . .'

'I'm on my way.'

As she steps out onto the West Bow she hears the familiar sound of a diesel engine labouring on the steep bend and sure enough a black cab, whose catalytic converter can't possibly be legal, slips into view. Soon she's at Fettes, pays the driver and races up the steps. Red is already in the reception area and looks furtively right and left before shuffling Viv in through a door.

'You do realise if I had balls they'd be for the chop?'

Viv smiles. 'I'm grateful, I'm grateful.'

Red unlocks the door of a room with a huge window on one wall. Two tubular seats face the window but Viv can't see anything until Red lowers the lights by turning a switch on the back wall. As Red is heading back out, the door of the room on the other side of the window opens and an officer leads in Pete and another bloke, who must be his solicitor. Viv recognises the guy in the suit as a partner at the same firm as her chum Margo. He'll not be cheap. It's weird watching an interview without being able to hear anything. Pete is blethering, panicked, his eyes darting around the room as if he's expecting the Archangel Gabriel. His counsel keeps tapping his arm and shaking his head. Pete's not listening. It doesn't take long before he's being lead back out. As he reaches the door, and as if he knows she's there, he turns and stares at the wall. His eyes are not the eyes of an innocent. For years Viv has been watching people's behaviour in the mirror; it's given her insights. Pete's body language was a terrific give away. No specific eye contact, arms crossed over his abdomen, hands gripping his elbows. She doesn't feel like cuddling him now.

Five minutes later the door of Viv's room swings open and Red, shaking her head, says, 'Well, what did you make of that last gesture? I've been in here when someone has done that. Completely unnerving or what? It's not gonna be too tough to crack but . . . we'll get there.' She rubs her hands over her face and into her hair. A gesture which Marconi does all the time.

Viv notices Red's hesitation. 'You'll get there. Look, I'm meant to be somewhere but can we talk later?'

Red draws in a deep breath. 'Sure thing, Doc. Sure thing. But Pete's telling better stories than the Brothers Grimm. Says he's confused about who, where and what he was doing on the night of the murder. The forensics report said that Andrew was already dead before the car was torched. This one isn't going to be easy to untangle. Because he was so charred we can't tell whether he had any wounds, and even the tests that might show whether he was toxic are going to be problematic with so little of the body uncooked.'

Viv gives an involuntary gasp and Red says, 'Sorry, I keep thinking you're one of us . . . I've got someone onto the net to check those Facebook accounts and we've brought Thomas and John in, but they aren't saying anything without their solicitors. Almost an admission of guilt in itself.'

Viv interrupts, 'Don't even go there. But listen. Don't suppose there's any chance I could see . . .'

Red's face contorts. 'For fuck sake, Doc. What are you trying to do, get me lynched? If I get caught with you in here . . .'

'I know. I know. I just thought . . .'

'What, Doc? You just thought what? It'd be nice to see the charred remains of a young lad? Trust me, it ain't no picnic . . . Look, how about I let you see some of the photographs from forensics?'

'I don't think that would work. I need to see the body.'

'Christ! I didn't take you for a resurrectionist.'

Viv starts off toward the exit but turns. 'It sort of isn't real until you see it in the flesh . . . but if I have to, photographs are better than nothing.'

Red marches up behind her. 'You can't get out until I scan my card.' Gently says, 'Honestly you really don't want to see what's left.'

Frustrated at being infantilised, Viv no longer wants to argue and just nods. When they reach the entrance doors Red says, 'Look, I'll have a go. I really appreciate the tip. If anything dramatic happens, or a nice neat confession, I'll let you know.'

Chapter Twenty

By the time Viv approaches the Outsider she's half an hour late and distracted by fantasy images of the remains of Andrew. When she reaches the door her belly begins an edgy dance. She slows her pace, takes her hand back off the handle, questioning what she's doing. Maybe Dawn was right; perhaps she can't go back to men, after all. She takes a couple of deep breaths before she rounds the corner, pushes open the double glass doors and wanders as nonchalantly as she can into the restaurant. He stands when he sees her and waves her over, kissing her on both cheeks. She flinches as his two-day growth scratches her cheek. Her hand touches the spot, still tender from last week's encounter with Croy. A memory of Dawn, the gentleness of her soft skin, rises in contrast. Viv swallows. Her mouth is dry, and she is aware of her sudden longing for a female touch. She tenses even more as the waiter helps her take her jacket off. This isn't the kind of establishment where, whatever they cost, they allow coats to hang on the backs of their designer chairs.

'Hi, Viv. This feels weird, nice weird, but weird.'

She smiles. He seems as nervous as she is. She's surprised he isn't cross that she's late. Maybe he was too.

She's hesitant but hears her own words, 'Hi . . . Mac, it is strange, I agree, and yes, nice strange.' She sounds as if she's underwater.

Pushing her chair in he says, 'Good kit.'

Distractedly she notices his lemony cologne and says, 'Thanks.'

'You didn't strike me as the type who'd wear a pelmet.' He registers the look of surprise on her face. 'I mean . . . you look fabulous. I've only ever seen you in jeans before.'

'You've only ever seen me on the job before.' Her tone is more defensive than she means it to be, and she catches a look crossing his face that she can't make out. He continues to be chipper. Too chipper.

'True, but we're not on the job now, so we should get work out of the way. Two things. First, Pete still hasn't spoken, but they had a match on the goat shit. Beats me how forensics do it, but I'm ever grateful for their efforts.'

She waits, hoping to get the chance to mention that she's spoken to Red already.

'And second, have a look at this number.'

He takes out his mobile and shows her a number on the display. She doesn't recognise it, but takes out her own phone and scrolls through the messages wondering if by any chance it's the same number as the strange late night call without a voice. It isn't. About to close the phone she remembers something else. Bingo! It's the same number as the 'U r safe' text.

'Look.' She holds her phone up for him to view the text. 'You want me to ring it?'

He glances around at other diners who look suitably engaged and says, 'Don't see why not.'

A male answers, and through a din of music says, 'Hi, Viv.'

She's baffled but recognises the voice. 'John? John Black?'

' Viv, I just wanted to tell you . . . I'm so sorry. I feel so guilty.'

Viv, still baffled, says, 'I can't speak now. I'll ring you later.' She stares at the phone, then at Marconi. 'Would you credit it? John bloody Black.' It takes her a second but she manages to put two and two together. 'Shit! So he's your man for the tip off at the Whitemans?' Marconi nods, and Viv lets out a huge breath. 'Well, well. What next?'

Marconi looks pleased. 'I like ticking boxes. By the way, on another note, Sandy's wife turned up at the hospital and took him home. He'd had a serious asthma attack. We've also searched Robbie's own flat and turned up evidence enough for a chemistry class, so we're bringing him in again and I imagine he'll give us more than we need to secure Whiteman. But listen, there's something else – unrelated. He hesitates. 'I had a call this morning from an interesting colleague who's keen to meet you. Asked if I could set up a meeting. I told them we were having lunch here, so there's a good chance they'll drop in.'

She picks up the menu. 'Curious.'

He looks confused.

'Not the menu, Mac – your colleague. Why don't they just ring me?'

'You'll find out. I bet every time the door opens you'll be wondering if it's them. Now the garlicky fries are exceptional, but not great for only one person . . .'

He looks over the top of his menu and smirks.

'I'm not sure I could eat fries.' She keeps her eyes on the menu. 'But I think we deserve some fizz. How about Prosecco?'

Viv is relieved at the idea of a visitor and wonders if it could be Sal. Chapman, but he starts by saying, 'Sal sends her best.'

So she knows that they are having lunch. 'How is she, and what is it she does exactly?'

'She's an academic who does profiling for us.' He adjusts the cuffs of his shirt so that they extend just so from his jacket.

'Yeah, but what is that? What exactly does it mean?' Viv feels her concern rising, wondering what Sal must think of her.

He exhales a deep breath. 'She looks at patterns of behaviour and predicts the possible next moves of the criminal. She's come up with some invaluable stuff for us.'

'But she's not working on this case, is she?'

He shakes his head, clearly disappointed at the direction the conversation is taking. 'Not officially, but with a brain like hers available it would be daft for us not to keep her in the loop. She hasn't led us a merry dance yet. Why are you so interested?'

'Just wondered about interviewing her.' A blatant lie, but now that she's said it it mightn't be a bad idea. The wine arrives and the waiter pours two glasses.

'You could try but I don't imagine she'd be up for it. She likes the quiet life. Anyway I'd rather hear about you, Viv. How come you're a hairdresser and a journalist? That sounds like a journey.'

'It's not as strange as people think.' She takes a sip of wine. 'Hairdressers are, or rather have to be, anthropologists. I went back to school as it were, while still doing hair. I had to pay my way through university somehow, and hairdressing financed it. Besides it's an addiction . . . and I'm as loyal as a cat. How about you? How did you get to where you are? Fast track or up through the ranks?'

He looks apologetic. 'Fast track, I'm afraid. Law. I looked at anthropology but much as I'd have loved to read *The Sexual Life of Savages*, I couldn't see how it would improve my career prospects. I should've known better!'

She laughs, relaxing into safe territory. 'You're taking the piss. I never met a single student in George Square who was doing law. The law faculty, or whatever they call it now, was an anthropologist's dream all on its own – a community in isolation, stuck out there in Old College. Says it all really.'

'You should have arranged to do your field work at Old College.'

'Actually,' Viv says, 'you're not too far off the mark. I did a gender study of the lawyers in Parliament Hall.'

He grimaces. 'That couldn't have taken long . . . Find anything worthwhile?'

'Yeah, I did, but it wasn't to do with gender so much as hierarchy.'

Their food arrives and she stops mid-sentence, but he prompts her to go on.

'It's not that interesting . . .' She leans forward and centralises the white, angular porcelain salt and pepper pots. Then noticing what she's done, continues, rather flustered, 'I was keen to observe the way the genders use space, but ended up obsessing about the way the doors into the Signet Library were used.'

She stops again, wondering if he's really interested or just humouring her, but again he says, 'I've used that Parliament Hall myself a few times when I was training, and never noticed anything except the way advocates are fearful of someone overhearing their case. That's why they keep on the move – pairs of them incessantly walking up and down the length of the hall.'

'Yeah, I noticed that too.'

Their conversation dots from one safe topic to another, without halting, until a shortish, stout man, in 'shoulder season' tweed, appears next to the table. 'Sorry to butt in like this.'

Mac stands and introduces the man, saying, 'Ah, this is the colleague I mentioned.'

He puts out his hand and says, 'Glad to make your acquaintance at last, Dr Fraser.'

So she has a name . . . and he doesn't. Strange. He has a plummy, slightly Scottish accent and sports what looks like a dead rat on his top lip, but otherwise his countenance is pleasant and ruddy, in fact not unlike the man in her recent dream. Mac pulls a chair from another table, eliciting a testy look from the waiter.

As the man speaks, Viv has a vision of Mycroft Holmes and lets out an involuntary snort. Mac gives her a funny look. Feeling the need to explain herself she says, 'I'm sorry, but you speak in a way that I imagine Mycroft Holmes would . . . that is, if he existed.'

He and Mac look at each other, then at her and break into broad smiles. The man says, 'Funny you should say that,' as he takes a seat.

Mac says to the man, still with no name, 'Would you like lunch?'

'No, thank you. Just passing and thought it best to speak to Dr Fraser directly.' He turns on full charm and grins at Viv. 'Now, I don't suppose Mac here has mentioned why I'd like to meet you. But I'll try and be quick. We need help. Your help, with a case we're working on.'

Viv looks bemused and shakes her head.

'No. Hear me out if you will. One of your clients is up to something and although we've been following his progress we could do with someone who has inside information. You, my dear, are the very person.'

The waiter interrupts and asks if they're ready to order. Mac gestures to Viv to go first.

'I'll have the sea bass and fries.'

'Ditto.'

The waiter says, 'Ordinary or garlicky?' And turning to the new arrival.

'May I get you a menu, sir?' He shakes his head in answer.

Mac replies, 'Garlicky. Thanks.'

Viv says, 'Ordinary,' and turns to the man in tweed, 'I may well be perfect for the job in your eyes, but there's the little matter of ethics. You see I have an unspoken code not to interfere with any business of my clients' beyond their hair. It's taken me a long time to build up their trust. Besides I'm unqualified for this.'

'I can see your point but if . . .'

'No buts or ifs. I'm not interested.'

He looks at Mac and says, 'I see what you mean.'

Viv looks at Mac then at the nameless man. 'Am I invisible? Whatever you two have had up your sleeve is out of my remit unless you'd like me to write a story on it.'

This certainly has their attention. 'That wouldn't be wise, Dr Fraser. If we told you it's in the national interest that we gain access . . .'

Viv laughs, 'For God's sake, we're surely beyond the days of 007? There's nothing you can't access. Sorry, I'm not your girl.' Then, looking regretfully at the waiter, as he approaches with an appetiser of bread and oil, she stands and gestures to him that she'd like her coat.

But Tweedy says, 'No need to go. I'll leave you to think it over.' He stands, and she realises he's not as small as she had thought. His girth must act like an optical illusion.

As she shrugs into her coat she says, 'I don't need time to think it over.' Then, turning to Mac, she says, '"Forks and knives. You'll have heard of them."' Her exit isn't as smooth as she'd like when she has to yank her coat free of the restaurant door, and blaspheming under her breath thinks so much for lunch lunch!

The only good thing about the situation, apart from the fact that it takes less than five minutes to power walk home, is that she didn't have to politely decline Mac. Cursing herself for being an idiot, her disappointment takes the form of criticism and she generalises about how exploitative men always are. Then consoles herself with the advice that she should stick to women. Once in the security of the flat she strips her new kit off and steps into a hot shower, definitely a form of penance. She scrubs her hair, applying too much shampoo, but standing inches deep in bubbles allows the heat to work its magic. Within five minutes she can no longer recall the frustration of the meeting. Her tension has slipped down her back and out through the drain.

Chapter Twenty-One

As she rubs at her hair with a towel she spots the answering machine light blinking. She hesitates imagining it'll be Mac with an apology. But no it was Sal very tentatively suggesting lunch. Viv keeps rubbing, but replays the message. A tingle of excitement rises in her gut and before she has too much time to think it through she punches number one to reply. Sal picks up immediately. When Viv hears Sals actual voice she gets flustered. 'Oh hi, it's Viv. I'd love to do lunch. When did you have in mind?'

'As soon as you like.'

At this very moment Sal's straight, no nonsense approach appeals to Viv and she smiles, toeing a ball of hair that's gathered on the rug beneath her bare feet. 'Well I haven't eaten lunch yet today.'

Sal interrupts her. 'I've got some transcripts to evaluate but I could do a very late lunch at say four?'

Viv's interest is piqued but she stops herself asking 'what transcripts'. Sal breaks the silence. 'We've had to go wider at the school...'

It's Viv's turn to interrupt. 'No, no I was just wondering... No four is great.'

'What were you wondering Viv?'

But already there's an idea tickling at the edge of her brain. 'No honestly four is great. How about Susie's Diner, I haven't been for ages?'

'Susie's it is. See you at four... and Viv you can relax we're only having lunch.'

Viv is slightly taken aback but the idea that's kicked in distracts her.'

'See you there.' She replaces the handset still grappling with the vague notion. She can't quite grasp it and is clever enough to know that the only way to retrieve it is to let it go. After flicking through the channels on the TV she decides that the only way to clear her head is to go for a run. But while she's pulling on a pair of joggers the piece that she was missing begins to surface again. She berates herself for not seeking out Pete's mother. His home life is bound to give her the edge on what he is capable of. In the sitting room she leafs through the pages of her notebook knowing that she must have written down Pete's address at some point. Nothing. She goes back on-line and searches. As usual there's not much she can't find on the net and she jots down an address in the Grange. Within a few minutes Viv is jogging over the Meadows, into Marchmont, then five minutes further south she reaches Lauder Road. The vast Victorian pile whose stable has become a double garage, nestles within a high walled garden. Open gates allow her access to the front door. Whether she'll get beyond that is down to luck. As she approaches she hears a voice coming through an open window. The closer she gets the more hysterical the person sounds. She tiptoes over the gravel to the front door and tucks herself beneath the porch. Her hand hovers over the bell. The voice is female and sounds as if it's speaking on the telephone. Viv can't make out words but the tone is distressed. After a few minutes of continuous ranting everything goes quiet. Viv waits another couple of minutes and presses the bell. The sound of heels clicking on wood, echo in the hallway inside. They stop and Viv imagines the person behind the door sorting her hair or her skirt, but instead a slim man in brogues, a pale blue shirt and chinos, swings the door back. He looks exactly like Pete. Must be his brother.

'Hi, I was wondering if I might speak to Mrs Brendan?'

He looks quizzical but gestures with his arm for her to enter. She steps onto the polished parquet and stares up at walls adorned with modern paintings. Viv spots a Vettriano and smiles. She is led through a door on the right into a large sitting room where a woman, recovering her composure, stands to shake Viv's hand. But when Viv says her name the woman looks confused and retracts her hand. 'Oh, you're not from the police then . . . they said they'd send a family liaison officer.'

'No, I'm not from the police but I have been working with them.'

For the first time the young man speaks, the frustration in his deep voice evident. 'Why are you here, then? You can see that this is a difficult time.'

'Yes, yes, I can see that. But I wondered if I might be able to help.'

Mrs Brendan stares at Viv. 'Do you know Peter?'

'Well, yes. I do. But . . . I wondered if you know the head girl . . .' Viv doesn't get the chance to finish her sentence. Mrs Brendan's contorted face almost has Viv reeling back on her heels.

'That little vixen. What would you like to know about her? She's . . .' She chokes back more tears and the young man turns away toward the window, as if he can't bear the sight of her distress.

'I suppose I had an idea that maybe she was involved with Andrew . . .'

The young man swings round. 'Involved with Andrew, he couldn't stand the sight of her. She's toxic. Always threatening him with . . .' He crosses his arms across his chest.

Viv prompts him. 'With what?'

'With outing him. Always threatening to 'out' Andrew.' His frustration mounting.

Viv screws up her eyes. 'But I thought . . .'

'You thought he was out and proud . . . yes, well, maybe with his close chums. Like Pete and Tom and Johnny, but not his family. That little bitch, 'Head Girl' as you call her, has been blackmailing him for months.'

Viv waits quietly taking in what they've said until he continues. 'All this because he wouldn't go to the year end dance with her. Tradition has it that head boy and head girl go to the year end dance but from the minute they were named she was on him and he wouldn't agree to go.'

Viv, trying to keep all the information she's already holding in her head, can't believe she's been so blind. How stupid could she be?

She turns as if to leave, but then asks, 'You don't happen to have a name, or even an address for her?'

He marches over to a desk and scribbles a few lines on a pad then hands it to Viv.

Mrs Brendan drops her head into her hands again and the man, shaking his own head, draws in a deep breath and leads Viv back to the front door.

'How is Pete?'

'As you'd expect. Distraught. In pain . . .' He shakes his head again, this time as if he's fighting back tears himself.

'What sort of . . .'

'His hands are burnt, he tried to pull Andrew . . .'

Then he does choke and nods as he closes the door behind her.

Viv stands beneath the porch again and shakes her own head. What a mess. She checks what's written on the paper and looking right then left starts to jog west towards Bruntsfield. The address she has is in Merchiston, West Castle Road.

When she reaches the Links she stops to catch her breath. Mrs Brendan couldn't have been more vehement when she spat out 'that little vixen'. What does a young girl have to do for people to hate her so much? And who was the young man? Was he Pete's brother?

West Castle Road is in one of Edinburgh's most elegant Victorian areas. As in the Grange, people built their houses for maximum privacy with high walls protecting grand houses, and with spacious, professionally tended gardens. Mature leafy trees shade drives with 'high end' four by fours which, beyond mounting the pavement on the school run, have never been off road in their lives. Viv checks the number on the paper but reaches the bottom of the street without identifying the house. The houses have names, no numbers. The postie must clearly know where to deliver what. She retraces her steps, scanning the glass above the doors and gates, and ever hopeful of spotting a wheelie bin with a number painted on it. Not a chance. As she approaches the top of the street for the second time she recognises a car and its driver coming round the corner. She ducks and pretends to collect a parking ticket from the machine. She glances to the side; the car halts midway down the hill. It's Johnny. He parks and steps out pulling up the hood of his sweatshirt as he closes the car door behind him. Furtively he looks right and left then begins to walk in her direction. Unsure what to do she bends down and presses the buttons on the machine as Johnny passes without giving her a glance. He looks determined, on a mission. Another three or four houses up he tries to open a gate but either it's stuck or locked. He shakes it and blasphemes. Just as she's about to step between two parked cars he looks back down the street and recognises her.

He approaches her with an ugly questioning stare. 'What are you doing here?'

'I might ask you the same thing.'

He digs his hands into his pockets and shakes his head again. 'I've got to find Ruthie.'

Viv nods, acknowledging with her eyebrows that he spits her name out in the same way as Mrs Brendan had called her a vixen.

'Shall we take a look?'

He glances towards the gate then shrugs. He turns to Viv resigned. 'Not much I can do to stop you, is there?'

Viv smiles. 'No. Not much . . . Safety in numbers, though.'

She takes off but he remains. She turns. 'You coming or what?'

He hesitates again then decides. As they approach Viv notices that the house has the same sort of high-security panel as Morgan Clifford and she wonders what's inside that requires this.

'So what is it that Ruthie's parents do?'

'Dunno really. She just says he works for the Civil Service.'

Viv snorts. 'A cover-all.'

Johnny throws her a puzzled look. 'What . . .' Then, as if he understands, he says, 'D'you think he could be in Special Services?'

'I just mean he could be anything from a road cleaner to prime minister. They're all civil servants. But I'd be surprised if the road cleaners have such high-end security.' She points at the panel. The gate is solid so she wedges her foot into the masonry at the side and steps up. She only gets a swift glance before she slips off.

'See anything?'

'No. But if you give me a hand up. . .'

Johnny blows out a huge breath then bends, clasping his hands together in a basket, Viv puts her foot in and he hoists her as if she's feather light. 'That rugby training certainly comes in handy, eh?'

'You're not exactly ten ton Tess. What's happening over that wall?'

'Well, I'm on camera for posterity that's for sure. The good thing is, I can't hear any dogs.'

She jumps down and brushes off her jacket. 'Thanks. Technology is easier to overcome than dogs.'

'Look there's no way I'm doing anything illegal. It's alright for you. We're all in enough trouble as it is. But Ruthie can't get away with what she's done. Someone's got to make her see sense.' He sounds calm and rational.

'And what has she done exactly?'

'She must have killed Andrew . . . or set him up to be killed. By the time we reached him the car was ablaze. There was nothing we could do.' His eyes screw up as if he can't bear to let the memory in.

'Whoa! Are you saying... No wait, how did you know where he was?'

'Pete got a text.'

'What did it say?'

He shook his head. 'Just where we'd find him. We'd no idea 'til we got there that she was the one who had torched the car.'

'There's a world of a difference Johnny between saying you want someone dead and actually killing them.'

'No, there isn't. She's responsible for his car bursting into flames. I don't know how she did it, but she didn't become head girl because she's thick . . . She thinks she's beyond the law.' He gestures to the house. 'All this?'

Viv cranes her neck at the height of the wall then steps back off the pavement. Cameras and security indicate fear of invasion. Little Miss Ruthie has had a life of incarceration.

'Why would she want to kill Andrew? I mean, it's one thing to have a spat with someone, but a whole other to want them dead.'

Johnny releases another huge sigh. 'You don't get it.' He sighs again. 'She's a fag hag. She thought all she had to do was destroy the other sides of the 'love triangle'. Pete loved Andrew, Andrew loved Pete but Ruthie also loves Pete, who has, by the way, played her like a fiddle . . . Andrew was in her way. She made a fuss of Andrew as a pretence. He wasn't the one she wanted.'

'She couldn't really believe that killing him would make things better for her? She's got to be too bright for that?'

As they speak a large, well–polished, dark blue Jaguar pulls up on the opposite side of the road. The driver steps out and opens the rear door, allowing Viv and Johnny a view of a female passenger dressed in an expensive trouser suit with beautifully coiffed blonde hair. No one speaks, but Viv and Johnny glance at each other then back at the vaguely familiar woman who beckons them over with a throw of her head. Johnny is about to step off the pavement when Viv puts her hand out to stop him. The driver's hand hovers over his trouser pocket. Although this is Edinburgh, Viv's had enough drama over the last few weeks to keep her alert and she's seen this gesture before. Guys in Special Services, although trained not to give the game away, keep a weapon close to hand. In addition he looks on the large and fit side for a bloke who spends his days at the wheel. The woman in the car concedes, swings her long legs out of the car and saunters across.

'I'm guessing you're here to see Ruth?'

Johnny's a quick learner because he follows Viv's lead and stays quiet.

The woman smiles. 'Okay. You're wasting your time. She's gone.'

Viv nods and says, 'And you are about to tell us where?'

The woman laughs, but not because she's amused. She sighs. 'They said you'd be difficult.'

A puzzled look flits across Viv's face, which Johnny catches.

He asks, 'Anyone going to let me in on this little game?' He turns his back to the woman and spots a curtain moving on the upper floor of the house. Viv, noticing his distraction, gives the slightest shake of her own head and widens her eyes in warning. He, at first confused, says, 'Well is anyone going to . . .'

The woman interrupts. 'Ruth has been taken somewhere for her own security.' She sneers. 'Am I likely to tell you where that is?' A laugh. 'I don't think so.'

'Well, piss off, then.' Viv is vehement. 'If you've got nothing useful to tell us just piss off.' The woman is taken aback but recovers her composure before stepping back towards the car. Once inside the woman turns her face to Viv. 'I'd be careful if I were you.'

Viv's response, 'But you're not me, are you?' Then adds an after thought. 'You're just a messenger.'

The flunkey closes the door and slips back round to the driver's side. Suppressing a smile, he shoots Viv a nod of approval before he climbs in and drives away.

Johnny plants his hands on his hips, stares at Viv and says. 'So who the fuck was that?'

'Someone's PUP.' Because of his raised eyebrows she continues. 'PUP means pumped up PA.' Then, gesturing to the upper floor of the house, 'So what did you see up there?' They both stare at the windows where all the curtains are still.

'There was someone at the window on the far left . . . could have been Ruthie.'

'Time for a bit of adventure. You give me a hoist up again, and once I'm in I'll get this gate open. It's bound to be easier from the other side.'

Johnny shrugs. 'Might as well be hung for a sheep as a lamb chop.'

Viv looks at him and smiles, thinking everyone has their own version of the world. If he wants lamb chop then where's the harm in that?

Johnny clasps his hands again and Viv is efficiently hoisted up to the top of the wall. She swings her leg over and lets out a squeal. 'Shit! There are shards of glass embedded on this side. I'll have to jump.'

Viv noisily hits the deck on the other side. Then comes the sound of scratching metal on metal.

'What the hell are you doing over there?' Viv doesn't answer but after a long few minutes, the gate scrapes back the opposite way from that which he'd expected.

'My God! You've unscrewed the hinges . . . how clever is that!'

Viv grins and snaps her Swiss army knife closed. 'Get your backside in here and we'll push it back into place.'

Viv thinks if Ruthie was at the upper window she won't have gone anywhere while all this has been going on, and sure enough, when she looks up again the curtain in the left window gives the slightest twitch.

The first thing she does is press the brass front door bell. There's no way Ruthie will have idly watched that scene. Viv tries to imagine what might be going through the head of a girl who was angry enough to kill one boy in the hope of getting to another, either to gain his affection or to make him furious. She certainly won't give herself up without a battle. She presses the bell again but there is no movement inside the house. They both step back and check the window again. No sign of anyone this time.

'What now?' says Johnny, not taking his eyes off the window. 'She's definitely in there. We can't get to her without breaking in . . . can we?'

Again Viv tries to imagine what's going on in Ruthie's head and what the parents might be willing to do to protect her. Then something strikes her. Ruthie may not be free to wander round the house. She could be a captive, held by one of her parents or almost anyone on behalf of her parents. Before she makes a decision on her next move she hears a car and then another pulling up outside the gates. The sound of eight doors slamming means there's a crowd. Whoever it is rattles the gate then pushes it, and it gives way at the wrong side. Viv indicates to Johnny to step into the shadows but she recognises Red's voice, sighs, shrugs and then beckons Johnny out towards the voice.

'I might have known I'd find you here, Doc. You've been holding out on me.'

Viv stutters, 'Eh . . . No way. I just thought . . .'

Red interrupts her. 'What, Doc? You just thought if you planted a chicken a hen would grow.'

Viv gapes at Red. 'What are you on about?'

'Well it seems to me that you do too much thinking. Got a problem with that mobile of yours? No signal, no battery.' Red rolls her hand in a gesture of etc, etc. 'Heard all the excuses.'

'There's nothing wrong with my signal or my battery. I just wasn't ready to call you in until I knew that my hunch was worth following up. Anyway you're here now, and Johnny and I think . . .'

Johnny frowns. 'Count me out of that . . . I don't think anything that she does.' Johnny thumbs in Viv's direction.

Red looks from one to the other. 'And here was I thinking you were a team. Okay, Doc, out with it.'

Viv glances up at the window and Red follows her eyes.

'You think she's in there?'

'Yep. But I was just thinking . . .'

'That's what I mean, Doc, you're way out there with all that thinking.' Red indicates to the horizon with both hands. 'You're thinking that she might not be alone.'

'Exactly.'

'And that whoever she's with might not take kindly to us interfering.'

Viv smiles and nods, 'Exactly.'

Red smiles. 'See you and me, Doc, we're of one mind.' Red indicates to some of the uniforms to go round the back. 'Hope there isn't too much of a fight; they're crying 'diplomatic immunity'. Murder doesn't really count in their world.' She grimaces. 'But it does in mine.' She looks at Viv. 'And I'm guessing that it does in yours as well.'

Viv nods. 'Can I do anything?'

Red snorts. 'You mean you're going to listen to whatever command I give? I know you. Why would I bother?'

As Red assesses the garden and the boundary walls, another car pulls up. She glances at her watch. 'Marconi. That didn't take him long.'

Viv turns and steps away from Red's side in an attempt to become invisible. She flushes as he throws her a 'what are you doing here' look, but he soon refocuses on the task at hand and ceases to pay her any attention.

Red speaks to Marconi her gentle lisp increasing. 'We think she's inside but we're not sure if she's on her own or with someone.' She stretches forward and presses the bell. They hear the sound echoing on the inside but no movement comes in response. Viv wanders off to the side of the house and through another tall iron gate. She finds a side door and tries the handle. It gives slightly. Although it isn't locked it has been barricaded by something heavy. She puts her shoulder against it but can't shift it. She beckons to a PC who, not realising he's doing wrong, comes to help. Between them they make it move about two inches. Viv returns to the front of the house where Johnny is standing with his arms crossed watching the upstairs window. Viv beckons him. If his muscle won't shift it nothing will.

Red spots Viv and Johnny skulking round the corner of the house and shouts, 'Oi! What are you two up to?'

Viv concedes. 'There's another door. It seems to be open.'

'You can't just go opening people's doors. There's a procedure.'

At this Marconi returns from checking out the back from the opposite side. He takes command. 'Sandra, you go and see if you can gain entry.'

Red gives him a questioning look.

Mac responds immediately. 'Of course I've got a warrant. Now get going.' His tone becomes grave. He really means business. 'Viv, you stand clear with Jonathan over there.' He points toward the gate. 'Don't move.'

She pulls a face but he ignores her. She shrugs and wanders toward the gate with Johnny at her tail. 'I think we're probably done here. If she's in there, there's no way she's getting out unless she's clamped to one of them.' She nods back over her shoulder. Just as Viv goes towards the gate there's a commotion behind her and Johnny jumps clear of a hooded body running at full pelt into Viv's path. Although Viv's instinct is also to jump clear, and as if she's in an Ealing comedy she sticks her foot out and the body goes head over heels onto the garden path. It scrabbles to regain its footing but Viv leaps on top and pins it down. The figure may be small but it puts up a significant fight, which has Viv dredging up tactics that she hasn't used for some time. No sooner has she knelt on the girl's arms, than they are surrounded by uniforms. Mac stands a few feet back. He gives his first comment. 'I might have known there was no chance of this concluding without you putting your oar in.'

As Viv dusts down her trousers she looks up, incredulous. 'Excuse me. I wasn't the one who let her escape.'

Mac throws up his arms. 'Okay, okay.' He turns to Red. 'Who did?'

One side of Red's face is swollen and she raises a length of pipe. 'Even my skull couldn't get the better of this pipe.' She looks sheepish. 'Thanks Doc, she was just too quick.'

Viv looks concerned. 'Is that okay?' She points at Red's face.

Red nods briefly and turns to Ruthie. 'Assaulting an officer isn't going to help your cause.' Ruthie's response is to spit in Red's face. Viv, horrified, steps forward but Mac has already given the nod to get Ruthie cuffed and into the car. Viv scrabbles about in her jacket, takes out a packet of tissues and hands one to Red.

Red declines the offer. But when Mac hands her what looks exactly like a tissue she accepts it, wipes her face then bags it. 'Not nice, Doc, but useful.' Mac takes the bag, folds it and puts it in his inside pocket.

'Think positive, Doc. That'll save me hassling her for a DNA sample . . . 'preciate the thought, so thanks all the same, Doc.'

Viv heads through the gate and Johnny skips to keep up with her. Viv glances into the police car where Ruthie sits defiant with her arms crossed, and a look on her face that could turn salt into stone. Flanked by two officers twice her size she won't be going anywhere anytime soon.

Johnny, clearly on an adrenaline high, says. 'Oh, my God! That was so disgusting. Can you believe that?' He glances towards the police car. Then he turns to Viv and sighs. 'Come on, I'll give you a lift.' He beckons her towards his car.

Distracted, Viv says, 'No. No, thanks. The walk'll do me good.'

Johnny continues. 'Look Pete's no angel . . .'

This gets Viv's attention. 'Go on.'

'Well I just mean he's added fuel to the fire. If he hadn't led Ruthie on . . . and . . . Och, no point in going over all Pete's misdemeanours. He's got a wicked streak, for sure, but he'd never kill anyone.'

Viv nods, hearing the lack of conviction in Johnny's tone. Having been on the receiving end of Pete's wrath she sensed he was capable of much worse.

The walk home over the Meadows gives her time to reflect on the machinations of the last few weeks. How off the mark she's been. Not once has she thought of a schoolgirl being tangled up in this story, let alone the cause of it. It was all very well to 'get there in the end', but what a lesson. If only she'd been less . . . naïve. The sun peeked out from behind a cloud and threw a shaft of light through the trees and across her path. She turned her face upward, pushed her hair back and for a few steps enjoyed hopeful warmth. What was the point in going down the 'what if' route? There was always so much more to learn. But now she checks her watch, time for lunch with Sal.

To find out more about upcoming releases go to www.vclifford.com

Made in the USA
Middletown, DE
11 March 2021